BETTER IF HE STAYS

ALLIE EVERHART

Better If He Stays

By Allie Everhart

Cover Design by by Qamber Designs

Model Photo by Lindee Robinson Photography

Models: David and Alyse

CHAPTER ONE

Riley

"Hey, Giada," I say, answering her call as I take the sack from Carlos.

He smiles and gives me a wave. "See you tomorrow!"

"Riley, can you talk?" Giada asks. "It sounds like you're at work."

"I am, but I'm not working. I'm just picking up dinner." I go out the door and walk to my truck. Luckily, I still have it. My mom's ex didn't get parole so his truck is mine for a few more months.

"Did you have the day off?"

"No. I worked the night shift at the gas station. Got off at six this morning. It was a ten-hour shift." I turn the key to start the truck but nothing happens. "Great. Now the truck won't start." I try it again. It attempts to start but then dies.

"Is the battery dead?"

"I don't know." I try it again and it starts. "Okay, I think we're good. So how's everything there?"

"I have exams this week and a paper due. That's why I haven't called."

Giada's in grad school in Austin, studying psychology. She wants to have her own business someday doing couples counseling. Given my situation right now, she's the perfect friend. I have my own personal couples counselor to help me with the situation with Brad.

"I've been busy too," I say. "Double shifts at the gas station all week and my regular shifts at the restaurant."

"Riley, you gotta cut back. You're working way too many hours."

"I need the money."

"What you need is rest. Pregnant women need lots of rest, especially in the first trimester."

I smile. "Have you been reading pregnancy websites again?"

"I have to, since you won't."

"I don't have time. And I don't have a computer. I'm not going to read all that stuff on my phone."

"Don't you want to know what's happening? Or what's going to happen next?"

"Not really. It kinda freaks me out knowing all that stuff. Besides, the doctor will tell me all that."

"How did your appointment go?"

"Missed it. I had to work."

"Riley, you can't miss appointments."

"Relax, I'm going tomorrow. And I'm only ten weeks along. The nurse said I can see the doctor anytime this month. There's no rush."

"Just don't go skipping appointments, okay?"

"Okay, Dr. Russo." I smile as I say it. I'm just teasing her. I love that she cares so much about the baby and me. My mom doesn't. She told me to get rid of it, but I refused. I also refused to tell her who the father is, but she knows it's Brad. She knows he's the only guy I was with last summer.

"You can't work all those hours, Riley. I'm serious. It's too much."

"I don't have a choice. I'm the only one working right now. Plus, I'm trying to save up for the baby. Do you know how much baby stuff costs? I'll try to find stuff second hand but still, it's going to cost a lot."

I'm at the trailer now but remain in the truck so I can talk without my mom listening in.

"I know you don't want to hear this, Riley, but I think you should tell him. He'd help you with the costs. I know he would."

"He doesn't have money and neither do his parents. They're broke. He said his mom is filing for bankruptcy next week."

"Okay, but..." she pauses, "do you think you'll tell him? Like maybe later, when the baby's here?"

"I don't know," I say with a sigh. "Sometimes I think I should and then other times I think it's best if he never knew."

"I think he'd want to know."

"And lose everything he's worked for?"

"Telling him doesn't mean he'll lose everything."

"Giada, there's no way he'll stay in med school if he finds out we're having a baby. Being a doctor has been his dream since he was a kid. I can't take that away from him."

"He could take time off and go back later."

"You know it never works out that way. People say they'll go back, but they never do. And if he left, he'd lose his scholarship. Going back later means he'd have to pay for it himself, which means he'd have to go to a cheaper school. One that's not as good. But I know he wouldn't go. He'd end up getting a job to support the baby and me, and his dream of being a doctor would be over. This is his only chance, Giada. He's at a top school, living in a city he's always wanted to live in and..." I take a breath. "He's happy. He's really happy."

That last part is why I can't bring myself to tell him the truth. Brad's happiness means everything to me, and right now he's having the time of his life. He's away from the mess of his parents and their financial problems and starting a new life in New York. The life he's always dreamed of and didn't think would happen when his parents told him they were broke. I still remember the look on his face when they told him he couldn't go to med school. It nearly killed me to see him crushed like that. Everything he'd worked for—all those hours studying to make sure he'd get in a good school—was all for nothing. He was so close to making his dream happen and then, in an instant, it was taken away.

I'm not taking it away again. I can't take his dream from him after he just got it back. It was a miracle he got that unexpected scholarship. A sign that this is what he's meant to do. I don't usually believe in that stuff, but in this case, I really believe Brad was meant to go to med school and live in New York.

"How do you know?" Giada asks.

"Know what?"

"How do you know he's happy? Did he tell you that?"

"He doesn't have to. I can hear it in his voice. Every time I talk to him, I picture him with this big smile. He loves it out there. He loves New York. He loves his school. His classes."

"And he loves YOU. Did you forget that?"

"Of course not but—"

"Do you still love HIM?"

"Yes." A tear slips down my cheek and I quickly wipe it away. "I love him more than anything."

"Then you two should be together, which you will be if you tell him."

"I don't want him being with me because of the baby. That almost never works out. You know my friend, April? Her sister broke up with a guy, then told him she was having his baby so they got back together, got married, and divorced a year later. Now they fight all the time and the baby's stuck in the middle."

"That's not going to happen with you and Brad."

"You don't know that, and neither do I. Brad and I only dated a few months. We have no idea if we could make it work long-term. Even if we could, what if he regretted it later? What if he regretted leaving med school and blamed me for it? Or blamed the baby?"

"He wouldn't do that. He's not that type of guy."

"He's also not the type of guy to be with a girl like me," I say, looking at the broken-down trailer with weeds growing all around it.

"Riley, it doesn't matter if you come from money. Brad doesn't care. He's told you that."

"I'm not just talking about money. I'm talking about our backgrounds. How we grew up. What we have in common."

"You have stuff in common," she insists.

"Like what?"

"You um..." She pauses. "You both like the outdoors."

"A lot of people like the outdoors."

"I'm sure there's other stuff. You guys just need to date longer to find out."

"But it's more than that, like how we grew up. Brad went

to private school. Spent summers at the country club. Traveled the world with his family. I never even left the state until that day Brad drove me to Texas."

"How he grew up doesn't matter. It's the past. You're his future. And together you two will figure out how you want your life to be. I'm sure Brad wouldn't mind if you want little Brad junior to go to public school," she says with a smile in her voice.

"It's a little soon to call him that. I don't know if it's a boy."

"Are you going to find out?"

"I haven't decided." I notice the curtains move on the trailer window and see my mom looking out. She sees me in the truck and lets the curtains fall back into place.

She was checking to see if Jerry was here. He's her latest boyfriend. He usually shows up around now, right after he gets off work. He works at the oil change place and doesn't bother to shower before coming over so he always smells like a garage.

"I should probably go," I say.

"You never answered my question."

I sigh. "Because I don't have an answer. Just this morning I was going to tell him, but then changed my mind when he texted me a picture of him smiling in front of the library along with a message that he got an A on his test. I don't want him losing this opportunity. He's doing really great in school and he loves it. How can I take that away from him?"

"Okay, how about this? How about you just go out there and see him? Check out the city and maybe see if you could live there?"

"I've already done the research online. There's no way I could afford to live there, especially with a baby."

"Just do it. Go out there and see him."

"Why? What's the point? Brad and I are over. I'm just not ready to tell him that yet." Another tear slips down my cheek. "But I think he might already know."

"Why? What happened?"

"Nothing. But it's not like he can't figure it out. We both know we can't keep this going if we never see each other."

"He'll be home for Thanksgiving."

"In Arizona, not here. He invited me there, but I can't go. I'll be showing by then."

"He loves you. He'll make sure he sees you. He'll probably skip Arizona and show up there instead."

"Which is why I need to make a decision. November isn't that far away."

"Riley, I really think you should go to New York, even if it's just for closure. You need to see him again. See if you still feel the same way when you're together. Maybe things will feel differently now that some time has passed and you'll see that there really isn't a future for you two. If so, you'll feel better about your decision to end it."

"It's not a bad idea. I just need to come up with the money."

"I could loan it to you."

"No. I have some money saved from working all those extra shifts. I could use that." A loud, rusty car pulls up behind me. "Jerry's here. I gotta go hide in my room before he starts talking to me. Call you tomorrow?"

"Yeah, but after seven. I have class all day."

"Okay, bye." I get out of the truck and hurry to the trailer.

"What's the rush?" Jerry calls out from behind me.

"Dinner's getting cold," I say, holding up the sack.

"You got us dinner?" he asks, catching up to me.

I swing open the trailer door. "If you have five bucks, then yeah. Otherwise, no."

I'm done letting my mom's boyfriends eat our food. I've even started hiding it in my room so they can't get to it.

"Charlene, did you hear that?" Jerry says as he follows me inside. My mom's on the couch watching TV, which is all she does now that she doesn't have a job.

"Hear what?" she asks, sitting up and letting her robe fall aside so that it shows off her bare legs.

"Your girl's making me pay for dinner."

"You weren't invited to dinner," I tell him.

"You should be taking me out," my mom says, getting up to give him a kiss. "C'mon, baby. Let's go out. I've been cooped up in the house all day."

He lets her go and walks over to the kitchen where I'm unpacking the food.

"Take her to dinner," I say. "That's what boyfriends are supposed to do."

"Your daughter's got quite a mouth on her," he says, shoving me aside to open the cupboard. "What happened to the Jack?"

"What do you think?" my mom says, sitting back on the couch.

"Woman, what did I tell you about drinking my booze?"

She just shrugs.

He walks back over to her. "Hurry up and get ready. I need a drink, and if we ain't getting one here, we gotta leave."

My mom jumps up from the couch and kisses him. "I'll go put on that dress you like." She looks him up and down. "You gonna change?"

He shrugs. "I guess I could. Don't want to ruin my uniform."

"Maybe you could shower too." She winks at him. "I could help."

I almost throw up, thinking of the two of them in the shower, the same one I have to use.

"Where you taking me?" my mom asks Jerry as they go to her room.

"We'll go to Don's place. It's rib night and he gives me free beer."

Don is Jerry's brother. He's a waiter at a barbecue restaurant close to Nate's house.

I haven't seen Nate since the day he left town. That was late August, right before the pool closed for the season. He got a job in Dallas at an ad agency. He said they're paying him a lot of money, or what's considered a lot for a graphic designer. He didn't tell me an amount so I thought maybe he was exaggerating, but he sent me pictures of his apartment and it's really nice so maybe he really does make a lot. Or maybe he went over his budget to try to impress me.

Ever since Nate found out about Brad and me, he's been trying to prove to me how much better I would've been with him instead of Brad. He sends me pictures of all the new stuff he's bought, like his new couch and big screen TV, and the car he keeps telling me he's going to buy. And he's always sending me pictures of Dallas and telling me I should move there.

My phone goes off and I see Nate's name pop up. We talk once or twice a week, but it's always him calling, not me. I don't like talking to him. He's not the Nate I was friends with all those years. He's changed. Now he's all about money and status, and he's jealous of anyone who has more than him. He's still mad at Brad for dating me. He hasn't even talked to him since Brad left town back in July.

"Hey, Nate," I say, taking my food to the table and sitting down. "What's up?"

"Just got off work. Had a meeting with my boss today."

"Yeah. How'd it go?" I ask, shoving some fries in my mouth. After working the night shift, I slept all day and missed lunch, so now I'm starving. Giada would have a fit if she knew how I was eating. She keeps sending me articles about nutrition during pregnancy. But with two jobs I barely have time to eat, and when I do, I go for something fast, which usually isn't healthy. I try to eat some fruit every day, but I don't have time to cook, so I usually eat fast food or stuff from the restaurant where I work.

"The meeting went great," Nate says. "I think I'm getting a raise."

"You've only been there a month and you're already getting a raise?"

"What can I say? I'm good at what I do. And I've been working 60-70 hours a week. Don said I'm the hardest worker there and that they reward hard work."

"Don's your boss?"

"He is for now, but at the rate I'm going, I could be *his* boss in a year or two."

There he goes again, bragging about himself. I'm really getting tired of it. I'm happy he's doing well, but I don't need to hear about how great he is every time we talk.

"So what else is new?" I ask, ripping open a packet of Ranch dressing for my chicken fingers.

"I'm going to a concert this weekend. You should come down for it. I could get you a ticket."

"Drive to Dallas?" I laugh. "With a truck that's technically not mine and no money for gas?"

"I'll give you money for gas."

"I can't take time off from work, and with two jobs I don't get a day off."

"Sounds like me. I've been working every weekend. But it's paying off. I'll get my raise and be able to buy my new car."

He always does that. I tell him something about me and he turns the conversation back to him.

"I'm really tired, Nate. I need to take a nap before my night shift."

"Try one of those energy drinks. I've been doing those when I work late and I've got energy all night."

"I can't drink those," I say, then realize I shouldn't have said it. Nate doesn't know I'm pregnant, and I don't want him to find out and tell Brad. It'll be hard to hide it from Nate since his mom lives in town, but I'm still going to try.

"You've never had one, have you?" he asks.

"I've tried a few. I don't like the taste."

"You've just got to find one you like."

"It's not just the taste. They make me jittery. So anyway, I should get going."

"Why are you racing me off the phone?" he says with a laugh. "I haven't talked to you in a week."

I slump back in my chair. "What do you want to talk about?"

"Did you look at those apartments?"

"Not yet," I say, rolling my eyes.

Nate keeps insisting I go look at the apartments near the mall. He even sent me a link to make an appointment for a tour. They're new apartments and really nice, but I can't spend my money on rent right now. I'm trying to save up as much as I can before the baby arrives. Hopefully, after that, I can move out. I don't want my baby growing up in this trailer with my mom and her disgusting boyfriends.

"Riley, it's time to move out of your mom's place. I know I've been saying it for years, but this time I'm not backing down. If I have to, I'll go there and move you out myself."

"Just let it go, Nate. I'm serious. I'm sick of talking about this. It's my life, and if I want to live here, I will."

"You *want* to live there? Since when? All you do is complain about it."

"I used to, but I don't anymore. I'm always at work. I'm hardly ever here."

"But it's not yours. Don't you want a place of your own? A place that's clean and quiet, where you don't have to deal with your mom?"

"Why would I pay for a place I'll never be at? You're always telling me to save money. If I stay here, I can save money. Maybe enough to buy my own car."

"And then you'll move out?"

"I don't know, and I really wish you'd stop asking. I'll move out when I'm ready."

"I'm sure Brad's not okay with that."

Nate almost never mentions Brad. When he does, he gets angry, which leads to us arguing and one of us hanging up.

"Nate, don't start. I thought we agreed we wouldn't talk about him. In fact, you're the one who came up with that idea."

"I suggested it during an argument. I wasn't thinking straight. Now that I've had time to cool off, I realize it doesn't make sense. Brad's a big part of your life. We can't avoid talking about him."

"Talking about him makes you angry, and then we fight. You really want to do that?" I pick up my glass of milk and take a sip. I've never liked milk, but Giada said it's good for the baby.

"Just tell me what he said. Is Brad really okay with you living there with your drunk mom and her loser boyfriend?"

"Brad supports me in whatever I want to do, even if he doesn't always agree with it."

Nate huffs. "Yeah. Whatever."

"What's that supposed to mean?"

"He doesn't want you living there. He just doesn't want to tell you and have you think he's some elitist snob. But believe me, he is, and if his friends found out he was dating a trailer park girl, he'd drop you so fast."

"What the hell, Nate?" I bolt up from my chair, hitting the table and sending fries flying to the floor. "Did you seriously just say that?"

"You really want me to lie? I'm being a friend. Telling you what you need to hear. Brad isn't the guy he pretended to be when he was there last summer. The real Brad grew up in a mansion, hanging out in country clubs. He wants that life again, and he wants it with a girl who will fit in that world. I'm sorry, but that's just not you."

"Okay, I'm hanging up now."

"Riley, wait! I'm not saying it's just you. I don't fit in Brad's world either. Most people don't."

"Oh, please. He wasn't *that* rich. It's not like his parents were billionaires."

"No, but they were millionaires. My mom said Uncle John made over a million a year as a lawyer. Brad was raised with all that money. The kind of money you and I can't even imagine."

"And now it's gone. That's not his life anymore."

"You really think he wants to live like the rest of us? After having all that?"

"Yeah, actually I do. Brad's not obsessed with money like his parents are. He doesn't need a mansion to be happy."

"And you've known him for how long? A few months? I've known him my whole life, and I'm telling you, once he's had a year or two of being poor, he'll do anything to go back to the way he used to live."

"Nate, we're done here. I'm hanging up."

"Why are you getting mad? I'm trying to be a friend. I'm trying to save you from being hurt."

"Too late. Bye, Nate." I end the call and slam my phone down on the counter.

"What's up with you?" my mom asks as she comes down the hall from her room, wearing a short pink dress. She slips her heels on as she walks over to me.

"Nate called." I sit back down at the table and eat my cold fries.

"Why do you still talk to that boy?"

"Because he keeps calling," I mutter.

"So stop answering." She opens the fridge. "Why do we have all this milk?"

"It's supposed to be good for the baby," I say, getting up.

"That's bullshit. I never drank milk when I was pregnant. Hell, I drank whiskey and smoked cigarettes when I was pregnant with you and look how good you turned out."

"Times have changed, Mom." I go around her to the trash and toss out the rest of my fries. They don't even taste good. Pregnancy has made everything taste different than it should.

My mom comes over and leans down to my stomach. "How's my little grandkid today?"

"The one you told me to get rid of?" I say, glaring at her.

I'm still angry at her for saying that. I didn't even want her to know I was pregnant, but my constant vomiting gave it away. I had horrible morning sickness until just last week. When I told my mom I was pregnant, she was furious. She told me to get rid of it or I'd end up just like her, single and poor, living in a trailer. Now she tells me she only said it out of anger and that she's actually looking forward to the baby.

"Stop that," she says, smacking my arm. "Junior will hear you."

"Junior already knows." I roll my eyes as I go over to the couch. "He—or she—was there when you said it."

"It didn't hear nothin'," she says, joining me in the living room. "It was just a little peanut back then."

I lay down on the couch and put my feet up. They're killing me from work last night, and soon I have to leave to work another ten-hour shift. At least Dave lets me sit for part of the time.

"How's the job search?" I ask my mom as she looks for something behind the TV.

"Same as always. You know how it is. You fill out the application and never hear back."

"Actually, no. They usually call me back. Any chance you're putting a fake number on there?"

"Found it!" She pops up from behind the TV holding a tiny bottle of vodka.

"Where'd you get that?" I ask, because I've hidden all the cash from her, and the checkbook. I've taken over paying the bills and I no longer give her money. If she wants something, she has to get a job. She hasn't yet because she keeps finding guys to buy her stuff.

She smiles. "I might've swiped it when you were paying for gas."

"You stole it? From the place I work? Mom, you could've got me fired!"

"Why? You weren't the one who took it." She opens the bottle and drinks it. "Had to hide it so Jerry wouldn't find it."

I get up. "That's it. You're never coming with me again. To get gas. Grocery shopping. I'm not taking you with me anymore."

She shrugs. "Whatever."

"Mom, I'm serious. This has to stop. The drinking. The stealing. The lying. It has to stop."

She saunters over to me. "Says who? My little girl who got knocked up? You were supposed to be the responsible one."

"I still am. And I'm moving out as soon as I save up the money."

She laughs. "You'll never move out. It's you and me, sugar. Forever."

"I'm ready," Jerry says, walking out of her room wearing jeans and a t-shirt, his hair wet from the shower. "Let's go."

"See ya, darling," my mom says, blowing me a kiss as they leave.

I'm too angry at her to say goodbye. She doesn't think I'll ever leave? She's wrong. As soon as I get enough money, I'm out of here. There's no way I'm raising my child in this trailer. I don't even want to be in this town.

I want to be with Brad. But that's just not possible.

CHAPTER TWO

BRAD

"Hey, man," Todd says, standing at the door as I go in my dorm room. "Got big plans for tonight?"

"Yeah. Hot date with the library."

"Are you serious? It's Friday night. You're in New York City. Get out there and do something. You want to go see this band with us? Charlie and James already left. I'm meeting them there."

"Love to, but I can't. I've got a test on Monday and I'm behind on the reading."

"You can study this weekend."

"I have a paper due next week. I want to get started on it. And I need to hit the gym. But we could meet up for lunch tomorrow."

"Can't. I have to drive home for my sister's birthday."

Todd's family lives in Connecticut so it's a short drive home. His father is a doctor and owns a family practice clinic, the kind I'm hoping to open someday. Todd's in his second year of medical school. When he's finished with school, he'll go to work at his dad's clinic and take it over when his dad retires.

Todd and I met at a coffee shop near campus my first week here. He knows a ton of people. Hanging out with him has helped me make a lot of friends in a short amount of time.

"So what's up with you and Riley?" Todd asks, leaning against the door frame.

"What do you mean?" I take my laptop from my backpack and set it on the desk.

"Are you two still going out? You haven't said much about her this week. I thought maybe something happened."

"Nothing happened. She's just been busy so I haven't been able to talk to her. She works two jobs and has been putting in overtime at one of them."

"Why doesn't she just move here?"

"She can't afford it. You know how much rent is around here. Even working two jobs she wouldn't be able to afford it."

"So you're just going to keep doing the long distance thing? For four years?"

"That's the plan." I check my phone to see if she sent me any messages. She didn't.

"You've dated this girl for how long? A few months?"

"Four, almost five."

"But you were only together for what, three of those months?"

I put my phone away and look at him. "What's your point?"

He shrugs. "I'm just saying it seems like you're giving up a lot to be with a girl you only dated a few months."

"I'm not giving anything up. I'm in school in New York,

just like I planned. I offered to stay with her instead of coming here, but she insisted I go."

His brows rise. "Maybe because she has someone else?"

I fold my arms over my chest. "She isn't cheating on me. And if you want us to stay friends, you better stop talking about her that way."

"I'm not saying she's a bad person. I'm just saying it's hard to be this far away from the person you're dating. You have to admit it's not easy."

"It's not, but we both knew this is how it would be. We talked about it and decided we'd make it work."

"And *is* it? Working?"

"We're still dating. I still love her."

"Brad, no offense, but spending Friday night in the library when you live in one of the best cities in the world is a sign this isn't working."

"Maybe not for you, but I'm fine with it. And I need the time to study. I can't let my grades slip." I get my phone out and text Riley.

"So if she lived on campus, you'd be studying tonight?" Todd asks.

"No, but she doesn't live here, so that's not an option."

He walks over to me. "I know you really like this girl, but dating her doesn't mean you can't go out and have fun now and then. Just come out with us tonight. Or meet up with us later. You don't have to study all night."

I smile. "You don't give up, do you?"

"Not when my friend is studying on a Friday night. That's just sad."

"Text me after the band," I say, giving him a pat on the shoulder. "Now get out of here so I can study."

When he's gone, I check my phone again. No new texts from Riley.

My phone rings and I smile when I see her name on the screen.

"Hey, I was just thinking about you," I say, answering the call. "Are you at work?"

"I was, but I left. I went home and slept. I just woke up and saw your text."

"It's good you're finally getting some rest, but I'm surprised you left work. You never leave early."

"I didn't want to. Dave made me go home. I wasn't feeling well and he told me to go home and sleep."

"You're sick?"

"No. I just didn't feel well. I'm better now."

"Riley, you gotta stop working all those hours. You have two jobs and now you're working overtime? It's too much."

"I need the money so I can move out."

"To New York?" I ask, wishing she'd agree to it but knowing she won't. I can't blame her for that. This city is so freaking expensive, and she's right when she says I wouldn't see her much. My classes are really hard. I have to study all the time just to keep up my grades. It wouldn't be fair to make her move here and then never see her.

"Brad, you know I can't move there."

"I know. I just really miss you."

"I miss you too," she says, her voice so weak I can barely hear her.

"Riley, I'm worried about you."

"Why?"

"You don't sound like yourself. You sound really tired."

"I just need to get a few more hours of sleep and I'll be fine."

"It's not just that. Lately, it seems like you never want to talk. You always say you're too tired, and when I call, you never say much." I pause. "Are you depressed?"

She laughs a little. "I'm not depressed, but I think my mom is. All she does is lie on the couch and watch TV."

"You think she'll ever get a job?"

"If I move out, she'll have to. I'm not going to keep paying her bills."

"Good. I'm glad you're not letting her take advantage of you anymore."

"I can't. Not with the—"

"The what?"

She clears her throat. "Nothing. I was just saying that with all the expenses I'll have living on my own, I wouldn't be able to help her even if I wanted to."

"Is she still with that guy?"

"Jerry? Yeah. He's here right now. They're in the living room watching a movie. He brought over a bottle of whiskey so I'm sure they're both drunk by now. I think she only keeps him around because he brings her booze. She can't afford to buy her own."

"Going back to you, I feel like you're not telling me something."

"What do you mean?"

"You haven't been yourself since I moved here. Actually, it was more like the week before I left. Did something happen that week?"

"No. Nothing," she says with a nervous laugh.

Maybe she *is* hiding something from me. What if Todd was right and she found someone else? But if she did, why would she keep dating me?

"Riley, what's going on?" I ask in a serious tone.

"Nothing. Why do you keep asking me that?"

"Because something feels off between us. It has for over a month. I keep telling myself it's because you're tired from work, but I think it's more than that."

"Brad, where this is coming from? If you've felt this way for over a month, why are you bringing it up now?"

"Because I'm realizing it's more than just you being tired. There's something else going on." I pause. "You didn't, um..." I don't want to say it. I know she wouldn't cheat on me, so why am I even going there?

"Didn't what?"

I don't answer, wishing I hadn't brought it up.

"Wait. Do you think I've been cheating on you?" she asks, getting angry.

"No. Just forget it. I shouldn't have said it."

"Brad, I would never do that. I can't believe you think I would."

"I didn't. It's just that someone said something today that —never mind. Let's stop talking about it."

She's quiet and so am I. This call isn't going well. The last one didn't either. It felt rushed, and in the few minutes it lasted, we didn't have much to say. I feel like we're not as close as we were, and it's worrying me.

I need to see her. I thought I could wait longer, but I can't.

"I'm flying you out here," I say.

"What?"

"I'm flying you out here."

"But I—"

"I'm not taking no for an answer. I don't care how busy you are with work. You can take a few days off to see your boyfriend. I'll pay for the ticket. I'll use the money I saved from last summer. I don't care what it costs. I have to see you, Riley. I can't wait any longer."

"You don't have to. That's actually why I called." Her voice sounds stronger now, and more excited. "I'm coming to see you!"

"Seriously?"

"Yeah. I already asked for the time off, but it's not for a couple weeks. Will that work?"

"Are you kidding? You can come here whenever you want."

"I just wanted to make sure you didn't have tests that week or—"

"It doesn't matter. I'll always make time for you." I feel myself smiling. "You have no idea how happy you've made me. I've been wanting to see you so fucking bad."

"I've wanted to see you too," she says, her voice getting quiet again.

"I'll pay for the ticket, or reimburse you if you already got it. And I'll pay for everything while you're here. I want your money to go toward getting out of that trailer."

"Is there a hotel nearby where I could stay?"

"You'll stay with me. I'll kick Anik out."

Anik is my roommate. He's from India and comes from a family of physicians. That's all I know about him. He's hardly ever here, and when he is, he's studying with headphones on.

"I don't want you kicking out your roommate."

"He won't care. He's never here anyway. He's always at the library. And his aunt and uncle live in Brooklyn. He can go stay with them for a few days. How long will you be here?"

"Just the weekend. I'll fly in Friday and leave on Sunday."

"That's not much time, but I'll take what I can get. I just want to see you."

"So what are you doing tonight?"

"Studying. And then later I'll probably meet up with Todd and his friends."

"Oh, yeah? Where are you going?"

"Not sure yet. They're going to hear a band. I'll meet up with them after that. I didn't want to go, but Todd won't get off my case if I don't. He thinks I spend too much time in my room."

"Why don't you go out more? Because you need to study?"

"That, and the fact I'm not looking for a date."

"Why would that matter?"

"Guys go out to meet girls. I'm not looking for a girl. I already have one."

"You can still go out. I don't want you not going out because of me. You've wanted to live in New York for years. Now that you're finally there, you should be out doing stuff. Going to new places. Meeting new people."

"I know. I just feel bad you're not with me. I want to do all those things with you."

"That's sweet, but I still want you to do those things."

"I can, but it won't be the same doing them without you."

I wait for her to say something, but she doesn't.

"I love you, Riley."

"I love you too." Her voice is quiet. Distant. Almost unsure. Is she questioning if she still loves me? I hope not, because I definitely still love her. I think about her all the time and miss her like crazy.

"Riley, are you sure everything's okay?"

"Yeah. I'm just really tired and I don't feel that great."

"Get some rest. I'll talk to you tomorrow, okay?"

"Yeah. Bye."

Despite what she said, I still feel like something's going on with her.

"WE'RE at the place down the street!" Todd yells into the phone. "The one with the red telephone booth?"

The bar he's at is really loud. I can barely hear him.

"Yeah, I know which one. Who else is there?"

"Just some guys. Girls." He laughs. "I'm too drunk to remember their names."

A guy yells something next to him and then some other guys start singing really loud.

"Maybe I'll just stay here," I tell him. "I don't really feel like drinking tonight."

"Too late. You promised you'd go out. C'mon. Just one drink."

"Yeah, okay. I'll be there soon."

Before meeting Riley, I wouldn't think twice about going out. In fact, I was always the one suggesting it. But now it feels wrong going out without her, especially to a bar.

When I get there, I can hear Todd's voice in the back of the room. I see James raising his glass in the air as a girl leans in to kiss him. Last I knew he had a girlfriend, but it's not the girl who just kissed him. This is why I don't feel right going to bars without Riley. Girls will assume I'm single and try to make a move, especially if they're drunk.

"Hey," I say, coming up behind Todd.

He turns around and smiles. "Hey, man, you made it!"

"Yeah. How was the band?"

"Awesome. You should've been there."

"Maybe next time."

"Here." He hands me a shot glass. "It's on James. He got his allowance early."

James is a spoiled rich kid who still gets an allowance from his parents even though he's 23. He gets $5000 a month, which he thinks is nothing. If I got an allowance like that, I'd use it to get Riley an apartment here. I'm so freaking excited I get to see her soon. I'm already counting the days until she gets here.

"Brad!" James says as he whacks me on the back. "Nice of you to join us." He points to my shot glass. "Drink up. That's premium tequila."

I drink it down, then set the glass on the table.

"Have another," James says, holding up a shot glass. "It's on me."

"No, thanks, I'm good."

"He won't stop until you have at least two," a girl says from beside me.

I didn't even see there until now. She's tiny, maybe five foot two, with short dark hair and wearing a tight black sweater, jeans, and very expensive heels, like the kind my mom used to buy before we lost all our money.

The girl leans up to talk in my ear. "Just take it and toss it."

I take the shot glass from James. "Thanks!"

"Have as many as you want. I'm gonna go take a leak." He stumbles to the bathroom.

"He's such an idiot when he's drunk," the girl says. "But he's actually quite brilliant when he's sober. How do you know him?"

"I'm friends with Todd," I say, looking to see where he

went. He was standing right next to me and now he's gone. "He introduced me to James. I've only been out with him a few times."

"Are you new to town?" she asks.

I nod. "Been here a little over a month. Going to med school at Columbia."

"So am I. Second year. I'm guessing you're a first year?"

"Yeah. It's been challenging so far. I feel like I can barely keep up."

"It gets better once you're used to it."

She's cute. Classy. Has a nice smile. She'd be just my type if it were a year ago. Back then I only dated girls my parents would approve of—smart, sophisticated girls who come from money, dress well, and would impress my parents. I don't know why I wanted their approval so much, but I don't now. Finding out my dad's a cheater and gambling addict made me stop trying to please him, or my mom.

"Corinne Carmichael," the girl says, holding her hand out to me.

I set the shot glass down and shake her hand. "Brad Whittaker."

"Nice to meet you." She smiles. "What are you planning to specialize in?"

"I'm not. I'm going into family medicine."

"Oh," she says, her smile now strained as she tries to hide her obvious disapproval.

"What about you?"

"Radiology. My father's a heart surgeon so he was hoping I'd do the same, but it's not for me."

"I see you met Corinne," Todd says, coming up beside me with a beer in his hand.

"Todd and I went to camp together when we were kids," Corinne says to me.

"It was science camp," Todd says. "We were in a building, not out in the woods."

"There were woods there," she insists. "And they let us outside during breaks."

"Yeah, we were really roughing it," Todd says with a laugh. He turns to me. "If you ever need a tutor, Corinne's your girl. She's at the top of her class. Beats me on every test, which pisses me off, but it's too much work to keep up with her so I've just accepted it now."

She rolls her eyes. "Don't listen to him. He makes me sound intimidating, which I'm not. I also don't like talking about my grades. But the offer is real. If you're having trouble with your classes, I'm happy to help."

"Thanks, but I'm doing okay. I just need to study more."

"The guy spends all his time at the library," Todd says to Corinne. "I had to practically beg him to come out tonight." Todd pats me on the shoulder. "I gotta go find James. I'm supposed to be keeping an eye on him tonight." He takes off.

"It's good to take breaks," Corinne says to me. "There's such a thing as too much studying."

"It's not just that," I say. "I also have a girlfriend so I don't really have a need to go out."

"Is she here tonight?" Corinne asks.

"No. She lives in Oklahoma."

"Is she moving here?"

"No. We're doing the long distance thing."

Her brows lift. "For four years?"

I shrug. "It'll go fast. We talk on the phone a lot and she's coming out here in a few weeks."

"Still, it's not easy being that far away."

"We're making it work," I say, although the more time that goes by, the more I feel like Riley and I are drifting apart. But I don't know how to fix it.

"You like art?" Corinne asks.

"Kind of. Why do you ask?"

"A bunch of us are going to MOMA tomorrow to check out the latest exhibit." She smiles. "Don't worry. We're not art snobs. It's just something to do. You should come with us."

"I really need to study."

"C'mon. It's just a few hours. And it'll give you a chance to meet some people."

"Who are you going with?"

"Some friends I know from school. Second and third years. They're all really fun. I think you guys would get along great."

"Are we talking all girls?"

"No." She laughs. "There's a mix. Todd might even go. He hasn't confirmed yet. Oh, and we're all going for dinner afterwards, but you wouldn't have to if you want to go back and study."

"I'll think about it."

She checks her phone. "I didn't realize it was so late. I need to get back. I have yoga at five tomorrow."

"In the morning?"

"Yeah." She looks around. "I think Charlie left. He was supposed to walk me back." She sighs. "I knew I couldn't count on him." She looks up at me. "Would you mind walking me home? I don't feel safe walking alone this time of night."

I know she's only asking as a friend, so why do I feel guilty for considering it? Riley wouldn't be mad. She'd want me to make sure this girl got home safe.

"Sure," I say to Corinne. "I can walk you back."

"Thanks. I really appreciate it. I hate that I even have to ask, but last year a friend of mine was attacked while walking to her apartment at night, so now I'm extra careful."

"I understand."

"Let me just settle my tab." She hurries off to the bar to pay her bill, then returns. "Okay, I'm ready."

"You're leaving already?" Todd asks as we're heading to the door.

"I'll be back. I'm just walking her home."

He smiles. "You're a good man, Whittaker."

We go out the door and head down the street.

"So tell me about your girlfriend," Corinne says. "What does she do?"

"She's a waitress. And she works the night shift at a gas station."

"She didn't go to school?"

"No, but she's a really hard worker. She works harder than anyone I know."

"She couldn't do those things here? I mean, there are plenty of waitress jobs here in the city."

"Living here costs a fortune. Waitressing wouldn't pay enough."

"It could if she worked at the right place. There are a lot of fancy restaurants around here where she could make good money in tips."

"I guess, but even if she lived here, I wouldn't see her much. Between classes and studying, I don't have much free time."

Corinne glances at me. "Are you sure this is what you want?"

"What do you mean?"

"I mean this girl. Do you really want to be with a girl you never see?"

"I love her. I'm not breaking up with her just because I can't see her."

"But if she loved you, wouldn't she move out here? If it were me, I'd want to be with the man I love."

"She *does* want to be with me. But being with me means leaving her hometown. Leaving her mom behind. Her friends."

"Aren't you more important than all that?"

"Corinne, don't take this the wrong way, but I'm not comfortable talking about this with you. We just met, and you don't know the situation. It may not work for you, but it works for Riley and me. Let's just leave it at that."

She nods. "So about tomorrow, you think you can make it?"

"I'm not sure."

She gets her phone out. "Give me your number and I'll text you in the morning to let you know when we're leaving in case you decide to come."

I give her my number, then feel the guilt creeping back again. *She's just a friend*, I remind myself. I can give a friend my number.

We arrive at her building and I wait for her to get her key out and unlock the door.

"Thanks for doing this," she says, standing in the doorway.

"No problem."

"You going back to the bar?"

"Probably not. I think I'll just go back to my room and call Riley."

"Tell her she's a lucky girl," Corinne says with a smile.

She goes inside and I head back to my building. When I get to my room, I start to call Riley, then realize she's at work. It's nearly impossible to reach her when she works so much. She's my girlfriend and yet I only talk to her an hour or two a week. I need more than that, and so does our relationship if it's going to survive.

I really want to believe Riley and I can make this work, but sometimes I wonder if we really can.

CHAPTER THREE

Riley

The moment I see Brad at the airport, I run to him. It's loud and crowded and I'm sure I'm bumping into people as I try to get past, but the only thing I'm focused on is him. God, I've missed him. I've missed him so much.

"Riley!" he yells when he sees me. His smile is bigger than I've ever seen it. I'm sure mine is just as big.

"Watch it!" some guy yells as I bump his arm, trying to squeeze through the crowd.

I see an opening and race through it to Brad's waiting arms. He wraps me in a hug and picks me up off the ground.

"Brad," I say, laughing. "Put me down."

"Never," he says, giving me a kiss. "I'm not letting you go until you have to leave."

"I missed you," I say, resting my head on his shoulder and breathing in his scent. It's different. I recognize his cologne, but the other part is new. He smells like the city now. Whatever that is, I'm not sure, but it's not the smell of home.

"I missed you too," he says, kissing my head, his arms still wrapped around me.

My eyes squeeze shut as I try not to cry. This trip, this visit, has a purpose. I'm here to either tell Brad the truth, or end things between us. I haven't decided what I'm going to do, but either way, I know it won't end well.

Telling Brad the truth means taking away his dream and everything he's worked for. He'll quit school and get a job and we'll move some place we can afford to raise our child. If I don't tell him about the baby, my only choice is to break up with him. This is my last chance to see him before I'm showing. I already have a slight bump to my belly, but it's small enough to just look like I'm bloated or put on a few pounds. I doubt Brad will even notice. But if he saw me in a few months, or even just a few weeks, he would know.

I don't want to lose him. I love him and want a life with him, but not if that means taking away everything else that's important to him. Last summer, he told Nate he wasn't sure he even wanted kids, and that if he had them, it wouldn't be for a long time. So how would he react to the news if I told him? Would he be angry? What if he didn't want the baby?

"Are you hungry?" Brad asks, setting me down.

"Starving. I didn't have a chance to eat breakfast this morning and I didn't know they charged for food on the plane."

"Riley, you should've got something. I would've paid for it."

"It's fine. I was too nervous to eat."

"So how'd it go?" He looks at me like he hasn't seen me in years. I'm doing the same to him, but for a different reason. I'm memorizing how he looks so I'll never forget him in case this is the end. "How was your first trip on an airplane?"

"It was okay. I was really nervous at first, but the lady next to me calmed me down. She had her baby with her." I smile. "A really cute little girl."

"Ugh, babies."

"What do mean?" I ask, my pulse ticking up at his reaction. "You don't like babies?"

"I like babies, just not on planes. I know they can't help it, but all that crying can get to a person, especially if you're nervous about the flight. But you were okay?"

"I was fine. And this baby didn't cry. She fussed a little, but then she fell asleep."

"That's good. So how about lunch? We can grab something by campus or I can take you somewhere touristy, like Times Square. You pick. What sounds best?"

"Somewhere by campus is fine. I don't need to see anything touristy. I'm here to see you, not tourist stuff."

"Okay, but if you change your mind I'm happy to take you wherever you want to go." He slings my duffle bag over his shoulder and takes my hand. "Let's get out of here."

As we leave the airport, I'm hit with more smells. Car exhaust. Bus fumes. The smell of roasted nuts from the stand across the street. Pregnancy has made me super sensitive to smells and sometimes they make me sick, like right now.

"You okay?" Brad asks as I stop suddenly.

"I think so." I take a deep breath just as a bus goes by, leaving behind a trail of exhaust fumes. I cough and almost throw up.

Brad gets in front of me. "Riley, what's wrong?"

"I don't feel good," I say, clutching my stomach. "Is there a bathroom nearby?"

"Just the one in the airport. You want to go back in?"

"Yeah. And fast."

He takes my hand and pulls me through the crowds of people back into the airport terminal. "There's one right there." He points to it, then stops. "Shit, it's closed for maintenance."

I'm sweating now and my mouth is dry. "I need to find a bathroom." I break from his hand and go the opposite direction, heading toward baggage claim.

Why is this happening? Why now? I've gone a whole week without getting sick. I thought the morning sickness was starting to go away, but I guess it's not.

"Riley, wait up!" Brad grabs my hand, stopping me. "Don't race off like that. I'll lose you."

"I need a bathroom," I say, frantically searching for one. "There's gotta be one by baggage claim."

"Let's head down there and find out."

As we're hurrying to find it, a man walks by holding a hotdog that's loaded with onions. The smell is all it takes for my stomach to decide it can't wait any longer. I spot a garbage can and push through the crowd to get to it, barely making it in time.

"Riley!" I hear Brad calling my name as I hurl into the trash can.

I didn't want Brad to see this. It's gross, and now he's going to wonder what's wrong with me.

"Riley, I'm sorry," he says, rubbing my back as I remain bent over the trash can. "I didn't know you were so sick. Was it the plane? Did it make you nauseous?"

I nod, then throw up again.

"Disgusting," a man says as he walks by.

I look up and see him shaking his head.

"Forget him," Brad says. "Just do what you need to do."

I slowly stand up, wiping my mouth. "I think I'm done."

"Let's find a bathroom so you can clean up." He goes up to the security guy who's standing by the exit door. "Can you tell me where the closest bathroom is?"

"Keep walking," he says, pointing to the baggage claim area. "It's past baggage and around the corner."

"Thanks." Brad hurries back to me. "It's not far. Think you can make it?"

"Yeah," I say, but I'm not sure I can. I'm feeling sick again.

We manage to make it to the bathroom and I race to the stall. After another round of vomiting, I go to the sink and wash out my mouth and splash water on my face.

"Isn't pregnancy great?" the woman next to me says as she looks in the mirror.

I glance at her. Was she talking to *me*?

"I heard you getting sick," she says. "I was the same way with my first two, but the last one was a breeze. Didn't get sick one time."

How did she know I was pregnant? I could've thrown up because I have the flu, or food poisoning. Why does she think I'm pregnant? Do I *look* pregnant? I'm not showing, so what gave it away?

If a stranger can tell that I'm pregnant, there's a good chance Brad will too. Or maybe it was just a lucky guess.

"It's your first, I assume?" the lady asks with a smile.

I just stare at her, too confused to respond any other way.

"Congratulations. Oh, and for the nausea I recommend ginger tablets. They worked wonders for me." She gives me a smile as she leaves.

When I come out of the bathroom, Brad's waiting there. "You okay?"

"Yeah. I'm better now. I'm really sorry about this."

"Don't be. You can't help it if you're sick. Did you get sick on the plane too?"

"No. And I'd rather not talk about it. Talking about it makes me feel sick again."

"Got it." He takes my hand. "Why don't we just go back to my place and you can sleep?"

"I think I need to eat something. I haven't eaten since last night."

"Riley, you can't go that long without eating. It's not good for you."

It's not good for the baby either, but I was too nervous to eat this morning. I was nervous about the plane and nervous about seeing Brad. I want to tell him about the baby, but still don't know if I should. He seems really happy here and I don't want to take that away.

We go back out to the street and Brad hails a cab. "I'd normally take the subway, but that's not the place to be if you're feeling sick. The smells alone are enough to—well, let's just say it's better to take a cab."

The cab takes us past streets packed with people. They all look very serious as they weave through the crowded streets, talking on their phones. The buildings are old and some look really run down. There's garbage lined up in front of them and I notice something running along the curb.

"What's that?" I ask, pointing to it.

"A rat," Brad says like it's no big deal. "They're everywhere."

"That was a rat?" I ask, horrified. "It was the size of a squirrel."

He laughs. "They get pretty big."

The cab driver slams on the brakes and says something in a foreign language.

"Traffic's backed up," Brad says. "Could take a while."

I look up and see a line of cars that aren't moving. More cars surround us on both sides. I'm feeling claustrophobic. I've never been in a city this big and crowded. I'm used to rural Oklahoma with its wide open spaces and small towns.

"We can get out and walk if you're not feeling well," Brad says, rubbing my hand.

"How much longer do you think it'll be?"

"Maybe another half hour?"

"And if we walked?"

"Probably about forty-five minutes."

"We can stay here. Is there something going on, or is it always like this?"

"It's always like this. This is actually not that bad for a Friday."

Not that bad? Is he kidding? We're not even moving, and nobody around us is either.

I just got here and I already don't like this city. It's too big, too crowded, and there are giant rats running around. Why would Brad want to live here? Why does he like it so much?

A half hour later, we're moving, but barely.

"Probably ten more minutes," Brad says, squeezing my hand. "You still okay?"

"I could use some fresh air. You want to walk the rest of the way?"

"Sure." He leans toward the driver and gets his attention. "Hey, we need to get out of here."

"It's a few more miles," the driver says in a heavy accent.

"Yeah, but she's not feeling well. She needs to get out and walk."

The driver glances at me in his mirror, then quickly veers into the other lane, pulls up to the curb, and slams on the brakes. He jumps out and goes to the trunk to get my bag. Brad helps me out of the car, then goes up to the cab guy and gives him a fifty-dollar bill.

The guy takes it and gets back in the car. I assume he's going to get change, but instead he drives off.

"He just took off with your money!" I say to Brad.

"What do you mean? I had to pay him."

"Yeah, but he didn't give you your change."

"There isn't any. I gave him the fare and a tip."

"It cost fifty dollars? Are you serious?"

He laughs. "I told you this city is expensive. Don't worry about it. Everything is on me this weekend." He takes my hand and starts walking. "Check out the buildings around here. The architecture is amazing. Sometimes I just go on walks to look at the buildings."

I'm not sure what's so great about them. They all look pretty much the same to me, not that I'm looking too closely. I'm trying to keep my eyes on the sidewalk so I don't bump into anyone.

"This place is good," he says, pointing to a narrow restaurant wedged between two buildings. "Todd and I go there for pizza sometimes."

"I could eat pizza. You want to go in?"

"No. They don't have places to sit. Just long tables to stand at." We keep walking and pass by a bar. "That's the place I went to a few weeks ago."

"Where you met Corinne?"

When Brad told me about Corinne, I was immediately jealous, but he assured me they're only friends and I believed him. Brad wouldn't cheat on me. And Corinne has a boyfriend, which made me feel better.

"Yeah, it was the night James was buying drinks for

everyone in the bar. His tab had to have been at least a couple thousand. Maybe more."

"Wow. I could buy a car with that kind of money."

"Speaking of that, when do you lose your truck?"

"I'm still not sure. The parole hearing keeps getting delayed."

"How soon before you'll have enough saved to buy your own?"

"Probably another year. I don't have enough money to get an apartment and a car. It's one or the other."

"Maybe you should get the car first."

"I can't. I have to get out of that trailer. I'm not living there after the—" I cough on my words, panicking because I almost mentioned the baby. I'm so used to talking to Giada and April about the baby that the words almost slipped out.

"After what?" Brad asks.

"After the winter. That's my goal. I promised myself I'd be out by March, but I'd like to be out sooner than that if I can. If I lose the truck, I'll take the bus and keep working extra shifts until I can buy a car."

"So you're really going to do this?" Brad asks, smiling at me.

"Move out? Yeah. I told you I was. You didn't think I was serious?"

"I wasn't sure. I know how much you worry about your mom."

"I'll still worry about her, but I can't keep living with her. I need my own space. My own life. I'll go and check on her, but she's going to have to learn to take care of herself."

"It's good to hear you say that."

"Hey, Brad," some guy says as he walks toward us. He looks rich, wearing black pants with a gray sweater, a leather messenger bag slung over his shoulder. He stops just in front of us. "You going tomorrow night?"

"No, I've got a visitor." Brad puts his arm around me. "This is my girlfriend, Riley."

The guy looks at me and smiles. "So you're the Riley he's always talking about. We were starting to think you didn't exist." He holds out his hand. "I'm Charlie. I live on Brad's floor."

"Nice to meet you."

He turns back to Brad. "Why don't you guys just stop by for an hour or two? Todd will be there, and James. And of course me, which is reason enough to go," he says with a laugh.

"Sorry, but I want this weekend to be just Riley and me. I only have her for a couple days and I don't know when I'll see her again."

Maybe never if I break up with him this weekend. I don't know if I can do it. Even if it's for the best, I don't know if I can actually say the words.

"I understand," Charlie says. "Corinne won't be happy about it." He smiles. "Who's going to walk her home?"

"You. Like you should've done all the other times. Don't go getting drunk and taking off again. It's not safe for her to be walking home alone."

"Yeah, yeah, I'll walk her home," he says, rolling his eyes. "I'll see ya later, man."

"Yeah, see ya."

We continue down the street.

"You've walked Corinne home more than once?" I ask, wondering why he never told me that. I thought he only walked her home the night they met.

"I have to, because Charlie keeps ditching her. I don't know why she puts up with it."

"She can't find anyone else to walk her home?"

"They're all too drunk. They wouldn't be much help if someone tried to attack her."

"She could just wait until her friends leave and they could all go as a group."

"She doesn't stay out as late as them. She does early morning yoga."

"How many times have you walked her home?"

"I don't know. Maybe three or four?"

He's walked this girl home three or four times? Why does this keep happening? And why Brad? Is she trying to date him? But she knows he has a girlfriend, and she has a boyfriend. She's dating Charlie.

"Charlie's still her boyfriend, right?" I ask.

"She doesn't call him that. He's more like a friend with benefits."

"And it's the same for him?"

"Yeah. They have an open relationship. They're not exclusive."

Meaning she might be interested in Brad. Why else would she keep inviting him to do stuff? It's always with other people, but still, he's gone with her to parties, museums, art exhibits, bars. It didn't bother me when I thought she had a serious boyfriend, but now I'm getting angry. She didn't need Brad to walk her home all those times. She just did that to be alone with him. And he didn't tell me!

"Can I ask you something?" I say as we walk hand-in-hand.

"Go ahead."

"Do you like her?"

"Who?"

"Corinne. I mean, if you were single, is she someone you would date?"

He shrugs. "I don't know. Never thought about it."

"Then think about it now. Would you date her if both of you were single?"

"I'd have to get to know her better, but I guess it's possible." He stops and turns me toward him. "You don't have to be worried about Corinne. Or any other girl. You're the one I love. I'm not interested in anyone else." He kisses me. "Let's go inside. We'll drop your stuff off at my room and then we'll go eat."

I look up at the tall brick building. "This is where you live?"

"Yeah. What do you think?"

"It's not what I expected."

"What do you mean?"

"I guess I pictured more of a college setting. This looks more like a hotel in a big city."

He chuckles. "The dorms are actually more like apartments. This isn't the typical college campus. It can't be. Not when it's in a city like this." He opens the door for me. "I love it. It feels more grown-up, like I'm in the real world now, not just some kid going to college. I'm still going to classes, but it's different, you know?"

I don't, because I never went to college. I've never even been on a college campus. That's a world I know nothing about. I just know I wouldn't like this. I wouldn't want to live here.

"You coming?" Brad asks, waiting at the elevator.

"Yeah." I walk over to him.

He pulls me into his side and kisses me. "I love having you here. I wish I could convince you to stay."

And I'm wishing he were back home with me. Back in a small town that's quiet and safe and affordable. A place that's good for raising a baby.

I can't live here with a baby. Just getting around is a nightmare with all the people and the traffic. I don't like it here. I don't feel comfortable. But Brad does. He loves it. So how could we possibly make this work? How could we find a solution that works for both of us? And that's best for the baby?

I'm starting to feel sick again. Not because of the pregnancy, but because my decision is becoming clearer. And it's not the one I want to make.

CHAPTER FOUR

BRAD

"I need to take a shower," Riley says as we go in my apartment. "Could you put my food in the fridge?"

"Hey." I grab her hand and come around to face her. "You sure you're okay?"

She forces out a smile. "Would you stop asking me that? I'm fine. I just feel gross after being on a plane all day." She looks around. "Your roommate's not here, right?"

"No, he texted and said he'll be back Sunday night." I give her a kiss. "Go shower. Maybe it'll make you feel better."

She goes down to my room while I go to the kitchen and put her food in the fridge. I took her to dinner, but she only ate half her meal.

I'm worried about her. She seems really tired and keeps saying she feels queasy. Any motion sickness from the airplane should've worn off by now so I'm wondering if she's sick with the flu or something.

"Everything okay in there?" I ask from outside the

bathroom door. She's been in there a half hour with the water running.

"I'm almost done," she says.

"No rush. I was just making sure you're okay."

The shower shuts off. "I'm fine, but I think I forgot a towel. Should I use yours?"

"I'll get you a new one. Hold on." I go to my closet and grab one, then return to the bathroom. "Can I come in?"

She opens the door, looking more awake now and wearing that beautiful smile I love so much.

"Thanks," she says, taking the towel from me.

"Let me help you with that." I push the door open the rest of the way and join her in the bathroom.

"I think I'm good," she says, wrapping the towel around her.

"You sure? Because it looks like you could use some help drying off."

I slowly unwrap the towel from around her, my eyes drinking her in. I don't know how it's possible, but her body looks even more beautiful than I remember.

When we were together last summer, I memorized how she looked. How her body felt. Her silky skin. Her soft curves. But I must not have captured the memory as well as I thought because her curves seem rounder now. Maybe she's put on a little weight. If so, I like it. She was too skinny before. She looks more like a woman now. Her hips are more curved. Her thighs have more shape. And her breasts...damn, they're gorgeous. Fuller. Rounder.

I reach up to touch them and she flinches.

"What's wrong?" I ask, taking my hand back.

"Nothing." She softly smiles. "Just a little tender."

"Why are they—"

"Period next week," she quickly says.

That explains the larger breasts and the fuller appearance of her body. She's retaining water.

"So I can't—"

"You can," she says, bringing my hand back to her breast.

I drop the towel and kiss her. "God, I've missed you."

"I missed you too."

I kiss her again, then drop to my knees and wrap my hands around her waist. I suck her nipple into my mouth and she gasps, grabbing my shoulders, her fingers digging into my t-shirt. I sit back and rip it off, then move to her other breast as my hands slide slowly down her ass to her thighs.

"I love your body," I say, kissing my way down her center. I stop at her belly, noticing its slight curve. I like her body fuller like this. I wish it wasn't just temporary.

"Don't," she says, pushing me away.

"Don't what?" I ask, looking up at her.

"Don't kiss me there."

"Why?"

"I don't like it."

"Since when? You used to love it when I kissed your stomach."

"I don't anymore." She grabs the towel and covers herself.

"Riley, what's wrong? Why are you covering up?"

"I just...I feel really fat right now and I don't like you seeing me like this. Can we just go in the bedroom and turn the lights off?"

"We can, but I'd rather stay here and finish what I was doing." I reach up and gently remove her hand from the towel. "And you're not fat. You're beautiful."

The towel drops to the floor.

"Brad, no." She covers herself with her arms.

"I want to look at you," I say, lowering her arms to her sides. "I want to touch you." I run my hands over her body, my eyes following their path over her breasts, her belly, the gentle curve of her hips, her ass. I pull her closer and lean down to kiss her stomach.

She tenses up. "Brad." She goes to cover her stomach, but I take her hands and put them back at her sides.

I look up at her. "Don't think for one second you're not beautiful. You're perfect. You're absolutely perfect."

Her eyes are red and I notice the tears in them.

"Riley, what's wrong?" I reach up and cup her face.

"Nothing," she says, shaking her head. "I just really miss you."

"I'm right here."

She nods and sniffles. "But then you'll be gone."

"Only until we see each other again."

She shuts her eyes as a tear runs down her cheek.

"We'll make this work, Riley," I say, wiping the tear from her cheek. "I know it's hard but we'll make it work."

She opens her eyes, her eyes locked on mine. "I love you, Brad. For always."

"I love you too."

Her eyes fall shut as my hands move over her skin. Her luscious curves. Her breasts. She has me so turned on I can't wait another second to be with her.

I stand up and take her hand as I kiss her. "Let's go."

We go to my room and I lead her to the bed. She gets under the covers as I strip off the rest of my clothes. I slide in beside her and kiss her, then reach over to the nightstand to get the condom.

"I remembered this time," I say, ripping open the package.

"Oh, um, we don't need it," she says.

"But last time you said you—"

"I know, but I'm on the pill and we've only been with each other so we can skip it."

I look at her. "You sure? Because I don't mind if it makes you feel better."

"No," she says, shaking her head. "We don't need it."

"Okay." I toss the condom aside, more than happy to go bare. Riley's the only girl I've ever been with like that.

I grab her around the waist and pull her body flush against mine. She wraps her leg around me, bringing us even closer. My cock is primed and ready, wanting her more than ever. I lower myself just enough to position it between her legs. I tease her with it, sliding it over her slick center.

"Brad," she moans, almost as if she's in pain from the wait. I totally get it. I'm the same way. I'm aching to be inside her.

I gently roll her onto her back and nudge her legs apart. I slide my cock inside her, slowly inching my way in so I can memorize how she feels. I'll need that later when she's gone.

"I love you," she whispers as I go to kiss her.

"I love you too." I cover her mouth with mine and push all the way inside her, as deep as I can go. She feels amazing. Slick and wet. We fit together perfectly, like we were made for each other.

I want to just stay like this, buried deep inside her, never letting her go. I want her to stay with me. I don't want her to leave.

"Oh, God," she screams, panting and moaning and writhing beneath me. We've only been at it a few minutes, but I'm covered in sweat, more from willing myself not to come than physical exertion. I'm right at the edge...so close. But I want Riley to get there first.

She bites her lip and I feel her muscles clench around me. She's there, and it's beautiful. I watch her, her body trembling, the slow sweet smile that takes over her face as she comes down from her release.

I kiss her lips, then down her neck. I pick up my pace again before finally getting my own much needed release. I've been waiting months to do that, but it was worth the wait.

Still catching my breath, I lay back on the bed. Riley lays beside me, resting her head on my chest.

"You good?" I ask, stroking Riley's hair.

"Yeah. I think we should just stay here and keep doing that until I have to leave on Sunday."

"Didn't I tell you? You're not leaving."

She pops her head up to look at me. "What?"

"I'm going to hide you in my room and not let you go."

She lays back down on my chest. "If only that would work."

"Maybe we could figure something out. Have you tried looking online for jobs here?"

"Brad, you know I can't live here. It's too expensive. And I...well, I don't really like it."

"You don't like New York? You haven't even seen it yet."

"I've seen enough to know I don't like it. It's loud and crowded and it has a funny smell."

"All big cities smell. Not just New York. Same for the noise and the crowds. That just comes with living in a big city."

"Then I guess I'm not a city girl."

"You get used to it. It took me a few days to adjust, but now I barely notice the crowds, or the smell. And I figure it's a tradeoff for all the great things this city has to offer. It's one of the greatest cities in the world, which you'd see if you had more time here. The museums. The restaurants. Central Park. There are so many things to see and do. I have four years here and won't even be able to do half of the stuff I want to do."

Riley runs her hand back and forth over my chest. "You really love it here, don't you?"

"I do. It was always my dream to live here and it turned out to be better than I imagined. The only thing that would make it even better is having you here."

"I'm sorry," she says with a sigh. "I wish things could be different."

"You don't have to be sorry. It's not your fault. I'm the one who moved here."

"I want to be with you, Brad." She raises up to look at me. "I really do. And if things were different, then maybe..."

"Maybe what?"

"Nothing." She looks down.

"No, finish what you were saying. If what was different? If you could afford it?"

"Well, yeah, but...never mind. It doesn't matter." She lays back on my chest.

"Riley, it *does* matter. If there's anything I could do to get you to move here, I'd do it. So tell me what it'll take."

"There's nothing you can do. It's not going to happen."

"But you said if things were different. What things?"

"Nothing. I don't know why I said that. Let's not talk about this anymore."

I run my hand up and down her back. "You know if I had the money, I'd move you here in a heartbeat. I'd put you in a nice apartment. Pay for whatever you need."

"I know you would."

"I'm so damn pissed at my dad. If he hadn't gambled all our money away, we'd be able to do this, Riley. We'd be living together right now."

"Your parents never would've paid for an apartment. Not if you were living with me. You can deny it all you want, but I know they don't like me."

"It doesn't matter. I'm not going to date a girl just because my parents like her. I've tried that. It doesn't work."

"They'll never accept me."

"Yeah? So? I don't need their acceptance."

She moves off me and lays on her side, facing me. "How did your mom and Nate's mom turn out to be so different? Nate's mom loves me. She would've been thrilled if I ended up with him. But her sister hates me. How could they be so different?"

"My mom doesn't hate you. She's just obsessed with what other people think. She thinks they'll look down on her if her son doesn't date the right girl. It's her own insecurities making her that way. It has nothing to do with you. My dad made her that way. If she and my biological dad were still together, things would've been different. She wouldn't have had all that money and would've turned out more like Aunt Kathy."

"I saw her at the store last week."

"Aunt Kathy?"

"Yeah. She invited me over for dinner, but I didn't feel right about going so I told her I was busy."

"You can still be friends with her. You don't have to avoid her because of Nate."

"I'm not avoiding her. I just think it's better if I keep my distance from anything Nate-related until more time has passed. I don't want to slip up and say something to Kathy that might get back to Nate."

"Like what?"

"Stuff about you. Us."

"You still talk to Nate. Doesn't he ask about us?"

"Not really, and if he does, he keeps it vague. He'll ask how you're doing, but that's it. I think he only asks to see if we're still together."

"He could find that out through my mom."

"I guess, but he still asks. You think you'll ever talk to him again?"

"Nate? Sure. I have no problem talking to him, but he won't return my calls." My phone rings. "Maybe that's him now."

"I doubt it," Riley says.

I reach over for my phone and check it. "It's Todd. I'll call him tomorrow."

"You can answer it. I don't mind."

"I've got my girl here." I slip my arm under her waist and slide her over to me. "I'm not taking time away from you to answer the phone." I kiss her and pull her body against mine. "I like your idea of staying in bed all weekend."

She smiles. "It doesn't have to be the whole weekend. We can go out. You can show me this city you love so much. Or maybe I could meet some of your friends. Didn't that guy say there's a party tomorrow night?"

"Yeah, but I don't want to go. Tomorrow's our last night together before you leave."

"We wouldn't have to stay long. I really want to meet your friends."

"Then we'll go, but not for more than an hour." I kiss her. "I want more of this."

"Me too," she says with a sexy smile as she pushes me back on the bed.

"What are you doing?"

"One time wasn't enough." She keeps the smile going as she gets on top of me.

"I can never get enough of you," I say, smiling back.

She pulls the sheet over her, covering as much of herself as she can. She's being really self-conscious of her body, which is unusual. Last summer her body was on display at the pool all the time, and she had no problem letting me see her when we'd make out. But now she keeps covering up, even when she doesn't need to. It's so dark in my room I can barely see her, the only light coming from a small lamp in the corner.

"Riley, stop," I say as she pulls the sheet around her waist. "Don't cover yourself up. Why do you keep doing that?"

"I was cold."

"Then I'll warm you up." I take the sheet from her and pull it down, then rub my hands over her arms. "You don't feel cold."

"I just had a chill. I'm better now." She grabs the sheet again and brings it up around her waist.

"Riley, what's going on with you?"

"What do you mean?"

"You're worrying me. You're not eating. You're throwing up. You're saying you're fat. You keep covering up your body. Is there something you're not telling me?"

"Like what?"

"Like an eating disorder."

"Eating disorder?" She laughs. "No, definitely not. You saw me eat dinner."

"But you only ate half of it. Normally you'd eat the whole thing. And you said you hadn't eaten all day."

"Because I was nervous about flying and I felt sick. It's not because I was trying to lose weight. I've been eating so much I've actually *gained* weight, which I'm sure you noticed."

"I did, but it's good. You were too skinny before. I love your body even more now. And I think those extra pounds went straight to your breasts." I smile as I reach up to touch them. "I think these doubled in size."

"Not double, but yeah, they've grown a little."

"More than a little. They barely fit my hand anymore." I pull her down to me. "You're beautiful, Riley. Don't ever doubt that. And don't ever try to change yourself for me. You'll be beautiful to me no matter what." I kiss her forehead.

"I love you," she whispers.

"I love you too."

We kiss, which leads us back to what we were doing before we got sidetracked by the weight discussion. I hope what I said got through to her. She has the most beautiful body I've ever seen, and those extra pounds have made her look even better.

We make love two more times that night, and again in the morning. Around ten, we get up and get ready and I take her out for a late breakfast. She asks me to show her around, so I take her to Times Square and Central Park. Afterwards, I'm wishing we'd just stayed home because those two things took up most of our day. It's already late afternoon, and by this time tomorrow she'll be gone. I need more time with her. Two days just isn't enough.

"What time is the party tonight?" she asks as she sits on the couch.

"We're skipping the party. I only have you for a few more hours. I'm not going to waste time at a party."

"It's not a waste. I really want to go. I want to meet your friends."

"You can meet them some other time," I say, sitting next to her. "Let's just spend tonight here. We can watch a movie. Cuddle on the couch. Go to bed early." I smile at her.

"We can go to the party and still do all that, C'mon, Brad. I really want to meet these people. This is your life now and I don't feel like I'm part of it when I don't know the people you're always talking about."

I sigh. "Okay, we'll go, but we're not staying long." I get out my phone and call Todd. "Hey, it's Brad. What's the deal with the party tonight?"

"You're going?" he asks, sounding surprised.

"Riley wants to meet you, so yeah, we'll stop by, but we're not staying long."

"That's great! I want to meet her too. We'll be there around eight at that bar down the street from James' apartment. Shit, I can't remember the name. The one with the red awnings, where we went for Dan's birthday?"

"Yeah, I know the one. I thought the party was going to be at Kendra's house."

"It was, until she found out James was cheating on her. He claims they weren't exclusive, but she didn't agree. Anyway, she's not hosting the party anymore so we had to move it to the bar. What time you think you'll be there?"

"Probably around eight so we can get home early. I have to get Riley to the airport in the morning."

"Short trip. Seems like she just got here."

"She did." I put my arm around her. "I'm not ready to let her go."

"Sorry, man. That sucks. I don't know how you guys do it. I could never date someone that far away."

"We're making it work. So anyway, we'll see you tonight."

"Yeah, see ya." I set my phone down and say to Riley, "We'll go there at eight, spend maybe an hour, then leave. Sound good?"

She doesn't answer, and when I look at her, I see her eyes are closed.

"Riley, are you asleep?" I gently shake her, but she's out cold. I lower my arm around her, holding her against me, and kiss her head. "I love you, Riley. I don't want you to go."

CHAPTER FIVE

Riley

When we arrive at the bar, two guys in the back wave at us.

"Brad!" one of them yells.

"That's Todd," Brad says, keeping hold of my hand as we make our way over to them. "The other guy is James. There's a good chance James is already drunk. He gets really stupid when he's drunk, so you have to ignore everything he says. Half the time it doesn't make sense."

"This must be the famous Riley," Todd says, getting up to shake my hand. I imagined him being big and tall, like Brad, but he's average height and thin. His hair is light brown and parted on the side, and he's wearing tan pants with a blue button-up shirt and a plaid tie. He looks like he should be going to a meeting, not a bar.

"You're kind of famous too," I say to Todd. "Brad talks about you all the time."

Todd laughs. "Sorry about that."

"No, it's good. I like hearing about his friends."

"He ever talk about *me?*" James asks, before downing a shot of something. He's dressed like Todd but without the tie, and his hair is longer and messier and a dark blond.

"He told me a little, not much," I say.

"James isn't that interesting," Brad kids.

"What the hell?" James says, getting up to hit Brad's arm but missing as he wobbles on his feet. "I'm a lot more interesting than the guy who never leaves his room."

"I'm kidding, man. Relax." Brad pats him on the shoulder. "You might want to sit down there, James, before you knock over a chair."

"I'm good." James reaches for the table to steady himself before sitting back down. It reminds me of my mom when she's drunk. She swears she's fine even when she's too drunk to stand up.

"I get why you keep this going," James says, smiling as he looks me up and down. "She's hot."

"Hey!" Brad says.

"What? I'm giving you a compliment. Your girlfriend's hot."

"Can't disagree," Todd mutters with a smile.

Brad smiles back as his arm goes around me. "She's more than hot. She's beautiful. And mine, so stop looking at her."

I look up at Brad and he gives me a kiss and smiles.

I love him so much. This trip has made me love him even more. I thought maybe I'd get here and realize the magic was gone. That whatever we had last summer wouldn't be there anymore. I was almost hoping for that so it'd make my decision easier. But unfortunately, that wasn't the case. The magic is still there, even more than before. I felt it the moment I saw him at the airport.

Brad is everything I could ever want in a guy and more. He's loving and sweet and smart and super hot. And the sex? Off the charts. When we did it last summer it was great, but yesterday? It was great times a thousand. Maybe it's the pregnancy. Does being pregnant make sex better? I need to look that up. Or ask Giada. I'm sure she's read about it in one of her books.

"Riley, what are you drinking?" Todd asks. "First one's on me."

"Oh, um, I'll just have a pop."

He laughs. "Pop?"

"Soda," Brad says. "They call it pop where she's from."

Todd smiles at me. "So what do you want in your pop? Whiskey? Vodka? What do you like?"

"Nothing. Just the pop. Soda. Whatever."

"You sure?" Brad asks.

"Yeah. I don't feel like drinking tonight. I don't want to risk having a hangover in the morning. I don't want to feel sick on the plane."

Brad looks back at Todd. "Riley was really sick when she got here. That was her first plane ride."

"Really?" James asks, lifting his head from the table. I thought he'd fallen asleep. "I practically lived on planes growing up. My father took us all over the world."

"And you never felt sick?" I ask.

"Never. But I wasn't crammed in a seat either. We took my father's jet. I'd die if I had to fly commercial," he says dramatically.

I look at Brad, who's shaking his head. "Rich people problems."

"I'll get the drinks," Todd says. "Brad, you're having bourbon, I assume?"

"Yeah, and don't skimp on me."

"Got it." He smiles. "The good stuff. Double. On the rocks."

As he leaves, I turn to Brad. "I didn't know you drank bourbon."

"I don't unless it's the good kind, which I can't afford right now unless someone else is buying."

"You should order a drink," James says to me, slurring his words. "Todd doesn't usually buy. He usually makes me do it. This is a rare occasion."

"You don't pay for the drinks," Brad says. "Your dad does."

James shrugs. "He owes me. He's a shitty father." He gets up. "I'm going to go call Deidre. See what the hell's taking so long."

"Who's Deidre?" Brad asks.

"My girlfriend," he says, like Brad should know that.

"What about Kendra?"

"Broke up with her," he says, steadying himself as he stands.

"When?"

He checks his watch. "Like an hour ago. Hey, when Todd gets back, tell him I want another whiskey."

James stumbles through the bar to the outside.

"Is he always that drunk?" I ask Brad.

"I've never seen him sober."

"And he's in medical school?"

"Second year."

"How does he pass his classes?"

"Apparently, he's a genius. Doesn't need to study much."

"Hey, Brad," I hear a girl say from behind us. I turn

around and see Corinne, or a girl who looks like her based on Brad's description.

He turns to face her. "Corinne, good to see you." He gives her a hug, which instantly makes me jealous. I know friends hug each other, but I don't like seeing my man hug a girl who I'm not convinced is only interested in being his friend.

"Corinne, this is my girlfriend, Riley," Brad says.

"Riley, it's so nice to meet you," Corinne says in a syrupy sweet tone as she shakes my hand.

"Nice to meet you too." I look around. "Is Charlie here?"

She seems confused. "How do you know Charlie?"

"We ran into him on the street yesterday," Brad says. "Is he coming tonight?"

"No, he decided to go downtown with some friends."

"How long have you and Charlie dated?" I ask.

"We're not really dating. We go out now and then, but it's nothing serious. Charlie isn't husband material the way this guy is." She smiles at Brad and my temper flares. Now I know why she made him walk her home all those times. She wants my boyfriend!

"Not sure I'm there yet," Brad says, not even noticing she's flirting with him. How could he not know? She's so obvious.

"C'mon Brad," Corinne says, smiling at him. "I'm sure if the right girl came along you'd be more than ready to get married."

I clear my throat.

Her eyes dart to me. "Oh, God, sorry," she rushes to say. "I didn't mean to imply you're not that girl. I just meant he might be ready for the husband role sooner than he thinks." She pauses, looking between Brad and me. "You two haven't dated that long, right? It's been a couple months?"

"We've been dating since May," I say in an angry tone.

"And it's October, so..." she stops to think. "That's barely six months. Far too soon to talk about marriage," she says with a laugh.

"Corinne, what are you drinking?" Todd yells from the bar.

"Vodka martini," she yells back.

"Did you wear this just for me?" James says, coming up behind Corinne and wrapping his arms her waist.

She turns to face him. "James, you know I'd never go out with you, so why do you keep trying?"

"Who said we have to go out?" he asks, leaning down to kiss her neck.

She smiles as she pushes him away. She's loving the attention and she's getting plenty, not just from Todd and James, but the other guys in the bar. She's wearing a really short, black skirt along with black tights and tall black boots. Her white sweater, which I'm sure is cashmere, is a plunging v-neck with nothing under it but a lacy push-up bra I could see when she leaned over to Brad.

"Martini," Todd says, handing Corinne her drink and kissing her cheek. "Glad you could join us."

"Always a pleasure to spend an evening with my boys," she says, before taking a sip of her drink.

"Soda," Todd says, handing me a glass. "And bourbon for Brad." He sets the glass down on the table.

"You're not drinking?" Corinne asks me.

"Not tonight." I sip my soda from the tiny straw as I keep my eye on her. Why would Brad be friends with this girl? Can't he see how fake and conniving she is?

"Todd," she says. "Walk me home tonight?"

"That's Brad's job," he says, which makes me even

angrier. Why is it Brad's job? Why can't she find someone else to walk her home?

"Don't you have girlfriends?" I ask.

She looks at me like she's offended. "Of course. Why do you ask?"

"You should bring them along when you go out. Then you'd have people to walk home with you."

"It never works out that way. They find guys when we're out and end up going home with them."

"Then maybe you should take a cab." I loop my arm around Brad's. "It's not my boyfriend's job to take you home."

She looks at Brad. "He's just being a nice guy. That's hard to find."

"Why don't we go sit down?" Brad says, leading me over to the table where Todd is sitting. James is next to him, sipping his drink. Corinne takes the open spot next to Brad. Could she be more obvious?

"So you're a hairstylist?" James asks me.

"She's not a hairstylist," Brad answers. "She just worked at a salon. It's where we met."

"I thought you met through your cousin," Todd says.

"That wasn't the first time we met, but yeah, she was friends with my cousin, Nate, for years. He told me about her, but I didn't meet her until last summer."

"Brad said you work at a gas station," Corinne says with a smirk before taking a sip of her martini.

"And a restaurant," I say.

"She's the hardest worker I know," Brad says, pulling me closer to give me a kiss. It's good he's being affectionate with me in front of Corinne. Maybe she'll get the hint he's taken.

But he may not be for long. If I break up with him, will he end up with Corinne? I hope not.

Ten minutes later, more people arrive. They all know Brad and gather around our table to talk to him. I'm not surprised he's made friends this quickly. He's outgoing, fun, and easy to talk to. And he seems to fit better with the people here than the ones he met last summer. Everyone here has a similar background to Brad. They grew up with money, went to private schools, and have traveled the world. They use big words and talk about art and politics and books they've read. Brad fits right in. I don't, not in the least. I'm nothing like these people, which makes me wonder why Brad continues to date me. Could we really work long-term with so little in common?

"Hey, man, you're leaving already?" a guy says as Brad gets up from the table. We've been here for two hours now. Brad's introduced me to so many people I've lost track of their names. I think this guy's name is Pete.

"We need to get going," Brad says, taking my hand as I get up. "Riley's leaving in the morning."

"When are you coming back?" the guy asks.

"I'm not sure," I say, noticing Corinne's smile. Is she smiling because she doesn't think I'll be back?

She stands up. "Nice meeting you, Riley."

"Yeah, you too," I say, but without a smile. I want her to know I'm on to her.

Todd appears in front of us. "I'm glad we finally got to meet," he says to me. He turns to Brad. "Play some hoops at the gym tomorrow?"

"I don't think so. I need to catch up on some reading."

"Give me a call if you change your mind. Have a safe trip back, Riley."

"I will. Thanks."

More people come up to us as we try to leave, so it takes ten minutes before we're finally out of there.

"Sorry about that," Brad says as we walk down the street.

"About what?"

"Being there so long. I told you we'd be there an hour and it ended up being over two."

"I don't mind. It was good to meet your friends. You have a lot of them."

"Yeah, people have been friendly so far."

"You guys seem to have a lot in common."

"We all kind of grew up the same way. Sometimes I get annoyed with them constantly showing off their money, but I'm learning to just ignore it."

My phone rings. I don't recognize the number, so I send it to voicemail.

"You need to get that?" Brad asks.

"No. I think it's a wrong number. So anyway, I didn't know you and Todd played basketball."

"It's not very often. If I see him at the gym, we'll do a quick pickup game, but it's only once or twice a week."

"I like Todd. He seems nice. He was one of the few people who actually talked to me."

"Riley, don't read anything into that. The place was loud and I don't think everyone heard me when I was introducing you."

I think it was more about me not fitting in. After people realized I wasn't one of them, they gave up talking to me.

"So what do you think about Todd's offer?" Brad asks.

"What offer?"

"You didn't hear him?"

"I don't know what you're talking about."

"His dad's retiring in a few years and giving the business to Todd."

"Yeah? And?"

"Todd wants to expand it. Right now, it's just his dad and some nurses. Todd wants to hire four or five doctors. Make it more like an actual clinic instead of just a doctor's office. His dad's willing to help with the construction costs to make the place bigger."

"What's that have to do with you?"

"He offered me a job there. He said we could be partners, meaning I'd get a say in how we run the place. Todd and I have similar ideas and we get along well, so it'd be a good fit."

"You just started med school. Why is he bringing this up now?"

"Because he's excited about it. He wants to start planning it and he wants me to help him."

"You guys already talked about this?"

"We have, but tonight's the first time he asked if I wanted to be involved." Brad's getting more excited the more he talks about it. I think he really wants to do this.

"So where's the clinic?"

"In Massachusetts, just north of Boston."

"But it's cold there. I thought you wanted to live somewhere warm."

"I do, but an opportunity like this doesn't come up very often, if ever. I thought I'd end up working for some big corporate-owned clinic where I'd have no say in how anything is run and have to work my way up from the bottom. If I do this thing with Todd, I can practice medicine the way I want instead of following some corporate guidelines."

My phone rings again and I send it to voicemail.

"So what do you think?" Brad asks.

"I think if you want to do it, you should. If it doesn't work out, you could always get another job, right?"

"It wouldn't be that simple if we form a partnership. I'd have to sell my half of the business."

"Oh. Well, I guess you should probably give it more thought before you tell him yes."

He stops me. "Riley, this isn't just about me. I need your opinion on this. It affects both of us."

"I think it's too soon to be making plans that far off in the future."

"I still want your opinion. Do you think I should do this?"

I start walking again. "I can't answer that. This is your decision. I can't tell you what to do."

He catches up to me. "You're not telling me what to do. I just want to know if you'd be okay living there if by some chance we ended up still being together. There's an ocean nearby, so it's kind of what you were hoping for. It's just not very warm, except in the summer." He pulls me from the crowded sidewalk to sit down on a bench. "Just give me your honest opinion. I know it's still years away, but he's already making plans and—"

"Do you want to do it? Yes or no?"

"Yes. It's exactly what I wanted. My own clinic where I can have a say in how the place is run. I didn't think something like this would happen until I was in my forties or fifties, but now here I am getting an offer while I'm still in med school. Maybe it won't pan out, but if it did, it'd be an amazing opportunity."

"Then do it. Tell him yes."

"You really think so?"

"Why are you even questioning this? You keep saying it's

an amazing opportunity and I've never seen you this excited. You have to do this, Brad. Tell him yes."

"But what does that mean for us?"

"It's too soon to say. We're still trying to figure out how to make this long distance thing work."

He stands up. "Let's go."

We continue to his building and up to his apartment, neither of us saying anything. I'm sure he's upset with me for not being more excited about Todd's offer, but if he knew the truth, he'd understand why I don't share his excitement. It's a great opportunity, but seems like just another sign telling me to let him go. First the unexpected scholarship, and now this. The signs keep telling me Brad's meant to follow the path that was intended for him. The path that leads to his dream of being a doctor and owning a clinic. It's all falling into place, but could be taken away in an instant if he found out about the baby.

My phone rings again as we walk into his apartment. It's the same wrong number that's called three times now. It's my home area code so maybe it's someone I know.

"I'm going to get this so they'll stop calling," I say to Brad.

"Go ahead."

"Hey," I answer. "I think you have the wrong number."

"Riley? It's Renee."

I haven't talked to Renee in weeks. Now that we don't work together, I never see her unless I run into her at the store. But my mom calls her and sometimes they go out. My mom said she'd never forgive Renee for selling the salon to Kandace, but within a week of the sale, Renee and my mom were friends again. My mom doesn't have many friends. She can't afford to lose the few she's got.

"I've been trying to reach you," Renee says, "but you wouldn't pick up."

"I thought it was a wrong number. Who's phone are you using?"

"Mine. It's a new number. My old one was the salon number, so I had to get a new one. Anyway, I'm calling about your mom."

"What about her?"

"She was supposed to come over so I could do her hair for her date with Jerry, but she never showed up."

"She probably just forgot or changed her mind. Did you call her?"

"Yes, and she didn't pick up. Then I texted her, but didn't hear back."

"She's probably at Jerry's place. I'm in New York right now so I don't know where she stayed last night, but I wouldn't worry about it. You know how she is. She always changes her plans."

"Maybe just check in with her to be sure."

I'm not going to check on her. She's a grown woman, and I'm tired of playing the role of her mother.

"So how's New York?" Renee asks.

"It's okay. It's really big. And crowded."

"How's your boyfriend?"

"Good. I just back from meeting his friends."

"I'll let you go. I just wanted to know if you'd heard from your mom. I'm sure she's with Jerry, like you said. Have a safe trip home!"

"I will. Bye, Renee." I walk over to the couch and sit down next to Brad.

"Renee? Your old boss?"

"Yeah. She was supposed to do my mom's hair last night,

but my mom didn't show up. That's typical for her, which Renee knows, so I don't know why she's freaking out about it."

"She thinks something happened to your mom?"

"Yeah, but I'm sure my mom just forgot about going to Renee's or changed her mind and didn't bother to tell her."

"Have you heard from your mom since you got here?"

"No, but I didn't think I would. I'm sure Jerry showed up as soon as I left."

"You want to call her just to check in?"

"No. This time of night I'm sure she's passed out drunk. Jerry encourages her drinking and pays for it. It wouldn't surprise me if she's been drunk since I left." I take a breath. "Can we not talk about my mom?"

"Sure." He turns to me. "So about what we were talking about earlier. The long distance thing. You don't think it's going well?"

"What? I never said that."

"You didn't have to. I can tell. Every time I try to bring up the future, you either change the subject or tell me it's too soon to talk about."

"Because it *is* too soon. We've only dated for six months, three of which we weren't together."

"And now you're starting to doubt if this will work. You don't think we can keep this going for four more years."

I don't answer. I wasn't ready to have this conversation. I knew we needed to before I left, but I was hoping to put it off as long as possible.

"I feel the same way," Brad says.

"You do?" I ask, surprised.

"Of course I do. Being away from you is one of the hardest things I've ever done. I try to stay busy so I don't think about you, but I still do. I want to be with you, Riley, and when I can't, I get frustrated, wishing it didn't have to be this way. Sometimes I wonder how we can keep this going. It's only been a few months and I'm already tired of it."

"So what are you saying?" I ask, my heart thumping against my chest.

"I think we need to figure out a different way to do this. Maybe you get a place just outside the city so you're closer to me but able to afford it. You'll need roommates, but I can help with that. I'll ask around school. See if anyone knows someone who needs a roommate. I'll—"

"Brad, stop." I take his hand. "I love you for trying to make things better for us, but I'm not ready to move. To leave my friends. My job. My mom."

"Then I don't know how this is going to work." His eyes lock with mine. "I didn't expect this to happen, Riley. Falling in love with a girl right before I started med school? It wasn't supposed to happen. All through college I avoided getting serious with a girl because I knew I wouldn't have time for her with everything else going on in my life. I didn't want a relationship slowing me down or getting in the way of my goals. But then you came along and I wanted to do everything possible to keep you in my life."

"Even if it meant giving up your dreams?"

"But that's the thing. I haven't given anything up. I'm still doing everything I set out to do and you've supported me in that." He holds my face as he looks in my eyes. "I love you even more knowing you support me. I was willing to put everything on hold in order to be with you, until we could figure out a way for us to be together while I'm in school. But you wouldn't let me do it. You told me to take the scholarship. To stick with the plan. To keep following my dreams. You have no idea how much that meant to me, Riley. You're the only person in my life who's truly supported me, and I can't thank you enough for that."

My head is a mess right now, thinking about what he just said and what he doesn't know.

What do I do? Telling him about the baby will change his life forever. And it won't be the life he wanted.

I need to make a decision. I'm running out of time. This isn't a secret I can hide for much longer. And if I do decide to hide it, it means I can never see Brad again.

CHAPTER SIX

Riley

"I don't want to say goodbye." Brad keeps me in a hug as we stand outside the airport.

I didn't tell him last night. I didn't tell him about the baby and I didn't break up with him. When we had that talk about the future, that would've been the time to speak up, but I couldn't make myself say the words. I couldn't make a decision.

So now here we are at the airport, still a couple, with Brad still unaware I'm carrying his baby. I wish I'd just made a decision and gone through with it, but I didn't, and now it'll be an even harder decision to make because seeing Brad again made me realize how much I love him and want to be with him.

But if I love him, how can I take away everything he's worked for? His dreams? His future?

"I'll miss you," I whisper as tears run down my face.

"I'll miss you too," he says, squeezing me tight. "But I'll

see you at Thanksgiving. You have to be there, Riley. I'm not taking no for an answer."

I wipe my eyes and pull away. "I should go."

He looks at me with those deep brown eyes. "I love you."

"I love you too."

He gives me one last kiss. "I'll see you soon, okay?"

I nod, biting my lip.

"Hey." He takes both my hands in his. "I know this is hard, but we'll make it work."

"Yeah." I attempt to smile.

He pulls me in for a hug. "Last one and then I'll let you go."

It might be the last one *ever*. Last hug. Last kiss. The last time I see him.

"Call me when you get home, okay?" he says.

"I will." I give him a wave as I hurry into the airport. I race to the bathroom, go in a stall, and let myself cry, knowing I may never see him again.

A text pops up on my phone from Brad. *Miss you already! I love you!*

It makes me cry even more. When I'm all cried out, I go to the sink and clean up my face, then head to the check-in area. There's a huge line and people keep bumping into me, not even saying they're sorry. I was hoping after a couple days of being here I'd start to like it, but I don't. Even if I lived here for years, I don't think I'd ever get used to the crowds and the noise and that city smell.

As I'm waiting to board the plane, I call Giada.

"Hey, Riley," she answers, "Are you back home?"

"Not yet. I'm waiting to board the plane."

"So? How'd it go?" she asks in an anxious tone.

"I didn't tell him."

"Oh," she says, sounding disappointed. "Wait—so you guys broke up?"

"No. I couldn't do that either."

"Riley, the whole point of going out there was to tell him in person. Tell him about the baby or tell him it was over."

"I know, but I couldn't do it. We were having such a great time, and then last night and this morning we were um...well, saying goodbye, and I couldn't do it."

"You're using sex as the reason you didn't tell him? Riley, that's—"

"That's only part of the reason. I had a chance to tell him when we got home last night, but I couldn't do it. I couldn't make a decision. I love him so much, Giada. This trip just made the decision harder, not easier."

"I thought that might happen."

"Then why did you tell me to go?"

"Because you needed to see him again. You had to confirm that your feelings for him hadn't changed."

"And I found out they're even stronger. I love him even more! Giada, what am I going to do? How do I give him up when I love him this much?"

"You don't give him up. You tell him about the baby and live happily ever after."

"If only it were that simple. I can't live here with a baby. It'd be hard enough just to live here on my own. I can't believe how expensive everything is. Even if I had the money, I can't imagine living here."

"You didn't like New York?"

"Not at all. But Brad loves it. He loves everything about it. And he loves his school. His friends. Oh, and he already has a job lined up for after he graduates."

"A job? He just started school."

"Long story. The point is, everything's coming together for him. He's happy. Happier than I've ever seen him. And he's so excited about his future. I can't take that away from him."

"So what are you going to do?"

"I don't know. I don't think I'm ready to make a decision."

"Then don't. He won't be home until Thanksgiving, right? So you have some time to think about it."

An announcement blares from the airport speaker. "Boarding will begin soon for..."

"Giada, I have to go. My plane's boarding."

"Okay. Text me when you get home."

"I will. Bye."

When I'm on the plane, I text Brad that I love him. He texts back with a picture of us he took in Central Park. We look really happy, because we *are* happy, but would we still be happy if he left that life behind?

Hours later I get off the plane, tired and feeling sick to my stomach. This time it feels like airsickness more than morning sickness.

"Riley!" I look up and see April just outside the security check-in, waving at me and smiling.

As much as I miss Brad, it feels good to be home and back with my friends. I go up to April and give her a hug. "Thanks for coming to get me."

"How'd it go? Did you tell him?"

"No. It's a long story. Can we talk about it later? I'm really tired from the flight."

"Sure. You want to stop anywhere on the way home?"

"I really need to eat. Maybe we could go through a drive-thru?"

"Yeah, definitely." She glances at my stomach and smiles. "You're starting to show."

"Really?" I look at my stomach. She's right. My normally flat stomach now has a slight curve to it.

"I started planning the baby shower. I got a ton of ideas online." She takes my duffle bag from me. "You shouldn't be carrying this."

I'm still looking at my stomach. "Do you think people can tell?"

"Relax. It just looks like you gained a few pounds."

"That's what I told Brad."

"He noticed?"

"He could tell I'd put on weight. He said he liked it." I roll my eyes. "Especially since most of it's in my boobs."

She laughs. "They *are* getting really big."

We leave the airport and she takes me to a fast food place that's on the way to the trailer park.

"Your mom hasn't been around," April says as she takes some fries from the bag on her lap. She stuffs them in her mouth as she turns the corner.

"Yeah, Renee called me in New York." I take a bite of my burger and grab some fries from the bag. "She said my mom didn't show up to get her hair done. I'm guessing she was passed out drunk at Jerry's place."

"They both must've passed out. Jerry didn't show up for work this morning."

"Really?" I look at her. "How do you know he wasn't at work?"

"I went to get the oil changed in my car this morning and heard the manager complaining about Jerry not showing up."

"Huh. I guess I'm not surprised. He was probably too hungover to go to work."

"You think they're at the trailer?"

"I hope not. I need to sleep."

"You could come to my place and sleep."

"Thanks, but I really need to get home. I have a lot to do before work."

"You have to work tonight?"

"Not until eight."

She parks next to the trailer and jumps out to get my bag.

"April, you don't have to carry it for me."

She ignores me and takes it to the door. "It's locked. They must not be home."

My phone rings. "It's Renee calling again." I hand April my key. "Go ahead and go in."

I answer the call. "Hi, Renee, what's up?"

"Are you home now?"

"Yeah. Just got here. What's going on?"

"There's been an accident."

I go in the trailer, holding the phone to my ear. "What accident? What are you talking about?"

"Your mom and Jerry were out last night and Jerry lost control of the car. I don't know all the details but—"

"Wait, what about my mom? Is she okay?"

April hears me and rushes over. "What's going on?"

"She's at the hospital," Renee says. "I don't know what her condition is, but Jerry..." She clears her throat. "Jerry didn't make it."

"What?" I'm breathing hard and feeling lightheaded. I go to the couch to sit down. "Jerry's dead?"

"He died at the scene."

"What about my mom? How is she?"

"Honey, I'm sorry, I don't know all the details. I'm

heading to the hospital now. You want me to come pick you up?"

"No. I'll go." I get up, searching for my keys.

"What do you need?" April asks, holding me steady as I sway a little. I'm really dizzy and it's getting worse.

"I need a ride. My mom's in the hospital."

"Okay, let's go." She keeps hold of my arm and walks me to the door.

"Who's with you?" Renee asks.

"April. She picked me up at the airport. Renee, do you know anything about my mom? Anything at all?"

"All I know is the ambulance got there and took her to the hospital."

"How do you know all this?" I ask as I get in April's car. "Who told you?"

"Jen. She was driving home from the store and the road was blocked. The police told her they were cleaning up an accident and that she'd need to go a different way."

Jen is Renee's cousin. She used to work at the salon but couldn't stand working for Kandace, so she quit and got a job at a different salon.

"Did they tell her anything else?" I ask.

"No, but she said the car was pretty messed up."

"Messed up *how*?" I ask, my heart pumping so fast I'm feeling dizzy again.

"It was wrapped around a telephone pole. The whole front end was smashed."

"Oh my God." I cover my mouth and notice I'm shaking.

April reaches over and rubs my arm. "We're almost there, okay?"

I nod.

"Honey, don't assume the worst," Renee says. "For all we

know, she just has a few cuts and scrapes. I'm at the hospital now. I'll see you soon."

My phone falls from my hand and I search the floor trying to find it.

"Just leave it," April says. "I'll get it when we stop."

I turn and look at her. "Jerry's dead. What does that mean for my mom? She was in the car with him. What if—"

"Riley, just try to relax. Stress isn't good for the baby."

The baby. I look down at my stomach. April's right. I need to stay calm for the baby, but right now I'm finding that really hard to do. My mom might be dying at this very moment.

"Okay, we're here." April pulls into a parking spot, then jumps out of the car and races over to help me.

"April, I can walk just fine."

"No, you can't. You almost fell down earlier."

"Because I was dizzy. I'm tired from the flight and I didn't drink enough water today."

"We'll get you some water when we get inside."

Renee is waiting for us just inside the door. She races up and gives me a hug. "I'm sorry."

I pull back. "What do you mean? Is she..." I can't even say it.

"No," she says, shaking her head. "She's not..." Even Renee can't say it.

"Then *what*? What is it? What's wrong with her?"

"She's in critical condition. They wouldn't tell me anything more. They were waiting for you."

I look around for a doctor, panicked, and feeling like I can't breathe. "Who do I talk to? Who can tell me something?"

"Over here." Renee takes my arm and leads me to the nurses' desk. "This is Riley, Charlene's daughter."

"How is she?" I ask. "Can I see her?"

The nurse stands up. "Not right now. Your mother's in surgery. She arrived with multiple injuries, including a punctured lung and damage to her spine."

"Her spine? Does that mean she's—she's paralyzed?" I choke on the words.

"We won't know until later. If you'd like to have a seat, we'll update you when she's out of surgery."

"That's it?" I say louder than I intended. "That's all you can tell me?"

"Miss, I'm sorry, but that's all we know."

"Let's go sit down," Renee says, taking my arm and leading me to the waiting area. April's holding my other arm like she's afraid I'm going to collapse. When we get to the chairs, they sit me down, then take the seats on either side of me.

"They'll tell us more when they know," Renee says, rubbing my arm.

"They already know," I say, nervously tapping my foot on the floor. "They're just not telling me."

"Just try to relax," Renee says. "It could be awhile before we find anything out."

"I'll go get you some water," April says.

I watch as she goes to the water cooler that's across the room. Glancing around, I notice people staring at me. They probably think I'm crazy because I yelled at the nurse, but I couldn't help it. I need to know about my mom and the nurse wouldn't tell me anything.

"Do you know when it happened?" I ask Renee. "The accident?"

"It was sometime last night. I don't know what time."

"Last night? But didn't they just bring her in?"

"Yes," she says with a sigh. "Honey, I think it's best if we don't talk about this right now."

"Renee, I want to know," I say, turning to her. "Tell me."

She hesitates, then says, "All I know is what the officer told Jen this morning when she got to the road closure. He said the accident happened sometime last night and wasn't discovered until this morning."

"So she was alone there all night. In pain." I choke back tears.

"We don't know that," Renee says. "It's possible she was unconscious the whole time."

"Did the officer say what caused it? Why the car went off the road?"

"No, but..." She looks down, then back up at me. "Riley, don't jump to conclusions here."

I search her face and know what she's about to say. "They were drinking."

"I can't prove it. But Jen said she saw liquor bottles scattered near the car, like maybe they were thrown from it when the accident happened."

An image of the scene pops in my head. I can see them drinking, then Jerry losing control of the car and hitting the pole. But then what? Was Jerry instantly killed? What happened to my mom? Was she lying there hurt and in pain? All night?

"I shouldn't have told you," Renee says, rubbing my arm. I'm shivering now, not because I'm cold, but because I'm horrified by the thought of my mom suffering for hours with no one there to help her.

"That's why she didn't show up," I mutter. "When you called to tell me she didn't show up at your house, that's why."

"I can't say for sure, but yes, it's possible."

I collapse back in the chair, feeling dizzy and shaky.

April comes back and hands me a cup of water. "Riley, you really need to try to calm down. The baby—" Her eyes shoot to Renee.

"Baby?" Renee says. "What baby?"

Only April, Giada, and my mom know about the baby. I was trying to keep it a secret as long as possible because once people find out, they'll be trying to guess who the father is. But I don't know if they'd figure it out. Brad and I kept our relationship a secret for most of last summer. Few people even know we dated. And given that everyone assumes I'm like my mom and sleep around, the father could be anyone.

It's Nate I'm worried about. He knows I was only with Brad last summer. If Nate finds out I'm pregnant, I'm worried he'll tell Brad.

Renee turns to me. "Riley, are you pregnant?"

I nod.

"Did you just find out?"

"I've known for a few months."

"Months? Why didn't your mother tell me?"

"I told her not to. I don't want people knowing until I'm ready."

"She doesn't want people asking," April says.

"Asking what?" Renee says.

April answers. "About the father."

I look at April. "Would you just let me answer?"

"Sorry," she says, sinking back in her chair.

I look back at Renee. "I haven't told the father. And I don't want people trying to guess who it is. That's why I've kept it a secret."

"I understand. I won't tell anyone." She lowers her voice. "Just between you and me...is it Nate?"

"Nate?" I say like she's crazy. "Why would you think it's Nate? We're friends. We never dated."

"That doesn't mean you never, you know, did anything. There was definitely an attraction between you two."

"I wasn't attracted to him. I only see Nate as a friend. He wanted more, but I told him I didn't feel the same way."

"So...never?"

"Never. Not once."

She scoots back in her chair, staring straight ahead like she's trying to figure out who the father could be, which is exactly why I didn't want to tell people about the baby.

"It isn't that boy from last summer, is it?" she asks.

I burst from my chair, realizing I didn't call Brad. "I'll be right back."

As I leave, I hear Renee say to April, "What ever happened to that boy?"

When I'm outside the hospital, I call Brad.

He answers right away. "Hey, are you home?"

"Yeah. Sorry I didn't call earlier. Something happened."

"What?" he asks, sounding concerned.

"My mom was in an accident last night. She's in really bad shape. I'm at the hospital, but they won't tell me anything."

"Have they let you see her?"

"No. She's in surgery. They said her spine is damaged and something about her lung." My voice cracks.

"Riley, I'm so sorry. What can I do?"

"Nothing. I just needed to talk to you. To hear your voice. I'm so scared, Brad. I don't want her to die."

"I'm coming out there."

"No. Brad, don't. I'll be fine. I have April here and Renee. I don't want you missing school."

"I'm your boyfriend. I need to be there."

"Not right now. I don't even know what's wrong with her yet. Wait until I figure out what's going on. Maybe she'll come out of surgery and be okay. I need to get back in there. I'll call you later."

"Riley, wait."

"Yeah?"

"I love you. Anything you need, you call me, okay?"

"I will. Bye, Brad."

Back in the hospital, I feel Renee's eyes on me as I sit down.

"I don't want to talk about it," I say.

She puts her arm around me. "I just want you to know you can do this on your own. I did. Your mother did. My daughter's raising her two boys on her own."

"Renee, please. I don't want to talk about it. I don't want to talk about anything right now."

She sits back in her chair and the three of us quietly wait for three very long hours. Finally, the doctor comes out and asks to speak to me. We go through a door and he takes me in a room that looks like an office.

"Take a seat." He points to the chair.

"I'd rather stand," I say, nervously clenching my hands. "Is she going to be okay or not?"

"We've got her stabilized, but she's suffered injuries that she won't likely recover from."

"What does that mean?"

"We can't say for sure yet, but we believe she'll be paralyzed from the waist down."

My mom is paralyzed. I'm the only one who can care for

her. Within a matter of hours, both our lives have changed forever.

I feel dizzy and search for the chair he just pointed at.

"Over here," he says, helping me to the chair.

"What else?" I ask, staring at the floor as I try to breathe.

"She's suffered some brain damage, but we won't know the extent until she's alert and able to interact with us."

"I don't know what that means."

"She might have trouble remembering how to do basic tasks, like feeding herself. She can relearn those things through therapy, but it'll take some time."

"What other injuries does she have?"

"Cuts, bruises, a collapsed lung, two broken ribs. She had some internal bleeding which we dealt with during surgery."

I look up at him. "Do you know if she was conscious? After it happened?"

"I really don't know. She wasn't when she arrived here. Based on the officer's description of the accident, the force of the impact most likely rendered her unconscious for most, if not all, of the night. She might have woken up briefly but not been aware of it."

"Can I see her?"

"Not now. She just got out of surgery."

"When will she be able to go home?"

He clears his throat. "Your mother won't be going home. She'll need to be in a facility with round-the-clock nursing care."

"For how long?"

"Possibly indefinitely. It'll depend on her progress and the extent of the brain damage."

"But I..." I look down. "I don't have money for that. She doesn't either."

"She'll need to rely on public assistance. We have people here to help you with that."

I swallow. "So she's not coming home."

"I'm sorry, but no." He pauses. "Do you have any other questions for me?"

I shake my head. I'm sure I'll have questions later, but right now I'm too shocked to think of any. My mom's paralyzed. She has brain damage. She's never coming back to the trailer.

"I suggest you go home for now and come back later," the doctor says.

"I can't go before seeing her."

"She can't see you for several more hours. Go home and get some rest. And try to relax. This kind of stress isn't good for someone in your condition."

"What condition?"

"The pregnancy?" He motions to my stomach. "I assume that's why you keep rubbing your stomach. Many mothers do that as a way to calm themselves."

"Oh," I say, not realizing I was doing it.

"If you have any questions, just let us know. Would you like me to walk you out?"

I nod and follow him down the hallway to the waiting room. Renee and April jump up from their chairs when they see me.

"What happened?" Renee asks. "What did he tell you?"

"It's bad," I say, the tears I held back now breaking loose. "It's really bad."

LATER THAT NIGHT, as I'm sitting by the bed of my

unconscious mom who's hooked up to machines and so swollen and bruised I no longer recognize her, I realize this is my life now. For just a brief moment in time, I thought things could be different. I imagined a life with Brad. Raising our child together. Getting married. Living in a house.

None of that can happen now. I can't leave my mom. I'm all she has, and there's no way I'm leaving her to live out the rest of her life alone in some place that's not even her home.

Around midnight, I get back to the trailer. It seems so empty without my mom. I've spent plenty of time here alone over the years, but it's different knowing my mom's never coming back. It almost feels like she died, which in a way she did. The mom I know is gone.

Taking a deep breath, I call up Brad. His phone rings twice before he picks up.

"Riley, are you okay?" he asks, sounding concerned that I'm calling so late.

"No." I squeeze my eyes shut and rub my pounding head. "We need to talk."

"About your mom?"

I already told him about my mom. I called him earlier and told him about her condition and what was going to happen to her. This call isn't about that.

"It's not about my mom. This is something I needed to say when I was out there but didn't. I wish I had, because this isn't something that should be said over the phone."

"Riley, what are you talking about?"

Tears are streaming down my face, but I manage to keep my voice steady. "I can't do this anymore. I love you, but I can't do this."

"Do what?"

"This relationship. It isn't working. I thought I'd be okay

with you being there, but I'm not. I don't want to date someone halfway across the country."

"Then move here. It doesn't have to be New York. You could live in New Jersey or Connecticut. Anywhere outside the city will be cheaper. I'll get a job. I'll—"

"Brad, no. You're not hearing what I'm saying. It's not just the distance. It's us. It's not working between us."

"Why would you say that? We just had a great weekend together."

"*You* did. But I felt out of place. The city. Your friends. Your school. They're all perfect for you. But not for me. We had a great summer, Brad, but that's all it was. It was never meant to be anything more."

"Riley, what the hell? You're breaking up with me?"

"I'm sorry, Brad, but I just don't want to do this anymore."

He sighs. "You don't mean it. You're upset because of your mom. Just give it some time and—"

"It has nothing to do with my mom. I was going to tell you this when I was in New York, but I couldn't do it. I didn't want to hurt you."

"But doing it now is better?" he says, a hint of anger in his voice.

"It's not better, but I can't keep putting it off. I'm sorry, Brad. It's over."

"It's not over! Riley, just—"

"Goodbye, Brad." I end the call, then collapse to the floor, sobbing.

My life with Brad is over. Any dreams I had of us being together are gone. My life is here now. Caring for my mom. Caring for my baby.

I'll never see Brad again.

CHAPTER SEVEN

Riley

It's been over a month since I broke up with Brad. He's called me, texted me, and sent me letters, but I didn't respond to any of it. I can't. It's over between us, which I think he's finally accepted. I haven't heard from him for a week.

I think about him constantly. I miss him so much. Sometimes I find myself getting my phone out to text him and then remember I can't. April said I should delete his number, but I can't do it. Not yet.

You'd think with everything going on with my mom, along with my two jobs, I'd have no time to even think about Brad, but my mind just keeps going back to him. And my heart is still his. I think it always will be. I can't imagine giving it to anyone else.

"Why don't you get out of here?" Dave says, nudging my side.

We're working the night shift together at the gas station.

When my mom dated Dave, I thought he was so annoying, but the past few months, we've become good friends. He's like a big brother, always looking out for me, especially now that he knows I'm pregnant. He won't let me lift anything or stand for too long.

"I just got here," I tell him.

"Yeah, and you forgot to give the last two customers their change."

I turn to him. "I did?"

"Don't worry about it. I took it from the other register." He folds his arms over his chest. "I think it's time you quit."

"Quit? I need the money. I'm not quitting."

"You never sleep. You barely eat. You're a mess, Riley. If anything, you need to do this for your kid."

"My kid is going to need diapers and food and a million other things. All things that require money."

"Go after the kid's dad. Make him cough up some money."

Dave doesn't know Brad's the father. He thinks it's some guy I hooked up with after Brad left town. That's the rumor someone started, and I never denied it, so now everyone thinks it's the truth.

"He's gone. And he's not coming back." I look down at my belly, which is definitely showing now. "I need this job, Dave. I can't quit."

"Okay, but I can't have you out here when you're not awake enough to do your job. Why don't you go in the back and take a nap?"

"I can't sleep. I have too much on my mind."

He looks around the empty store. We don't get many customers in the middle of the night on a Sunday.

"Then at least sit down," Dave says, pulling a chair up for me.

"But—"

"If someone comes in, I'll deal with them." He waits for me to sit, then says, "When's the last time you ate?"

"I don't know. Maybe lunch?"

He sighs. "I know you're messed up because of your mom, but you gotta eat." He grabs a banana from the counter. "Take this. It's good for you."

I don't like bananas, but I do need to eat. I keep forgetting to because I'm never hungry and the hours go by without me even noticing. The days do too. I can't believe it's already November. This Thursday is Thanksgiving. I wouldn't have even known if Renee hadn't called and asked me over for dinner.

I need to wake up from this fog I've been in, but I haven't been able to. Losing Brad and my mom all at once is too much for me.

I haven't actually lost my mom. Her body is still alive, but the rest of her is gone. She looks different, acts different, and has no life left in her. She knows it's me when I go see her, but her eyes are distant, like she's seeing right through me. Her voice is soft and weak, so when she says my name, it comes out like a whisper. She was always a loud talker, to the point I'd have to tell her to quiet down. Now I can barely hear her.

Dave leans back against the counter, facing me. "That guy come pick up his truck?"

"This morning. I didn't see him. I was at work, but it wasn't there when I got home."

My mom's ex finally got out of prison. When he called

saying he was coming over to get his truck, he didn't ask about my mom, so I didn't tell him. I just thanked him for letting me use the truck and told him I'd leave the keys in it for him to pick up.

"Your car's running okay?" Dave asks.

It's actually my mom's car. She'll never drive again, so I took it to replace the truck.

"I think so. It makes a rattling noise when it idles, but that's probably just because it's old."

"I'll have my brother take a look at it. Make sure it's nothing serious."

Dave's brother is a mechanic. He fixed my tire for free a few weeks ago after Dave told him my situation.

"How about a sandwich?" he asks as I toss the banana peel in the trash.

"I'm not really hungry."

"Ham or turkey?" he asks, going to the cooler.

"Ham," I tell him.

He comes back with the sandwich and a bottle of milk.

"Thanks." I take a five from my pocket and hand it to him.

"Put your money away." He sits on the stool in front of the register, looking out the window at the gas pumps. "Your mom's gonna pull through this, Riley."

I peel the plastic wrapper from the sandwich, ignoring Dave's comment. He's trying to make me feel better but it's not working. And it's not true. My mom will never go back to how she used to be. She's going to be like this forever.

"She was a good lady," he says. "I mean, she *is* a good lady." He shakes his head. "Sorry."

"Dave, we don't have to talk about this. I'd actually prefer that we didn't." I take a bite of the sandwich. "So what are you doing for Thanksgiving?"

"Going to Kristy's mom's place. There's gonna be like thirty people there."

Kristy is his girlfriend. They've been dating a couple months now.

"Are you bringing anything?"

"Yeah." He chuckles. "One of those pies." He nods toward the bakery table.

"You're bringing a gas station pie to Thanksgiving?"

"Why not? It's not like it was made here."

"I guess." I open the milk and take a drink. I still don't like milk, but at least Dave gave me chocolate, which is a little better.

"How about you?" he asks.

"Renee invited me over, but I might go to the hospital instead."

He looks back at me. "And eat hospital food? C'mon, Riley. It's Thanksgiving. Go have a nice meal."

"And leave my mom all alone?"

"You can go to Renee's and go see your mom. You'll have time for both."

"I'll think about it." I finish the sandwich and the rest of the milk.

"I'm tossing those donuts soon," Dave says, pointing to them.

I smile as I go over to the case to get one. "What kind do you want?"

"Jelly filled if there's any left."

I bring him one and keep one for myself.

"Got a customer," he says, getting up from the stool.

I remain seated and eat my donut.

The door swings open and I hear someone say, "Is Riley here?"

I stand up, dropping my donut when I see who's there. "Nate?"

His eyes fall to my stomach. My round protruding stomach. "Riley?"

"Hey, aren't you that kid she used to hang out with?" Dave asks.

Nate ignores him, his eyes going from my face to my stomach and repeating the pattern like he can't believe what he's seeing.

"Nate, what are you doing here?" I step up behind the counter to hide my belly.

"I'm back for Thanksgiving."

"I thought you weren't coming home."

"I wasn't going to, but plans changed and I decided to come back."

"Why didn't you tell me?"

"I wanted to surprise you. I was going to wait until tomorrow, but then I remembered you were working tonight so I thought I'd stop by."

"It's really late. Why don't we talk tomorrow?"

His eyes meet up with mine. "I think we need to talk now."

Glancing at Dave, I see the confusion on his face. He has no idea what's going on and I don't want him finding out.

"Dave, do you mind if I take my break now?"

"Go ahead."

"Nate, let's go in the back." I motion for him to follow me.

We go in the break room and I close the door. When I turn around, he's right in front of me.

"You're pregnant."

"Yeah."

"Why didn't you tell me? Why didn't my *mom* tell me?"

"She didn't know."

"How could she not know? She brought you meals every day for a week after your mom's accident."

"I wasn't showing back then. And I wore baggy sweatshirts."

He looks down at my stomach. "How far along?"

I go around him. "I don't want to talk about this."

"Are you kidding? Of course we're talking about it. Why didn't you tell me?"

"Because I didn't want you to know." I stand with my back to him, facing a stack of boxes.

He comes up beside me. "It's his, isn't it? It's Brad's."

"Nate, please. I don't want to talk about it. It's none of your business."

"It is if this kid is part of my family. Why the hell would you hide this from me? We're best friends."

I look at him. "We haven't been friends since the night you told me you love me. When I didn't say it back, everything changed. You became someone else. Someone I didn't want to be around anymore. And you got even worse when you found out I was dating Brad."

"Yeah, fine, but I got over it. I thought we were friends again. Are you saying we're not?"

"I don't know what we are. We talk on the phone, but it's not like it used to be. And honestly, I don't know why you keep calling me. You have a new life now. A new job. New friends."

"You're still my friend. I still care about you."

"I care about you too, but it's different now. We have our own lives. We both need to move on."

His eyes lower to my belly. "I can't believe he just left you. I can't believe he'd fucking do that."

"Who? What are you talking about?"

"Brad. He finds out you're pregnant and leaves? Just goes off to New York like nothing's happened? He obviously didn't tell his parents about it. So he's just going to pretend it's not happening? Is that the real reason you guys broke up? So he wouldn't have to step up and be a man?"

"No." I turn and walk away. "That's not it at all."

"I'm gonna call that asshole up tomorrow and tell him he better at least be sending you money."

"Nate, no." I whip around to face him. "Don't call him. Please. Just stay out of it."

"And let him get away with leaving you to raise a baby with no support? No money? You're working two freaking jobs while he goes to class a couple hours a day. Why doesn't *he* get a job? He should be the one working all night at a—"

"Nate, stop!" I take a breath. "He doesn't know."

"What?" He steps closer to me.

"Brad doesn't know."

"That doesn't make sense. You spent the weekend with him last month."

"I didn't tell him. I was going to, but I changed my mind."

"How could he not tell? I'm sure you guys...you know."

"I told him I'd put on some weight. He didn't question it."

Nate rubs his hand over his jaw. "You have to tell him."

"No. I don't."

"Riley, why would you keep this from him? He needs to know he's having a kid."

"Not if knowing will ruin his life."

"Why would it—" Nate sighs. "He'd give up school."

"And he'd never go back. He'd leave New York. He'd give up everything he's worked for."

Nate walks away from me, shaking his head. "So what are you saying? You're just going to raise this kid on your own? Never tell him about it?"

"That's my only option if I want him to stay in school." I go over to Nate. "Please don't tell him. This doesn't involve you, Nate."

"It *does* involve me. He's my cousin. We grew up together. We were like brothers until...well, until I found out he was dating my best friend."

"You still haven't talked to him?"

"No. How about you? Have you talked to him since you guys broke up?"

"He's called, but I won't return his calls. Or his texts."

"Is this why you broke up with him? So he wouldn't find out?"

I nod. "It was the hardest decision I've ever had to make. Part of me thought we could make this work, but then the accident happened and I knew what I had to do. I can't leave my mom. I'm all she has. Even if I wanted to be with Brad, I couldn't."

"What's the latest on your mom?"

"She's supposed to leave the hospital next week. I don't think she's ready, but she can't stay there. It's too expensive."

"I thought she was getting aid."

"She is, but they have rules about how long you can stay. They also have rules about where she can go for rehab."

"So where are they sending her?"

"To a nursing home." My voice cracks. "I don't want her there, Nate," I say, wiping my eyes. "She's not old. She shouldn't be there."

He hugs me. "I'm sorry."

"Why is this happening? I keep thinking things will get better, but then they don't."

The door opens and Dave pops his head in. "Everything okay in here?"

"Yeah." I pull away from Nate and wipe my face. "I'll be out in a minute."

He closes the door.

"I need to go back to work."

Nate stands in front of me. "Can I see you tomorrow, or do you work all day?"

"I work here until six in the morning, then I'll need to go home and sleep, but we could try to meet for lunch. I have to work at the restaurant from three to ten, then come back here for another shift, so lunch is my only free time."

"Riley, that's crazy. You barely have time to sleep. You need to quit this job."

"I'm not quitting. Do you want to meet or not?"

"Yeah. Where do you want to meet?"

"At the hospital. It's the only time I'll have to see my mom. We can eat in the cafeteria."

"Okay." His eyes lower to my stomach. "You're gonna be a mom. That's gonna take a while to sink in."

THE NEXT DAY, we meet up at the hospital. I'm already in my mom's room when Nate arrives.

"Hey." He stands at the door. "Ready to go?"

"Yeah. You can come in."

Nate was avoiding looking at my mom, but his eyes slowly move to her as he walks in the room. His jaw drops, then quickly snaps shut as he looks away. His reaction is a reminder of how different she looks now compared to when he saw her last. I'm used to it, but Nate's not. He's used to the woman with long blond hair and overdone makeup, wearing outfits that showed off her body. Now she's covered in blankets, her skin is pale and lifeless, and her hair is shorter than Nate's. They had to shave off her hair for the surgery they did on her brain and it's just now starting to grow back.

"Hey, Charlene," Nate says, standing beside me.

Her eyes slowly move to him and her lips part. "Nate," she says in that breathy whisper that's now her voice.

"She knows you," I say under my breath. "I didn't think she would."

"I'm home for Thanksgiving," Nate says to my mom.

"Thanksgiving." She mouths the word, but barely any sound comes out.

"Thursday is Thanksgiving, Mom. See the turkey I put up?" I point to the paper turkey I taped to the wall across from her bed.

Her eyes follow my hand to the turkey. Then her head falls back on the pillow and her eyes shut.

"What just happened?" Nate whispers.

"It's the meds," I tell him. "She has a hard time staying awake." I stand up. "Let's go eat and I'll check on her again before we go."

When we're seated in the cafeteria with our food, Nate reaches across the table for my hand. "I'm so sorry, Riley. I didn't know."

"Didn't know what?"

"I didn't know she was that bad. I know you told me on the phone, but it wasn't until I saw her that..." He looks down, shaking his head.

I pull my hand from his and pick up my fork. "We should eat. I don't have a lot of time."

Hearing him talk about my mom like that will only make me cry, so I'm not going to let him do it. I'll talk about anything but that.

"So what's new with your mom?" I ask, picking at my watery mashed potatoes. The food here sucks, but we don't have time to leave the hospital to go somewhere else.

"She's fine. Still dating that guy."

"They've been dating for months. You should probably start using his name."

"I'm hoping they'll break up. He's so damn boring. I don't know why she likes him."

"As long as she's happy, that's all that matters." I salt my potatoes, hoping it'll make them taste better. "So why'd your plans change? Why'd you end up coming home?"

He looks down at his plate, picking at his salad, which looks even worse than my potatoes. "I was supposed to go to Thanksgiving with a...a friend, but she ended up going to the Bahamas with her parents. It was a last-minute thing."

"She?" My brows rise. "I get the feeling this girl is more than a friend."

"She is." He sets his fork down. "I need to tell you something. Something you're not going to like."

"What is it?"

He takes a deep breath as his eyes meet up with mine. "I'm dating Kari."

"Kari who?"

"Kandace's daughter."

"What?" I burst up from my chair.

"Riley, sit down," he says in a hushed tone as he notices people staring.

I slowly lower to my seat. "You're dating Kari? The girl who tortured me in junior high? The girl whose mother is the reason my mom and I lost our jobs at the salon?"

"Well, technically you both quit but—"

"You know what I mean," I snap. "Why the hell would you date Kari?"

"She's not that bad once you get to know her."

"Uh, yeah. She is. And she gets *worse* the more you know her, not better. How did you two even get together?"

"I went out to a bar with some guys from work and saw her there. It was about a month after I moved to Dallas. I thought she was living here to run the salon, but she said she missed Dallas and moved back."

"And you've been dating her since that night?"

"Yeah, it's been a couple months now. I knew you'd be mad if you found out, so I didn't tell you. But things are starting to get serious, so I thought you should know."

"Things are getting serious? As in you're going to marry her serious?"

"I don't know. It's too soon to say, but we are talking about moving in together."

"You've gotta be kidding me," I say with disgust. "Out of all the girls in Dallas, you had to pick Kari?"

"Out of all the guys in town, you had to pick Brad?" he shoots back.

"Don't turn this back on me. This has nothing to do with Brad." I pause. "Or does it? Are you doing this for revenge?"

"No! Of course not!"

I pick up my tray and stand up. "I'm not hungry. I'm gonna go back to my mom's room."

"Riley, wait!" he calls after me, but he doesn't follow me.

And he doesn't show up in my mom's room. He probably left, which is fine with me.

Just when I think I can be friends with Nate again, I'm reminded he's not the guy I grew up with. That Nate would never date a girl like Kari.

I think it's time I stop talking to Nate. I miss what we used to have, but it's gone now and I need to accept that.

CHAPTER EIGHT

BRAD

I haven't talked to Riley for over a month, but I think about her constantly. And as much as it hurts, I still love her. I don't know what happened to make her end things between us. She said it wasn't working, but I don't think she really believes that. She definitely didn't act like she did when she came here to see me. That weekend was perfect. And then she dumped me.

"You sure you don't want to go with me?" Todd asks, getting up to leave. He came over to watch Monday night football. He's leaving in the morning to go home for Thanksgiving. He invited me to come with him, but I decided to stay here.

"Maybe next year. Tell your mom thanks for the invite," I say, walking him to the door. "I'll see you when you get back."

"It's not too late for you to go home. I'm sure you could get a flight."

"Go home so I can hear my mom fighting with my dad for a week?" I chuckle. "I think I'll pass."

My father's out of the addiction rehab program and living with my mom. They were planning to divorce, but decided to work on their relationship instead. So far, it's not going well. My brother was home a few weeks ago and said they fought the entire time, which is why he won't be going there for Thanksgiving. My mom is angry at us for not showing up, but what does she expect? We don't want to spend Thanksgiving listening to them argue.

"You could go see Riley," Todd says.

I shake my head. "She made it clear it's over. She won't even answer my calls."

"I don't get it, man. Everything seemed to be going great when she was here."

"Yeah, I don't get it either. Well, have a good trip."

He leaves, and I shut the door and look back at my empty apartment. Anik already took off for the week so I have the whole place to myself.

Going back to the couch, I flip through the channels trying to find something to watch. My mind keeps going back to what Todd said about going to see Riley. Maybe I should do it. Maybe I should show up there and make her talk to me and tell me what's really going on.

There's a knock at the door. I get up to answer it.

"Hey," I say, seeing Corinne there. "I thought you left."

"Not until tomorrow," she says, going around me to come inside. "You want to go do something?"

"Not really. I think I'm in for the night." I close the door and turn to see her sitting on my couch, her shoes tossed aside like she plans to stay awhile.

"Corinne, I'm really tired so..."

She doesn't take the hint. "Come sit down. Let's watch a movie."

I can't figure this girl out. She flirts with me all the time, but then claims she's dating Charlie, even though they don't really go out. I've told her many times I'm not looking to get involved with anyone, but then she does something like this. Showing up late at night at my apartment.

"Why aren't you out with Charlie?"

"He already left for home." She pats the couch. "Come sit down."

I go over there, but sit on the opposite end. "Corinne, just so we're clear—"

"You don't want to date me," she says, rolling her eyes. "I know. You've told me that a million times."

"So why are you here?"

She smiles and moves over until she's right beside me. "We don't have to date to..." She leans over and kisses my cheek. "Meet each other's needs."

I stand up. "Sorry, but I'm not interested in you that way."

She sighs. "God, Brad, I don't understand you. I'm offering you sex. No strings. What guy wouldn't take that?"

"Well, for one, you're dating my friend. And two, I'm not ready to go there. I just got out of a relationship."

"That was over a month ago."

"And I'm not over her," I say, sitting back down.

Corinne moves back to the other side of the couch, turning to face me. "No offense, but I don't get why you liked her so much. You two have nothing in common. You're going to be a doctor and she didn't even go to college."

"That doesn't matter. My mom doesn't have a college degree, and she married a lawyer."

"Your mom didn't go to college?"

"She did, but she dropped out to have my brother. She never went back."

"I'm just saying, I don't see you and Riley together. She doesn't like art or the type of music you like. When I told her she could go check out the new MOMA exhibit when she was here, she had no idea what I was talking about."

"None of that matters to me. We don't have to like the same things. Riley and I...we understand each other, in a way I can't really explain. It's rare to find someone you click with like that, and it's hard to let them go. You feel like you'll never find that again."

My phone rings. I check it and am surprised when I see Nate's name on the screen. He hasn't talked to me since I moved out of his mom's house last summer. I tried calling him, but he wouldn't pick up.

"I need to get this," I say, standing up as I answer the call. "Hey, Nate. What's going on?"

"I'm home for Thanksgiving and thought I'd give you a call."

"So we're speaking again?" I ask, sounding annoyed.

"Don't be giving me shit about that. I needed time to cool off."

"I'm going to go," Corinne says, putting her shoes on.

"Who was that?" Nate asks.

"Corinne. She's a friend from school."

"A friend, huh?" He chuckles. "Kind of late for a friend to be over."

"It's not like that."

"You don't have to pretend with me. I think it's good you're dating again."

"I'm not—"

"Bye!" Corinne waves as she leaves, then blows me a kiss and smiles.

I walk over to the door and close it, then lock it.

"Should I call back later?" Nate asks, a smile in his voice. "So you can be with your girlfriend?"

"She's not my girlfriend. Nate, why are you calling?" I go to the fridge to get a beer. I don't usually drink during the week, but I'm making an exception since I don't have classes.

"I'm just checking in," he says. "I don't want us to keep fighting. We used to be like brothers and I miss talking to you."

"You could've called anytime," I say, swigging my beer. "As far as I'm concerned, it wasn't a fight. I've been trying to call you for months."

"Yeah, fine. It's my fault. Can we just get past this now?"

I sit on the couch, the beer in my hand. "So what's new? How's the job going?"

"Good. How's med school?"

"A ton of work."

"But you like it, right?"

"Yeah, but I have to study my ass off to keep my grades up."

"I don't miss that shit. I'm glad I'm done with school."

"What else is going on? You dating anyone?"

"Yeah. Kari."

"Kari who?"

He laughs. "Funny. Riley said the same thing."

I was about to take a drink, but stopped when I heard Riley's name. "You talked to—"

"You remember Kari. The girl I set you up with last summer?"

"Yeah. The snobby bitch who bullied Riley."

"That was when they were kids. Kari's changed. She's not like that now."

"She sure as hell seemed like she was that day I saw her at the salon."

"She was just jealous seeing you with Riley. She admits she didn't react well that day."

"Did she apologize to Riley?"

"Well, no, but I'm sure Riley's forgotten about all that by now. It doesn't matter. It all worked out. Riley makes more money at the restaurant than she ever made at the salon."

"So you talked to her?" I ask in a casual tone, even though my heart's been beating out of my chest since the moment Nate said her name.

"Yeah, I stopped by to see her at the gas station when I got into town last night. And we had lunch today. I'm sure I'll see her again before I leave. I'm here all week with nothing to do. I was supposed to spend Thanksgiving with Kari but then—"

"What'd she say?" I ask, referring to Riley. I don't give a shit about Kari. That bitch is the reason Riley and her mom lost their jobs. I can't believe Nate would date her, knowing how she treated Riley.

"Kari?" Nate asks.

"Not Kari. Riley. What'd she say when you saw her?"

"I don't know. We just talked. We talk all the time."

All the time? When I was with Riley, she said she only talked to Nate once a week, if that. I get the feeling he's exaggerating to make me jealous, to get back at me for dating her.

"How's Riley's mom doing?"

"Not good. I went to the hospital today to see her."

"You went to see Charlene?"

113

"Yeah. Well, with Riley. We went there together."

It sounds like Nate and Riley are back to being friends. I'm surprised she'd be friends with him, knowing he's dating Kari.

"What do you mean she's not good?" I ask.

"She could barely talk. I'm not even sure she knows what's going on. She kinda just stared at the wall and then fell asleep."

"So she's not getting better."

"No. Riley said they're going to put her in a nursing home."

"Nursing home? She's not old enough for that."

"I don't think that matters. She just needs a place that has full-time nursing care. She can't pay for it, so it has to be someplace cheap. She's on government aid."

"Shit," I mutter. "I was hoping she was getting better."

"She's getting worse, if you ask me. I didn't even recognize her when I saw her. Her hair's chopped off, her skin is pale, and she's got this blank stare on her face. It's not the Charlene I know. It's like she's someone totally different."

"How's Riley handling it?"

"The best she can. She's actually doing better than I expected."

She's not. It's an act. She's putting on a smile and acting like everything's fine so people won't worry about her. She did the same thing when we were dating, but I saw through all that. I got her to talk about her problems and stop pretending everything was fine when it wasn't. Things are even worse for her now, but Nate doesn't see it. He was friends with her all those years, and yet I know her better than he does.

"Maybe I should go out there."

"Out where?"

"To Oklahoma. To see Riley."

"Yeah, I don't think so." He laughs.

"What's that supposed to mean?"

"She doesn't want to see you. Didn't you figure that out when she didn't return any of your calls or texts?"

"That's not about me. There's something going on with her."

"Sorry, man, but she dumped you, so actually it *is* about you. You just need to accept that and move on."

"It doesn't make sense. We were getting along great, and then she just ends it? I'm telling you, Nate, something happened. And it wasn't just this thing with her mom. Something else happened. Something she's not telling me."

"Like what?"

"I don't know, but I'm gonna find out." I get up and go over to my laptop, waking it up. "I'm going out there."

"Brad, no. Don't."

"Why not?" I say as I search for flights.

"She doesn't want to see you. I'm telling you this for your own good. Don't come out here."

"Why? What are you not telling me?"

"She um...never mind."

"What is it? What were you going to say?"

He hesitates. "She has someone else."

I chuckle. "Yeah, right."

"I'm not kidding. She's dating someone."

My chest tightens. "She told you that?"

"Yeah. I didn't want to tell you, but you kind of forced me to by saying you were coming out here. I don't want you coming all this way and then finding Riley with another guy."

"You're sure about this? She said she's dating this guy? They're not just friends?"

"She called him her boyfriend. She said they've been dating for about a month now."

"A month? She was with *me* a month ago. You're saying she cheated on me?"

"I don't think so. It sounds like they'd been friends for a while and it turned into more than that a few weeks ago. Maybe she went to New York to tell you she'd found someone else but then couldn't bring herself to do it."

"So she waited until she got home," I say, my voice trailing off.

I can't believe Riley would come to New York and pretend we're still a couple, knowing she had someone else back home. Knowing she was about to dump me. That doesn't sound like her at all.

"If you really want to know, I could ask her," Nate says. "I'm sure I'll see her again this week."

"No. I don't need to know." I rub my jaw as I stare at my laptop where I was just about to buy a plane ticket. Guess I don't need one now.

"So you decided not to go home for Thanksgiving?" Nate asks.

"To watch my parents fight? Yeah, I think I'll pass."

"What's the latest? Are they talking about divorce again?"

"I don't know. I didn't ask. I'm sure it's going to happen. I just don't know when."

"I heard your dad's working again."

"Yeah, he's back at the law firm, but everything he makes goes to pay off his debt. I'm gonna have to get a job here soon to cover expenses."

"What expenses? You're on scholarship."

"Going out in New York is expensive. I don't even go out much, but I've already used up most of what I made last summer."

"Where would you get a job?"

"I could find something at school. They have plenty of jobs. Or maybe I'll bartend. Who knows?"

"So you and this girl who was there...you sure there's nothing going on between you two?"

"I told you, we're just friends."

"Does she want to be more?"

"It doesn't matter. I'm not interested."

"Anyone else there you're interested in?"

"I'm still getting over Riley. I'm not ready to date again."

"You gotta move on from Riley. You two were never a good match."

"Says the guy who wanted her for himself. You'll never be okay with Riley being with another guy."

"Actually, I'm totally fine with it. When she told me she's dating someone, it didn't even bother me. I've moved on. I'm with Kari now."

"And you think that'll last? Kari seems like someone who gets bored easily."

"Things are going great between us," he says in a tone that's too over-the-top happy to be real. But I decide not to call him on it.

"That's great, man. Glad everything's working out for you."

"Yeah. Well, I should probably get going. My mom's taking me out for dinner."

"Tell her I said hi."

"I will. Have a good Thanksgiving."

"Yeah, you too. Bye, Nate."

I end the call, still gazing at the flights displayed on my laptop. Part of me still wants to go. I need to see for myself that Riley's moved on. That she's with someone else. Why would she start dating someone right after her mom's accident? Or was she dating this guy before that but didn't tell Nate because she didn't want it getting back to me? She didn't want me knowing she was cheating?

There's no way she would do that. I know Riley well enough to know she wouldn't cheat on me. I also know she wouldn't go on a date with some guy right after her mom's accident. So why did she tell Nate that? Did she want him to think things were serious with this guy so Nate wouldn't try to date her again?

None of this makes sense. I feel like I need to go out there to get the real story. Even if Riley's dating someone, I still want to see her. I need to say goodbye.

Our relationship ended too quickly. Too abruptly. It feels like it's not over. She told me it was, so maybe I should accept that and move on, but I can't. I don't feel like it's over between Riley and me. Maybe I never will.

CHAPTER NINE

APRIL

Riley

"I'm sorry, but there was nothing we could do." The doctor waits for me to respond, but all I can manage to do is look at my mom in that bed. Pale. Lifeless. Gone forever.

It's what she wanted. She didn't tell me that, but I knew. I knew when she didn't bother to fight. She may not have fully understood all that the doctors told her after the accident, but she knew the rest of her days would be spent in a bed, in this nursing home, and to her, that's not a life. She wanted to die, and so she didn't try to fight. She wouldn't do physical therapy. She'd spit out her meds. Whatever help they offered her, she wouldn't take it. She didn't want it. She gave up.

"I'll give you a moment to be with her," the doctor says before leaving the room.

I sit beside her on the bed, not sure if I should touch her. She's covered by the blanket, her eyes closed, her head resting on the pillow. If the doctor hadn't told me what happened, I'd think she's just asleep.

She passed away while I was driving here. I was late getting off my shift at the restaurant because I accidentally dropped a tray of plates and had to clean it up. It was almost like she knew. Like my mom didn't want me to see her die, so she passed just before I got there. Maybe it doesn't work that way, but if it did, that's what my mom would've done. She wouldn't have wanted me to see those final moments.

"Mom," I whisper, tears trickling down my cheeks. "I didn't want you to go." I look down at her limp hand on the bed and cover it with mine. "I know you didn't want this to be your life." I sniffle. "But I didn't want you to go." I put my hand over my huge belly. "You never got to meet her. If you just could've held on another week, you could've met your granddaughter. If you had, then maybe you would've..." I don't say it, because I know it's not true. Even if she'd met her grandchild, she wouldn't have wanted to live. She was tired. In pain. She could barely move.

She was done.

"I love you, Mom," I say, rubbing her hand. The baby kicks and I softly smile. "She loves you too. She didn't get to meet you, but she loves her grandma." I squeeze my eyes shut and take a deep breath to keep from breaking down. After a few moments, I look at my mom. "I have to leave here, Mom. I can't stay in this town. There are too many memories. Memories I'd rather forget. I always said I'd leave, but didn't think I could. But it's time now. There's nothing keeping me here. I want a fresh start. I want my baby to grow up somewhere else. A place where we can make new memories. Better ones." I sniffle. "I don't know where that is yet, but I'll figure it out."

A nurse knocks on the door and peeks her head in. "They'll be here soon to take her."

I nod. "Okay."

When the nurse leaves, I look back at my mom. "I'm gonna be okay, Mom. I know I haven't been myself since I broke up with Brad, but I'm gonna find my way back. I promise, I will." I put my hand over my belly. "I wish he could've been part of her life. I know I did what was best, but it still hurts. It hurts so much knowing it's over. Knowing I'll never see him again. Knowing he'll never meet his little girl." I take a breath. "He was it for me. Brad was the one." I rub my hand back and forth over my belly. "But I have to move on. I need to raise this baby on my own and be the best mom I can be."

Brad and I never spoke again after that night I told him it was over. I've considered calling him so many times I've lost count, but I never actually did it. I came close back in January. The phone was in my hand, his number was on the screen, but just as I was about to press call, my phone rang. It was Nate telling me Happy New Year. I'd been avoiding his calls since Thanksgiving when I found out he was dating Kari. I didn't want to talk to him after that. I was too angry at him for dating her. But that day in January, I was feeling really lonely so I answered Nate's call. He acted like we were still friends. I went along with it and we talked for an hour.

During the call, I casually asked Nate about his aunt and uncle, hoping it would make him tell me about Brad. It did. He told me Brad was doing well in school and had a job working at a lab on campus. Then he hit me with the news I didn't want to hear. That Brad had a girlfriend. And not just any girlfriend. He was dating Corinne.

Nate said Brad and Corinne had been dating for months and that he knew about it when he was home at Thanksgiving but didn't think he should tell me. I told him I assumed Brad had moved on, but actually I hadn't. I was holding out hope that Brad was still single. That maybe I still had a chance with him.

That day was the day I stopped hoping for something I knew could never be. What Brad and I had was over. We just weren't meant to be. I had to accept that, even if it broke my heart.

The door to my mom's room opens again. Two men are standing next to the nurse.

"I'm almost done," I tell them.

"We could come back," the nurse says, giving me a sad look.

"Just give me a minute."

She closes the door.

"I have to go now, Mom." I lean down and kiss her cheek. "I love you." I slowly stand up and look at her one last time.

As I make my way out of her room, I feel a sharp pain in my stomach. I grab the door handle and manage to open the door enough to talk to the nurse.

"Something's wrong," I tell her, as another sharp pain shoots through my belly. I cringe, doubled over in pain. "I need help."

"Dr. Tinsdale!" she yells as she grabs my arm, trying to hold me up. The man beside her takes my other arm and they lead me to a chair in the hallway.

"What is it?" the doctor asks, hurrying down the hall.

It's the same doctor who was in my mom's room. He's new. I've only met him one other time when he was here to check on my mom. I don't even know what kind of doctor he is, but right now, I don't care. I just want him to stop the pain.

"She almost collapsed," the nurse tells him.

He crouches down in front of me. "What kind of pain?"

"Sharp." I take a deep breath. "It's better now that I sat down."

"How far along are you?"

"My due date is next week."

He looks back at the nurse. "Call an ambulance. She needs to get to a hospital."

The nurse races back to her station.

"What's going on?" I ask him. "Why are you calling an ambulance? Is something wrong?"

"Just relax." He pats my knee as he stands up. "It might just be caused by the stress you're feeling over losing your mom."

"I don't think that's it. I think—" I stop as I feel something wet going down my leg. I look up at the doctor. "Um...Dr. Tinsdale?"

"Yes?" he asks as he steps aside to make room for the wheelchair.

"I think my water just broke."

The ambulance arrives and the next thing I know I'm at the hospital.

Two hours later, my daughter is born. A beautiful baby girl.

Within three hours, I said goodbye to my mom and hello to my daughter. I felt like my mom had something to do with that. She knew I was sad and did the only thing she knew would make me happy. Meeting my baby girl.

———

"I GOT HERE AS SOON as I could," Giada says, racing into my room.

It's the next morning and I'm holding Bree in my arms. She's so tiny. So sweet. I can't stop looking at her.

"Oh my God, she's adorable!" Giada gushes as she sits beside me on the hospital bed. "I'd give you a hug, but I don't want to crush her."

"You won't crush her." I smile at Giada. "You didn't have to do this. You didn't have to come all this way. Don't you have finals this week?"

Giada's almost finished with her first year of grad school. She also has a job and a boyfriend so she doesn't have much free time, but she still finds time to talk to me at least once a day.

"Finals aren't for two more weeks. And you're crazy if you thought I was going to miss this." She stands up and puts her hands on her hips. "You were supposed to wait for me. I was supposed to be in the delivery room with you."

"Sorry, but she came too fast. I barely made it to the hospital. I wasn't even sure what was happening. One minute I'm saying goodbye to my mom and the next I'm in labor."

Giada sits beside me again. "I'm really sorry about your mom. It didn't sound like she was that bad when we talked. Did something happen?"

"I think she just gave up. The doctor said all this medical stuff to explain what happened, but I wasn't really listening. I just kept looking at her and thinking that person isn't my mom. The mom I knew died the night of the accident. After that, she was someone else. She was never the same."

"I'm so sorry," Giada says, putting her hand on my arm. "Is there anything I can do?"

"I don't think so. Renee is going to take care of the funeral arrangements for me. She was here this morning."

"What about for you and the baby? Is there anything I can do? Do you need anything for when you take her home?"

"April came by and dropped off some stuff, so I think I'm okay." I hold the baby up. "You want to hold her?"

"Of course!" Giada takes Bree from me. "Hi Bree," she says, smiling at her. "Riley, she's beautiful."

"She really is," I say, gazing at her.

Giada lightly rocks her. "She looks just like you."

"Really? I think she looks like—" I don't say it. I shouldn't even be thinking it. Brad is out of my life. He's never coming back. Our daughter may look like him, but I'm not going to tell her that. I don't think I'll tell her anything about Brad. Why tell her about a man she'll never know?

"She does look like him," Giada says. "I just didn't want to say it knowing..."

"Knowing what?"

Her eyes lift to mine. "Knowing you still love him."

I look down at Bree. "I don't love him. Not anymore."

Giada hands me the baby. "You're still not going to tell him?"

"Giada, we've talked about this a million times."

"Doesn't mean you can't tell him. It's not too late."

"It *is* too late. He has a new life now." I run my finger over Bree's tiny hand as she sleeps. "He has a girlfriend."

"You don't know if it's serious."

"According to Nate, they're still together. If that's true, they've been dating for months now. I'd say that's serious."

"Or they could just be casually dating. You won't know unless you call him."

"Call him? And say what? Hey, Brad, how's your life going? How's your girlfriend? Any plans to marry her? By the way, you have a daughter. How's med school?"

125

"Yeah, obviously you wouldn't say *that*. You'd just ask how he's doing and see what he says."

"And not tell him about Bree? I couldn't do it. I'd get nervous and blurt it out. It was different last fall. Back then, it still didn't seem real, but now she's here and she's definitely real, and I have a feeling I'd tell him, even if I tried not to."

"Would it really be that bad if he knew?"

"You know it would. He'd give up everything. School. New York. Todd's offer to own the clinic with him. And telling Brad about the baby wouldn't get us back together. He'd be angry I didn't tell him sooner and hold it against me for the rest of our lives."

"You don't know that."

I sigh. "Giada, please don't do this. Don't make me second guess this decision. I've spent months agonizing over it, and I can't do it anymore. I need to move on with my life. I can't keep looking back, wishing I'd done things differently."

She nods. "Okay. I won't bring it up again." She jumps up. "Oh! I almost forgot."

"Forgot what?"

She races out to the hall and returns holding three big gift bags.

"What is all that?" I ask.

"Presents for the baby." She sets one of the bags beside me and pulls out a stack of onesies. "They were all so adorable I couldn't decide which one to get," she says as she lays them out on the bed. "So I got them all. And these blankets." She takes them out of the bag. One is pink with little white bunnies on it and the other is yellow with little white chicks.

"Giada, thanks, but it's way too much. You didn't have to get me all this."

"I'm just getting started." She picks up the other two bags and sets them beside me. "This one is full of toys and the other one has bottles and bibs and stuff like that. I don't know that much about babies so I had to call my mom and ask her what to get." She looks at me, annoyed. "Now, thanks to you, my mom wants a grandchild as soon as possible."

I laugh. "How does Nolan feel about that?"

She doesn't laugh, or even smile.

"Giada, what's wrong?"

"Nolan and I didn't work out."

"You guys broke up? When?"

"Yesterday. Right before you texted me you were having the baby. It was perfect timing, actually. It gave me an excuse to get out of there and come see my best friend." She touches the baby's head. "And this little one. Nothing like a baby to make you feel better, right?"

"Giada, I'm sorry. I know how much you liked him."

She shrugs. "It's fine. I kind of knew it wouldn't last. He's so focused on work. He really doesn't have time for a girlfriend."

Nolan works at some investment company. Giada's explained his job to me more than once, but I still don't understand it. I just know he makes a lot of money and works all the time.

"So what happened?" I ask. "Or do you not want to talk about it?"

"There isn't much to say. He took me to dinner, and during dessert he said things were getting too serious between us and that he wasn't ready for that."

"Why did he think it was getting too serious? Did you two talk about getting married?"

"No, he was just using that as a reason to get out of the

relationship. Whatever. His loss." She smiles at Bree. "Can I hold her again?"

"Sure." I hand her the baby. "How long are you staying?"

"Until you kick me out," she kids.

"I mean, when do you have to leave town?"

"Oh. I'm staying until the funeral. It doesn't make sense to leave and come back."

"The funeral probably won't be until Saturday. Are you sure you can stay that long?"

"It won't be a problem. All my assignments are online. I'll miss the lectures, but that's not a big deal."

"You're a really great friend," I say as I watch her hold Bree.

"And to think you hated me when we first met," she says with a smile.

"I didn't hate you."

She laughs. "You did when you thought I had a thing for Brad. And when I went out with him that one time? I thought you were going to punch me."

"I wasn't *that* jealous, and I tried to hide it."

"You didn't do a very good job. Everyone at the pool knew how much you liked Brad. Well, everyone except Nate. Speaking of Nate, have you heard from him?"

"No, but his mom texted me. She heard the news about my mom. And last night I texted her about the baby."

"Did you text Nate?"

"No. His mom will tell him the news."

"He still calls you, right?"

"Not as often as he used to. We talk maybe once or twice a month."

"And he's still dating Kari?"

"I don't know. I don't ask."

There's a knock on the door.

"Am I interrupting?" I hear his voice, then see Nate walking in, holding a teddy bear with pink balloons tied to it.

"Nate! I can't believe you're here," I say, completely shocked he showed up. He almost never takes a day off from work, and here he is on a Tuesday, all the way from Dallas. He must've left early this morning to get here.

He leans down and gives me a hug. "Sorry about your mom."

I nod.

He sets the bear with the balloons on the table beside me. "I left as soon as I heard the news. Then my mom called while I was driving and told me you had the baby." He glances at Bree, then up at Giada. "Hey, Giada."

"Hi, Nate." She hands me the baby. "I'm gonna go grab a cup of coffee from the cafeteria. You want anything?"

"No, I'm good. Thanks."

She leaves, and I look down at Bree. "She was born last night. I was at the nursing home, saying goodbye to my mom, and right after I left her room, my water broke."

"What's her name?"

"Bree," I say, keeping my eyes on her.

"Bree," he repeats. "Kind of sounds like—"

"Brad." I look up at him. "I wanted her to have a connection to him, even though she'll never know him."

"Are you going to tell her about him?"

"I don't know. Maybe. I haven't decide what I'm going to tell her." I pause. "Have you, um...talked to him?"

"Brad? Yeah. Last week."

"And he's...doing okay?"

"He's great. He decided to stay in New York this summer

instead of going home. His parents are getting divorced. I told you that, right?"

"I don't think so, but I figured they would. So he's getting an apartment there? In New York?"

"Just for the summer. Then he'll go back to campus housing."

"Is it just him or will he have roommates?"

"He'll have a roommate. It's um..." He clears his throat. "Corinne."

My eyes shift from the baby to Nate. "He's living with Corinne?"

"Only for the summer, unless things change."

"So things must be serious between them." My eyes go back to Bree, who's sound asleep in my arms.

"Riley, it's probably better if we don't talk about this."

"Is it serious or not? Just tell me."

He sighs. "He mentioned he'd been shopping for rings."

My gut clenches and I feel short of breath. Any sliver of hope I had of ever reconnecting with Brad was destroyed with those few short words. *Shopping for rings.* Brad's going to ask Corinne to marry him. He's going to have a life with her. Children. A house.

I should be happy for him, but all I feel is sadness. Sadness and loss for what I'll never have.

"Can I see her?" Nate asks, startling me from my thoughts.

"Yeah." I turn Bree toward him. "You can hold her if you want."

"No. I'm afraid I'd drop her." He smiles as he looks at her. "She's really beautiful, Riley."

"I wish my mom had been able to meet her. If she'd just

held on a little longer..." My voice trails off. I can't believe my mom is gone. That I'll never see her again.

"Any news on when the funeral will be?" Nate asks.

"Renee's trying to arrange it for Saturday. Probably in the morning. But Nate, you don't have to stick around for it. I know you and my mom didn't really get along and—"

"I'm doing this for you," he says, putting his hand on my arm. He's giving me that look again. The look he gave me last May when he told me he loves me.

I look back at the baby. "So how's Kari?"

"We broke up."

My eyes dart back to him. "When?"

"A few weeks ago. Apparently, I wasn't making enough money."

"She said that?"

"She said she deserved more than I was giving her. And by more, she meant more jewelry, more gifts. I couldn't keep up. I'm making good money, but I have bills to pay. She didn't seem to get that."

"Is she with someone else now?"

"I don't know. I haven't talked to her since we broke up. I should've listened to you when you warned me about her. I wanted to think she'd changed, but she hasn't."

"So are you dating again?"

"No. Right now I'm good being single. Focusing on work. How about you?"

I smile. "Kind of hard to date when you're pregnant. And I doubt I'll get many dates with a newborn."

"There's guys who'd be open to that. A lot of guys like kids."

"Their own, not someone else's."

"That's not true."

"It doesn't matter. I'm not interested in dating. All I care about right now is Bree and making sure she has the best life possible."

"Are you still planning to move out of the trailer?"

"Yeah. Dave knows a guy who'll buy it when I'm ready to sell. I'm not going to get much for it, but I don't care. I just want to get rid of it."

Giada returns with her coffee. "What are we talking about?" she asks as she sits in the chair by my bed.

"I was telling Nate about the guy who wants to buy the trailer."

"You should sell it while you can," Nate says. "That place needs a lot of work. You may never have another buyer."

"I can't sell it until I have a place to go," I tell him.

"What about those apartments you liked?" he says. "The ones you almost moved into?"

"They're nice, but I'm not staying here."

"Staying where?"

"In town. I'm moving."

"Where?"

"I don't know yet."

His phone rings. "It's work. I have to get this." He hurries out to the hall.

Giada moves over to sit on the bed, her gaze on the door Nate just went through. "He still loves you."

"No, he doesn't."

"He does. I could tell the minute he walked in. He still has that look. The one that says he wishes you were his." She looks back at me. "You can't tell me you didn't notice that."

"I kind of did, but I thought maybe I was imagining it."

Nate pops his head in the room, his phone in his hand. "My boss needs me to do something before he goes home for the night. I'm gonna have to go to my mom's house and work on this. Can I stop by later tonight?"

"Sure," I tell him. "Although they might send me home by then. I'll text you and let you know."

"Okay, bye."

When he's gone, Giada says, "Are you serious about moving?"

"Yeah. With my mom gone, there's no reason for me to stay here. I just don't know where to go.

"I think I have the perfect place," she says, sounding excited.

"Where? What is it?"

She smiles. "You like warm weather?"

"Yeah."

"The beach?"

"I've never been to one, but it's always been my dream to live by a beach. But I can't afford it. Those places would be too expensive."

"Would you be willing to waitress?"

"Well, yeah. It's what I do now. And I actually don't mind it."

She smiles even more. "This is so perfect. I can't believe I didn't think of it sooner."

"Think of what?"

"There's just one thing that could be a problem."

"What?"

"How do you feel about little Italian grandmothers who can be very loud, are strongly opinionated, and maybe a little bossy? Okay, a lot bossy. Any problem with that?"

"Um, no, I don't think so."

"Perfect!" She claps her hands. "I can't wait to tell her!" She gets out her phone.

"Tell who?"

"My grandmother."

"What are you telling her?"

"That she has a new tenant. And a new waitress." Giada starts texting.

"Wait!" I put my hand over her phone. "What's going on here?"

"You, and little Bree," she says, touching her tiny head, "are moving to Florida."

"Florida?"

"Gulf side. Right on the beach. What do you think?"

"I um...I don't know. I think I need to know more."

"You said you wanted a fresh start, right?"

I nod.

"Then don't question it. Just do it. You'll be working for my grandmother, who I admit can be a little crazy, but she's also really sweet. She LOVES kids. You'll have a built-in babysitter. And she loves cooking. You'll never be hungry. You'll get to live on the beach and you'll have a job. C'mon, Riley. I know it sounds scary to leave this place, but it's time. It's time to move on."

"Florida," I say considering it. I look down at Bree. "What do you think?" She's sound asleep, but I swear I see her lips turn up just the tiniest bit. "Bree thinks we should go."

"And how about Riley?"

"I'm with Bree." I smile. "We're going to Florida."

CHAPTER TEN

BRAD

"What do you think of this dress?" Corinne asks as she circles in front of me.

"It's fine," I tell her, barely glancing up from my laptop.

"You didn't even look!" she scolds. "Brad, this is important. I need your opinion."

I sigh as I take a moment to look at her. She's wearing a sleeveless black dress, black heels, and a pearl necklace. It reminds me of something my mom would wear, which to me isn't a good thing, but it's the look Corinne is going for. Classy and sophisticated. A look meant to appeal to old, rich guys.

"It's perfect," I tell her.

"It is, isn't it?" She smiles as she smooths her hair, which is tightly wrapped behind her head. "This dress cost a fortune, but it's worth every penny if it gets his attention."

"I'm sure he'll love it." I wake up my laptop and begin searching again.

Corinne sits beside me on the couch. "Give me some advice."

"About what?"

"About what to talk about. I don't want to come off as being fake. Or young."

"You *are* young. And he knows that."

"Yes, but I want don't want him focusing on it. Age is just a number. It shouldn't matter."

"It shouldn't, but it does. Even if this guy is able to look past your age, his kids won't let him forget it."

She huffs. "His kids don't want him to be happy."

"They're never going to approve of you. You know that, right?"

"I don't need their approval. I only care what Henry thinks, which is why this dress has to be perfect. This is a very important event tonight and I want to impress both Henry and his colleagues." She looks down at her dress. "Maybe I should wear the diamond necklace instead of the pearls. What do you think?"

"An award ceremony with a room full of old men?" I chuckle. "Pearls. Definitely."

Corinne is going out with this old guy professor who used to be one of the best heart surgeons in New York until he injured his hand in a boating accident and was no longer able to do surgery. Now he teaches and does research. Corinne is one of his research assistants for the summer. As soon as she started working for him, she fell in love with his intellect, and then him. He fell for her young, fit body, flirtatious remarks, and flattery, or at least that's what I'm guessing given what I know about old guys with money. It's something I'm familiar with given my dad is one of them. He cheated on my mom

136

with someone almost as young as Corinne. At least Henry's divorced.

"The men at tonight's ceremony are some of the world's top experts in medicine," Corinne insists. "And they're not old, at least not all of them. Certainly not Henry. He's only 55."

I glance at her. "He's over twice your age. That's old."

"It's not that old," she says, rolling her eyes.

"That right there." I point to her. "Don't do that around the old guy. Eye rolling is a sign of youth. Disrespect. It's something his kids would do, and they're older than you, so definitely don't do it."

Looking back at my laptop, I scan through the search results.

"Don't tell me you're still looking for her," Corinne says, sounding annoyed.

I turn so she can't see the computer. "Shouldn't you be leaving for your date?"

"Not yet. He's going to text me when he's ready." She puts her feet up on the coffee table. "So what are you going to do when you find her?"

"Nothing. I'm just curious where she ended up."

Corinne laughs. "Yeah, right. You're completely obsessed with her, Brad. I'm starting to worry."

"I'm not obsessed. This is only the second time I've searched for her and it's only because I have time to kill before work."

"You haven't dated anyone since she left. And I've offered you sex with no strings at least ten times the past year and you've never once taken me up on it."

"You and I are not having sex."

"Well, no, not now that I have the professor. You lost your

chance with me." She smiles as she runs her hand over her pearls. "But you could easily find someone else. Every girl I know wants a chance with you, but you're too obsessed with this Riley girl to care."

"For the last time, I'm not obsessed. Riley and I were friends. I want to know how she's doing."

"Then ask your cousin."

"I don't ask about Riley. We try to stay off that topic."

"Because he's in love with her and she picked you over him." Corinne rolls her eyes. "So much drama."

"You did it again."

"Did what?"

"Rolled your eyes. Old guys hate that. You've gotta stop that before your date tonight."

She takes her feet off the table and turns to me. "Why don't you just ask?"

"Ask what?"

"Ask your cousin all the questions you have about her so you can stop thinking about her and stop searching for her online."

"Asking about her will make Nate think I'm still interested in her, which will lead to us fighting. Nate and I are finally in a good place. I don't want to mess that up. And as for Riley, I'll never stop thinking about her. I loved her. Part of me still does. And I feel like things aren't finished between us. It was such an abrupt end. We never got to say goodbye."

"And you never will. I'm sure she's moved on with someone else by now. What's the last thing your cousin told you about her?"

"That her mom died. And what really pisses me off is that he was able to be there for her and I wasn't."

I wanted more than anything to be at that funeral. To be with Riley. To hold her in my arms and tell her everything would be okay. I almost did it. I almost flew out there, but Nate convinced me it wasn't a good idea.

"You could've called her," Corrine says.

"I was going to, but Nate talked me out of it. He said she was really upset and wanted to be left alone."

"And right after that she moved?"

"No, she moved at the end of May, so actually I guess that was the last thing Nate told me about her."

"And Nate doesn't know where she went?" Corinne asks. "Or is he just not telling you?"

"He says he doesn't know. Riley told him she wanted to leave her old life behind, which included him. He didn't think she was serious until he tried calling her and found she'd changed her number. Now he doesn't know how to reach her. I think her friend, Giada, knows where Riley is, but she won't tell Nate."

"It sounds like she doesn't want to be found," Corinne says.

"Yeah, maybe." I close my browser, thinking Corinne might be right. It might be time to finally accept that Riley is gone and I need to move on with my life.

Corinne's phone dings. "That's Henry." She stands up. "Last time. How do I look?"

"Great." I smile. "The old guys are gonna love you."

She rolls her eyes, then cringes. "Shit. I did it again."

"Maybe you should wear sunglasses," I kid.

"Why do I even ask you?" she says as she walks away.

When she's gone, I set my laptop aside and turn on the TV. My phone rings and I see it's Nate. I turn the TV down as I answer the call.

139

"Hey, Nate. Haven't heard from you for a while."

"Yeah, I've been busy with work. Finally got that promotion."

"Congratulations. That's great. More money, I assume?"

"Ten percent raise, so not great, but better than nothing."

"Will you have to work more?"

"Not sure yet. I get to manage someone now, so I'm hoping I can hand some of my work over to her. What's new with you? How's the bartending gig?"

"Not bad. I make more in a night than I did an entire week at the pool last summer."

He chuckles. "Yeah, we didn't make much, but it was fun. I miss working there."

"Yeah, me too."

It's hard to believe that was last summer. It seems like a lifetime ago.

Last year at this time I was dating Riley, spending every free moment I had with her while trying to hide it from Nate. When we weren't together, we were on the phone, calling or texting each other. We couldn't get enough of each other, which is why it's still hard to believe that it ended like it did.

Even though Riley and I only dated a few months, it seemed like so much longer. My time with her felt more like years than months, I think because we shared so much of ourselves with each other. We skipped that early dating stage where you hide all the bad stuff and pretend everything's perfect. Right away, she told me about her mom and their money problems and her issues with Nate, and I told her about my messed up parents and my dad's gambling addiction and his cheating on my mom. It was stuff I hadn't talked about with anyone, not even Nate, and yet I told Riley. I felt like I could tell her anything. It's why I fell for her, and why I went from seeing her as Nate's friend to seeing her as the girl I could spend my life with.

"How's your roommate?" Nate asks with a smile in his voice.

"Fine. And my roommate is all she is, and all she'll ever be. Corinne and I are friends. That's it."

"You didn't even test the waters? Not once?"

"If you're asking if I slept with her, the answer is no. I'm not interested in her that way."

"Are you interested in *any* girl that way? Because this dry spell you're having is starting to worry me."

"I'm not looking for a girlfriend. Between work and school and going to the gym, I don't have time for a girlfriend."

"You don't need a girlfriend to have sex. You work at a bar. I'm sure there are plenty of girls there who'd be more than happy to have sex with you."

"That's not I want."

"Why not? Since when have you not wanted—"

"How about you?" I ask, interrupting him. "Have you dated anyone since Kari?"

"No. I'm taking a break from relationships."

"Then why are you giving me shit about not having sex? You're not getting any either."

"I said I'm not in a relationship. I'm still having sex. Had it just last night, actually. Went to a bar with some friends from work and hooked up with this girl."

"Hooking up with a girl you just met? That doesn't sound like you, Nate."

"The old Nate, no, but the new one is all for it."

"And why is that?"

"Because I'm starting to think love doesn't exist. And if it does, it's impossible to find."

"You're only 23. You're giving up a little early, don't you think?"

"I'm no different than you."

"Meaning what?"

"You've given up. You haven't dated anyone since Riley."

"Because I haven't found anyone as good as her. Riley was...different. Girls like her don't come along every day."

"Yeah, Riley's one of a kind."

"So you, uh...still haven't heard from her?"

"No. And I doubt I will. Even if she wanted to be friends again, she doesn't have time."

"How do you know?"

He doesn't answer.

"Nate, what are you not telling me?"

"Nothing. Just forget it."

"If you know something about Riley, you better fucking tell me."

"Why? Things are over between you two."

"Doesn't mean I don't still care about her. I need to know she's okay."

"I'm sure she's fine. If something happened to her, Giada would tell me."

"You never talk to Giada."

"No, but if something happened to Riley, Giada would tell me."

"Give me Giada's number. Maybe if I talk to her, she'll tell me where Riley is."

"She won't. She said Riley doesn't want anything to do with her old life, which obviously includes me or she would've given me her number."

"That doesn't make sense. Did you guys have a fight, or why is she so insistent on never seeing you again?"

"Because I'm your cousin."

"Why would that matter?"

"She doesn't want shit getting back to you."

"Like what?"

"I don't know. Just forget it."

"You know where she is, don't you?"

"I don't. I swear. And I wasn't lying about her number. She changed it and I don't have the new one."

"What did you mean when you said she doesn't have time?"

"What are you talking about?"

"You said even if she wanted to still be friends with you, she wouldn't have time. What did you mean?"

"I don't know. I guess I just assumed she'd be working a lot."

"That's not what you meant. You know something. Something you don't think you should tell me."

He doesn't respond.

"Nate, I swear if you don't tell me I'll fly my ass down to Dallas and *make* you tell me."

He sighs. "Fine. But you're not going to want to hear this."

"Hear what? What is it?"

"Riley, um..." He pauses. "Riley has a kid."

"What?"

"She had a baby."

"Yeah, right," I say with a laugh. "C'mon, Nate, stop joking around and tell me what you know."

"I'm not joking. Riley had a baby. She had it in May, right before she moved. I called her to congratulate her and that's the last time we spoke. After that, she moved away and changed her number."

"Riley had a baby?" I mutter, still not believing it.

"I didn't think you'd want to know. That's why I didn't tell you."

"You said she had it in May?"

"End of May."

End of May. And I was with her in July.

"She got pregnant in August," Nate says, like he knows I'm trying to work the timing out in my head. "Sorry, man. You see why I didn't want to tell you?"

Riley cheated on me. She was with another guy after I moved away. I can't believe she'd do that. Why'd she keep dating me if she had someone else? Why didn't she break up with me back in August?

"When did you find out?" I ask.

"Last fall. When I came home for Thanksgiving, she was starting to show. It wasn't much, but it was enough that I asked her about it."

She was starting to show when she was here in New York. She told me she'd just gained some weight. She lied to me. Why would she even come here, knowing she was pregnant with another guy's baby?

Now it makes sense why Riley ended things so abruptly and ignored all my attempts to contact her. She knew if I ever saw her again I'd find out she was pregnant and she'd have to confess she'd been with someone else.

"Who was it?" I ask through gritted teeth. I'm so freaking angry. All these months I've been missing Riley, thinking she was the love of my life, only to find out she hooked up with someone else as soon as I left town.

I really thought we had something together. I thought she loved me. But I guess not.

"She wouldn't tell me," Nate says. "But the gossip around town is that it was a guy who was there a few months for a construction job. I think it was for that warehouse they built just outside of town."

That doesn't sound like Riley. Hooking up with some guy she barely knows? She didn't like her mom doing that, so it doesn't make sense she'd do it herself.

"You think it's true?" I ask. "About this guy? Did you ask her about him?"

"I did, but like I said, she wouldn't tell me. She just said I didn't know the guy."

"Do you know where he's from?"

"I don't know anything about him other than what I just told you. And nobody in town knew him. Like I said, he wasn't from there. He was just there to do a job."

"Maybe that's where Riley went. Maybe she moved to wherever this guy lives. Do you know if they're still dating?"

"She made it sound like it was over last fall, but who knows? It's possible they got back together after the baby arrived."

The baby. I can't believe Riley has a baby. A baby with another guy.

That guy should've been me. I'm not ready to have a kid, but if Riley had gotten pregnant when we were together, we could've made it work. I know we could have.

The first night we made love we didn't use a condom and I panicked for a moment, thinking we might have just made a kid. Later, I thought about it and imagined what would happen if Riley really had gotten pregnant that night. I was surprised when that panicked feeling didn't return. In fact, I

145

kind of liked the idea of Riley having my baby. Me being a dad. Before then, the thought of having a kid when I'm this young and still in school would've been my worst nightmare. But I didn't feel that way when I imagined it happening with Riley and me. If it had happened to us, we'd be together right now. Together with our baby. We'd have the life I wanted with her. It'd be sooner than I planned, but I'd take it. I'd love Riley and our baby more than anything.

But that's not what happened. She found someone else. Had his child.

It's time to move on. I've waited all these months for something that will never happen. Riley is never coming back. She has a new life.

And it's time I start living mine.

CHAPTER ELEVEN

THREE YEARS LATER

Riley

"Mommy, look!" Bree runs up to me, holding a tiny pink shell.

I bend down to see it. "Wow, that's really pretty."

"Nonna found one too!"

Sophia smiles as she follows behind. She can't keep up with Bree. Neither can I. Bree runs so fast I think she might be a track star someday.

"Thanks for taking her," I say to Sophia as I pick up Bree.

"Always my favorite part of the day." Sophia leans down to kiss Bree's head. "We love our morning walks, don't we little one?"

Bree nods really fast, then holds up her shell. "Can it go in the jar?"

"Yes." I set her down. "Go ahead. I'll be up in a minute."

She races through the kitchen to the stairs in the back that lead to our apartment. We live above the diner, which is where Sophia used to live until she decided she wanted a quieter place in town. She got herself a condo in a retirement community a few miles from here, but she still comes to work every day at the diner. She owns the place, including the apartment. It isn't much, but it's perfect for Bree and me. And since I'm best friends with Giada, her grandma gave me a great deal on rent—only $300 a month if I work at the diner. And the best part? It's right on the beach.

Every day I wake up, look out the window, and see the ocean. I smell the salty air. I hear the crash of the waves. For years, I dreamed of going to the ocean and now I get to see it every day.

I love it here. The warm weather. The beach. The beautiful sunsets. Living in a place that isn't a trailer. Raising my daughter here. It's my dream. All I ever wanted. The only thing missing is a husband, but I'm thinking that part of the dream may never happen.

Working full time and raising Bree, I don't have much time to date. And the few dates I've gone on didn't go well. As soon as guys find out I have a kid, they take off. Last year I went out with a guy who has a kid of his own, thinking that might work out better. He was a nice guy, but I felt nothing for him, not even a hint of a spark. So as of now, I've decided to just focus on being a mom and not worry about finding a guy.

"I'm coming to get you," I say as I race up the stairs. Bree is standing there looking at her shell. I scoop her up and cover her in kisses.

"Mommy, no." She giggles and tries to squirm away.

"You don't want kisses?"

"You break my shell," she says, hiding it in her hand.

"We'll put it in the jar where it's safe, okay?"

She nods.

I take her to her room, which is only big enough for her bed and the cardboard box I turned into a nightstand. I set her down on her bed and she carefully lowers the shell into the plastic jar. It's a giant mayonnaise jar from the restaurant that I cleaned out for her to store her shells. I had her decorate the outside of it with stickers.

"So pretty, Mommy." She sits on her bed and stares at the mayonnaise jar full of shells like it's the most wonderful thing she's ever seen. I love watching the world through her eyes. Even the simplest things, like a seashell, are magical to her.

"Should we go have a snack?" I ask, sitting beside her.

It's ten, which is when she has her morning snack. I try to keep her on a schedule as best I can. Sophia helps with that too. She takes care of Bree during my shifts, then works in the kitchen or orders supplies while I'm on break. I've offered to hire a sitter, but Sophia won't let me. She's been helping me care for Bree since she was an infant and thinks of her as her grandchild. If I even try to get a sitter for a night out, Sophia won't let me. She doesn't want a stranger caring for Bree. She's very protective of her, and me. I'm so lucky to have her. She's become like a mother to me.

"Bree, let's go. It's snack time."

"Mommy?" She looks up at me.

I pull her to my side and kiss her head. "What is it, sweet girl?"

"Why don't I have a daddy?"

She's never asked me that before. I knew the question was coming, but I thought it'd come later, when she's older.

I look at her big brown eyes, which are exactly like Brad's. Every time I look at her, I see those eyes and think of him. I wonder what he's doing. Where he's living. Who he's with. I've been trying for years not to think about him, but it's impossible when my little girl looks just like him. She acts like him too. Like right now, she's so serious, so intense, just like Brad. When he couldn't figure something out, he'd get this intense look on his face like he was thinking really hard, just like Bree is doing now.

"You have a daddy," I tell her. "He's just not here."

"Then where is he?" She turns to me, crossing her legs in front of her, her hands in her lap, like she does when I tell her a story.

"He um...he lives somewhere else."

"Where does he live?" Her eyes get wide, like she's eager for my every word.

What do I tell her? I don't know what to say. I wasn't prepared for this.

"I'm not really sure where he lives."

She frowns. "So I can't go see him?"

"No, sweetie." I hug her to my side. "I'm sorry, you can't."

"Nonna could write him a letter," she says, her eyes getting big again. "Like Santa!"

Sophia is always writing letters to her family back in Italy, and last Christmas, she helped Bree write a letter to Santa.

"I don't have your daddy's address." I pick her up and set her on my lap. "Your daddy isn't part of our lives anymore. He has a new life now."

"But doesn't he want to see me?"

"He would love to see you, but he can't. He can't be with us."

"But why?"

What do I tell her? How do I explain this to her?

"Where's my little Bree hiding?" Sophia asks as she comes up the stairs.

I sigh in relief. If anyone can get Bree's mind off her dad, it's Sophia. She's good at distracting her.

Bree slides off me and hides under her blanket, giggling.

"I don't know where she went," I say to Sophia. "She was here just a minute ago."

More giggling comes from under the blanket.

"I guess we'll just have to eat these cookies without her," Sophia says.

"Guess so." I get up and walk to the kitchen. "These are really good. Too bad Bree can't have any."

Just then, she comes running into the kitchen. "I want one!" she says, jumping up and down.

I smile at Sophia. "I'll go help Hector with lunch."

She nods, then leans down to Bree. "How about some milk with those cookies?"

As I go down the stairs, I have to stop a minute and take a breath. For months now, I've had this dizziness that seems to come out of nowhere. Or sometimes I'll feel lightheaded during my shift and have to sit down. Sophia says I'm dehydrated or not eating enough, but even when I drink water and eat every couple hours, I still feel this way. It reminds me of how I felt when I was pregnant, but I'm definitely not pregnant. I haven't had sex for almost a year. I still can't believe I did that. It was Fourth of July and I went to a party with one of the waitresses who works the dinner shift. I got really drunk and ended up having sex with her brother. She doesn't work here anymore, but her brother still comes here now and then. I pretend I don't know him, or hide in the back until he's gone.

Other than Julian, the guy I slept with that night, I've only been with one other guy since Brad. It was two years ago, and the guy looked just like Brad. When I saw him come into the

151

diner, I thought for sure it was him. The guy looked so much like Brad that I couldn't stop staring. The guy thought I was flirting with him and asked me out. We went on a few dates and ended up sleeping together. After that, I never saw him again.

"Riley, can you stir the sauce?" Hector yells from the kitchen. He must've seen me on the stairs.

"Yeah, I'm coming." I hurry down the rest of the stairs and go over to the pot.

"Where's your mini me?" he asks.

I smile. "Upstairs with Grandma. They moved their snack time upstairs today."

He nods. "Just signed my little one up for preschool."

Hector has a four-year-old son. His wife is in the military and stationed overseas so Hector's living with his mom. She watches his little boy when Hector's at work.

"Is he excited about it?" I ask.

"Nah. He'd rather be home with Grandma, playing with his cars while she watches her soaps."

"I'm sure he'll like it once he's there."

"How about you? You signing up Bree?"

"Not this year. Maybe next year, if I can afford it.

"Yeah, I hear ya. It ain't cheap."

Sophia comes down the stairs. "I was telling Bree a story and she fell asleep."

"Really?" I ask. "She's usually full of energy this time of day."

"She was tired from the shell hunting." She winks at me. "We had to find the perfect one."

For some reason Bree thinks fairies live in seashells, and when they don't need them anymore, they leave them on the beach. But they only live in pink shells, so that's what Bree searches for and collects. I don't know where she comes up with this stuff. I'm not creative like that, and as far as I know, Brad isn't either.

"Sophia, can I talk to you a minute?" I ask.

"Of course, dear." She motions for me to follow her. "In my office."

"Turn down the sauce before you go," Hector says.

I turn it down, then meet up with Sophia in the room she calls her office. It's really just a storeroom with a desk surrounded by boxes.

"What is it?" she asks, taking a pencil from her bun and writing something on her order pad.

"It's about Bree. I was wondering if she ever asked you about her dad."

Sophia looks up at me. "No, but I've noticed her watching other children with their fathers when we're walking on the beach."

"I've noticed that too, but she's never asked."

"And now she has?"

"Yeah. Right before you came upstairs. She asked where her daddy is."

"And what did you tell her?"

"That I don't know. I didn't want to lie to her and make up some story about him, so I told her the truth. I told her he has a new life now."

"What did she say?"

"She wanted to know more, but I didn't know what to tell her. I didn't think she'd be asking this soon. Before she could ask anything more, you came upstairs and distracted her, but I know she's going to ask again. What do you think I should say?"

"That's up to you. You need to decide how much you want her to know about him."

"I don't know if I want her to know anything. The more she knows, the more questions she'll ask."

"Do you think you'd ever want to contact him?"

"No. I decided a long time ago not to tell him about Bree, and that hasn't changed. I haven't changed my mind. For all I know, he's married and has other kids by now."

"Isn't he still in school?"

"He should've graduated last May."

"And then he'll have his residency for four or five years?"

"I don't know how long it lasts. It depends on what he decided to do. He always said he wanted to go into family practice, but maybe he changed his mind and decided to be some other kind of doctor. I really don't know."

She leans across the desk and looks me in the eye. "Why don't you call him?"

"What?" I laugh. "No. I'm not calling him. Why would I call him?"

"Because your daughter wants to know her father."

"But her father doesn't know she exists."

"You could at least find out where he's living."

"Why? I'm not going to go see him."

"Riley, you never met your father, correct?"

"No. My mom said she didn't know where he was."

"And how did that make you feel as a child?"

I sigh. "Yeah, fine, it made me sad, but finding him and finding out he didn't want me would've made me even sadder. I'm not calling Brad. It's better if he isn't part of our lives, especially if he has one with someone else."

She sits back. "Then you better come up with some better answers because that little girl of yours doesn't stop. She'll

154

keep asking you questions until she gets an answer that makes sense to her."

"I know."

Bree is the most inquisitive kid I've ever met. She's constantly asking questions, and if I don't have an answer, she makes one up. Like with the seashells. She asked where shells come from and why some are pink. I didn't have time to look it up when she asked, so I told her I didn't know. That's when she came up with the fairy story.

I don't want her making up stories about her dad, so I need to tell her something. I just don't know what. But I'm not calling up Brad or trying to find out where he lives. That part of my life is closed, and opening it again would just end with me getting hurt.

"I need to get back to the kitchen." I stand up, then quickly sit down.

"What's wrong?" Sophia asks.

"I got dizzy. I think I stood up too fast."

She tilts her head. "Did you eat this morning?"

"Yeah, but it was early. Around six."

"Go eat something. And drink water. You never drink enough water."

"I will." I stand up, slower this time, but still feel dizzy.

"Riley," Sophia says as I'm leaving.

"Yeah?"

"Are you pregnant?"

I laugh. "No. Trust me. It's not even possible."

She nods. "Go eat. And while you're out there, tell Hector not to overcook the pasta."

"Got it." I go to the kitchen and take some cheese from the fridge and a roll from the pan that just came out of the oven.

"I thought you were helping me," Hector says in a kidding tone.

"I was told I have to eat."

"Having those dizzy spells again?" he asks, stirring the pasta.

"Yeah. I can't figure it out. I'm not sick. I just get dizzy sometimes or lightheaded."

"You should go to the doctor."

"It costs too much. Don't tell Sophia this, but the insurance here sucks."

"That's why I'm on my wife's plan."

The water in the pot next to him boils over.

"Shit," he says, turning down the heat.

"Is he overcooking the pasta?" Sophia yells from the storeroom.

"No, ma'am!" he yells back, then he whispers to me, "She's small, but she scares me."

I laugh, because it's true. Sophia isn't even five feet tall and weighs about ninety pounds, but she takes her food very seriously and her temper flares when it's not prepared right. Hector's six-five and over three hundred pounds, but he jumps when he hears her yelling.

"I'm gonna go clean up the dining room for lunch," I tell him.

After grabbing my supplies, I go out to the dining area and start wiping down tables. I'm halfway done when Giada calls.

"Hey, Giada," I say as I continue to clean.

"Hey, can you talk?"

"I'm cleaning, but I can take a break." I take a seat at one of the tables. "What's up?"

156

"There was a fire at my office so they sent everyone home."

"How bad was the fire? Did anyone get hurt?"

"Everyone was fine. It was just a small fire, but they have to inspect the building before they let us back in. That could take all day."

"So you have the day off. What are you going to do?"

"Stay in bed. Read. Watch TV. Sounds boring, but I never get to do that stuff anymore. I'm always at the office or on the road."

Giada decided grad school wasn't for her, so she quit after a year and got a job selling medical equipment. It was only supposed to be temporary until she found something else, but she was doing so well they promoted her and now she's one of their top salespeople. She travels all over the country, including to Florida, so I get to see her every few months.

"How's mini Riley?" she asks. She calls Bree that sometimes because she thinks Bree looks just like me. I guess she does a little, but when I look at her, all I see is Brad. "Has she found any more abandoned fairy houses?"

"She did. She found one this morning with Nonna."

"She's such a sweetie. Oh, I got her a fairy doll when I was in San Diego last week. Is it okay if I send it to her, or do I have to wait until Christmas?"

"You can send it to her. I'll tell her it's a late birthday gift."

I try not to give Bree gifts outside of holidays. I can only afford to give her things on her birthday and Christmas, so I've asked other people to do the same. I don't want her expecting gifts or asking for things throughout the year.

"Did she like her birthday dress?" Giada asks. She bought

Bree a pink sundress for her birthday that is so adorable I'm keeping it even after she grows out of it.

"She loves it. She wears it all the time. She calls it her fairy dress because it's pink. She's convinced fairies only wear pink to match their pink houses."

Giada laughs. "Where does she come up with this stuff?"

"Just a good imagination, I guess." I pause. "She asked about her dad today."

"And? What did you say?"

"Not much. Your grandma came up for snack time and distracted Bree with cookies."

"So you didn't tell her anything?"

"I told her I don't know where he is and that he can't be part of our lives."

"He *could* be," she says.

"How? He has a new life now. A life with someone else."

"You don't know that. For all you know, he's still single and wishing he could see you again."

"A guy like Brad is not still single. In fact, I bet he's married by now, or at least engaged."

"Doesn't mean he's not still thinking about you."

"If he's engaged and still thinking about me, he shouldn't be engaged."

"You think about *him* but still go on dates."

"I haven't been on a date in months. And I don't think about Brad."

"Really? Hmm. When's the last time you thought about him?"

"Today, but that's only because Bree asked about him."

"So you didn't think about him yesterday?"

"Okay, yeah, I did, but only because Bree asked for chocolate chip ice cream, which is also Brad's favorite."

"And the day before?"

"This guy came in wearing swim trunks that looked just like the ones Brad used to wear so—" I sigh. "Okay, fine. I think about him, but only when I'm reminded of him."

"Which is every day, since you live with a miniature version of him."

"She has his eyes. That's it. You're always saying she looks like me more than him."

"But she acts like him. All the questions. That look she gets when she's thinking really hard. The way she tells you it'll all work out when you're sad. That's just what Brad used to tell you."

"She only says that because you told her that."

"I didn't tell her that."

"You didn't?"

"No. It must've come from you."

"I never said that to her."

"She just came up with it on her own?"

"Maybe she heard it on TV. Or from Sophia."

"The point is, it's another way she's like her dad. She always sees the positive."

"That's just kids in general. They aren't jaded like adults."

"You can try to deny it all you want, but Bree is just like her father. She may not have inherited his looks, but she definitely inherited his personality."

I smile. "Yeah. She did. Which is why I can't help but think about Brad. She's a constant reminder of him."

"It's not just that. You think about him because you still love him."

"I don't love him. Not anymore. Not after three years."

159

"It's been almost four since you've seen him," she reminds me.

"Okay, then four. Giada, I don't want to talk about Brad. Let's talk about you. How's work? Any plans to be in Florida soon?"

"Maybe in September. I have to check my calendar. I'll let you know. Hey, what's going on with these dizzy spells you keep having?"

"How'd you know about that?"

"Nonna. She said you've been getting dizzy again. Wasn't that happening a few months ago?"

"It comes and goes. I just need to drink more water."

"It could be more serious than that. You should get it checked out."

"And pay to have some doctor tell me I'm dehydrated? Sorry, but no. I'd rather spend the money on groceries. Or books for Bree. She really wants to read so I'm going to get her some books and read to her every night."

"That's great, but going back to you, I really think you should get this checked out. There could be something wrong with your heart. I just went through training for—"

"Nothing's wrong with my heart. I'm 26. People my age don't have heart problems."

"Sure they do. People of any age can have heart problems."

"Well, I'm not one of them. Hey, can we talk later? I really need to finish cleaning before we open for lunch."

"Okay. Tell Nonna I said hi and give Bree a hug and kiss from me."

"I will. Bye!"

I go back to cleaning tables, stopping every few minutes to drink some water. I should eat something too. I get busy and forget to eat. I'm sure that's why I've been feeling so dizzy.

"Mommy, Mommy!" Bree runs out of the kitchen and up to me.

"Hey, sweetie." I pick her up and give her a hug.

"I miss you," she says, resting her head on my shoulder.

"I'm right here." I kiss her head.

"Don't go," she says, her tiny arms around my neck.

"What do you mean? Where would I go?"

"Don't go like Daddy."

She thinks I'll leave like her daddy did. But he didn't leave. He just doesn't know about her. How do I make her understand that? And what happens when she's older? Do I tell her the truth about Brad? That he never knew she existed?

CHAPTER TWELVE

BRAD

"We need to leave soon," Elise says as she comes over to adjust my collar. "You should toss this shirt. It's so worn out, the collar keeps curling up."

"I'm not tossing it." I walk over to the mirror. "It's one of my favorite shirts."

It's a black polo shirt that's old and faded and probably should be tossed, but I can't bring myself to do it. I bought it the summer I lived in Oklahoma. The summer I worked at the pool. The summer I met Riley. She was with me when I picked it out.

Elise doesn't know that. She doesn't know about Riley. I don't talk about her, but I still think about her. I think about her all the damn time. I try not to, but every little thing reminds me of her. Like yesterday, I went to get my hair cut and it reminded me of the first time I met Riley. I felt an attraction to her the moment I saw her. Then she smiled and

I heard her voice, and that was it. I fell for her that fast. After our first date, I was hers. There was just something about her I've never been able to put into words, but I knew I'd never find someone like her again.

I've come to accept that, but I still can't stop thinking about her. When I met Elise, I immediately loved her energy, her intelligence, her enthusiasm for life. She came along at a time when I needed that. I was halfway through my second year of med school, exhausted and tired of school, wondering if it was even worth it. I met Elise, who had already graduated and was doing her residency, and heard all her inspiring stories about working with patients, and that's all it took to get me back on track. She made me excited about medicine again.

Sometimes I wonder if people are put in our lives at the time when we need them the most. But if that's the case, then why did I meet Riley? Why would I meet a girl I'd fall in love with, but couldn't be with? I wasn't looking to fall in love that summer, or even date. I was just there to make money and hang out with Nate. A girlfriend was the last thing I wanted, so why did it happen? Why did I meet her?

"Brad, hurry up," Elise says as she goes to get her purse from the bed. "Why are you just standing there?"

I wake from my thoughts and see I'm still facing the mirror. I turn to Elise. "Guess I'm just tired."

"Tired?" She laughs. "You're on summer break. Just wait until you start your residency. Then you'll know what tired feels like."

Elise has a year left of her residency. Mine starts in the fall. I applied to places in the area, but ended up getting assigned to a hospital in Charleston, South Carolina. Since

Elise's residency is here in New York, we'll be living apart next year. Our plan is to try to see each other a couple times a month, although that could be a challenge given our schedules. Elise is confident it'll work out, but I'm not so sure. Distance ended my relationship with Riley and I'm worried that might happen again with Elise.

"This woman is supposed to be the best caterer in New York," Elise says as we walk out to the street. I step aside as two guys on their phones race past me like they didn't even see I was there. Then a bike messenger goes by, bumping my arm as he flies past.

"Did you hear me?" Elise asks, holding my hand as we walk. "Brad, what's wrong with you today?"

"Nothing." I inhale a breath and notice the smell of the city. I never noticed it until Riley pointed it out. That was four years ago, and I've been aware of it ever since.

I used to love this city. The crowds, the noise, the constant activity. But now I'm tired of it. I don't even like being here anymore. When I found out I'd be moving to Charleston, I was happy about it. I'll miss Elise, but I won't miss the city. Four years here is enough. I want to go someplace quieter. Not as crowded. A place I can breathe without inhaling exhaust fumes. For now, Charleston will be that place, and then later, after my residency, I'm hoping Elise and I can settle down somewhere else. I'm not sure where yet. We can't seem to agree on a place. She likes big cities, but I want to live someplace smaller that isn't so crowded.

That's one of the reasons I didn't take the deal Todd offered me. The clinic he wanted me to own with him was too close to Boston, another big, crowded city. And it's cold there, and I'm sick of the cold. Todd and I are still friends. We just won't be business partners.

"This caterer is young, but getting a lot of press," Elise says, walking at her usual brisk pace. She's incapable of walking slow. Last winter we went to a resort in Mexico for a few days, and what were supposed to be slow romantic walks on the beach turned out to be fast sprints. She just can't slow down.

"If she's that popular," I say, "are you sure we can get her for August?"

"I've already booked her. I know we haven't met her yet, but I had to book her before it was too late."

"How much is this going to cost?"

"Don't worry about that. Daddy's paying for it."

Elise's parents are rich, as in multimillionaires. They live here in New York and attend all the high society events. They know a ton of people and have invited almost all of them to our engagement party. When I proposed to Elise last May, I thought we'd celebrate with some champagne and a few of our friends, but her parents insisted we have this huge engagement party that is going to cost more than most weddings. I haven't even asked what the wedding will be like. We haven't set a date yet, but Elise wants it to be sometime next summer.

"Your parents are both coming to the party, right?" she asks.

"Yes. And my brother."

"Anyone else from your family? Your aunt? Cousins?"

"No. Just my parents and brother."

My parents are divorced now and my brother is married and living in Oregon. I haven't talked to Aunt Kathy or Nate for over a year. Aunt Kathy married the guy she was dating when I lived with her. They moved to Houston last year and have been busy fixing up their new house. As for Nate, I'm not sure why it's been so long since we talked. I guess we've just both been too busy. Last time he called, he said he hadn't heard anything from Riley, which makes me wonder what happened to her.

Wherever she is, I hope she's happy. And if she's with a guy, I hope he treats her well. I wish I could've been the guy for her, but I guess it just wasn't meant to be.

"Taxi!" Elise yells as one pulls over to the curb.

"We can't walk?" I ask, following her into the cab.

"It's ten more blocks. I don't want to be late." She gives the cab driver the address.

Not being able to drive is another thing I don't like about this city. I'm tired of having to take the subway, or having to pay someone to drive me a few blocks. Even if I had a car, I'd have nowhere to park it. I miss driving. As soon as I get to Charlotte, I'm buying a car. Then I'm going to take a long drive, not caring where I'm going. It'll be like the day I went on a drive with Riley. I had no idea where we'd end up. I just wanted to get her out of Oklahoma so she could finally say she'd left the state. She was so happy that day. She couldn't stop smiling.

I miss her smile. I wish I could see it again. I wish I could see *her* again.

"It's this one," Elise says to the cab driver as she points to the building. "We can just get out here." She swipes her credit card as the driver pulls over.

Elise insists on paying for everything. It bothers me, and I've told her that, but she doesn't want to eat at cheap restaurants or live in a crappy apartment, which is all I can afford. In order to keep her lifestyle, she has to be the one to pay. She says once I'm working I can pay for things, but my residency salary won't be enough for the things she wants.

Right before I met Riley, I told myself I'd never date a rich girl again. I was tired of them never being happy with what they had. They were always wanting more; more clothes, more shoes, more jewelry. I didn't want to spend my life working in order to pay for it all. And I didn't want what little free time I had being spent at social events trying to impress other rich people. That was my parents' life. I didn't want it to be mine.

When I met Riley, I finally felt like I could be myself. I didn't have to buy her things to impress her, or dress a certain way in order for her to be seen with me. She didn't care what I wore, and she never expected me to buy her anything. The few times I bought her groceries she hugged me and almost cried, she was so happy. To me it wasn't a big deal, but to her it was huge. It was one of the many things I loved about her. She was so appreciative of whatever I did for her.

Now I'm dating a rich girl and going to society events where I have to wear a tuxedo and pretend to be interested in some rich guy's story about how he made a killing in the stock market last week. And I have to spend a beautiful summer afternoon inside some stuffy old building, tasting food for a party I don't want to have or go to.

I'm not sure how this happened. How did I end up doing the exact opposite of what I said I'd do? My parents are thrilled with how my life turned out. They love that I'm engaged to a girl from a wealthy, well-known family, and can't wait for us to buy a mansion and have two or three kids.

I don't want a mansion, or the excessive lifestyle that comes with it, but when I try to tell Elise that, she brushes me off. She tells me we'll talk about it later, but when's later? We're engaged. We need to be talking about these things now.

"Do you prefer shrimp or scallops as the first course?" Elise asks as we walk to the building. "Actually, if we have lobster for the main course, then maybe we should..."

Elise's voice becomes distant as I stare at a girl coming toward me. She looks just like Riley, but there's no way it could be her. I slow down as she gets closer, then watch as she weaves through a group of tourists who have stopped to take pictures.

She passes by me from a few feet away. She looks so similar to Riley. What if it was her?

I turn and watch her walking away. "Riley?" I yell. She doesn't turn back. "Riley!" I yell it so loud that several people look back, including her. She sees me and smiles.

It's not her. It's not Riley.

"Brad, what are you doing?" Elise yanks on my arm. "We're going to be late."

"Let's go." I take her hand and we walk back toward the building.

"Why were you yelling at that woman?" Elise asks.

"She looked like someone I knew."

"Riley?"

I look at her. "What did you say?"

"Riley. That's what you were yelling. Who's Riley?"

"Just a girl I used to know. She was a friend of Nate's." I open the door for Elise. "Go ahead."

We go to the caterer's office and Elise gets so wrapped up in the food and deciding what to serve that she forgets all about the incident on the sidewalk. But I don't. When I thought that girl was Riley, my heart was beating out of my chest. I thought I'd finally found her.

I wanted it to be her. And when it wasn't, I felt this huge loss, almost as bad as the loss I felt when she left me. What does that mean? Why am I feeling this way about a girl who's been out of my life for years? And what does it mean for Elise and me?

"What's next?" I ask Elise as we leave the shoe store. After the caterer, Elise wanted to go shopping. She dragged me to three stores and then didn't even buy anything.

"The bar. That one by the park? Why do I always forget the name? The one we had drinks at last week with Jane and Walter."

Jane and Walter are friends of hers from college. They're both actors and talk about nothing but the New York theater scene. At first I found it interesting, but now it bores me to tears. I dread going out with them.

"Why are we going there?" I ask.

"We're just going to have a quick drink with this woman I met at work last week."

"Is this a friend thing or a work thing?"

"So many questions," she says, wrapping her arm around mine as we walk. "You can never just go with it. You always ask a million questions."

"It wasn't a million. It was one." We stop in front of the bar. "Elise, I don't really want to sit there while you two talk. I'm just gonna go home."

"Oh, c'mon, it won't take long. One drink, and then you and I will go do something else."

"One drink will take an hour, and then you'll get another glass of wine and another hour will pass."

She laughs. "Not this time. I promise. I'll keep it short. Besides, she has to catch a plane so she can't stay long."

"I'd really rather just—"

"Elise!" someone yells.

I turn and can't believe what I'm seeing.

"Holy shit," I mutter.

It's Giada.

CHAPTER THIRTEEN

BRAD

Elise goes up to Giada and gives her a hug. "I'm so glad we could meet before you have to go."

"Yeah, I'm glad you suggested it."

"Oh! Let me introduce you." Elise turns to me. "Brad, this is Giada. She's a sales rep. We met at the hospital and really hit it off. Giada, this is Brad, my fiancé."

Giada didn't notice me when she saw Elise coming up to her, but now she's staring at me like she can't believe her eyes. I'm just as shocked. What are the odds my fiancé's new friend would be Giada?

Elise laughs. "What's going on with you two? Why aren't you saying anything? Do you know each other?"

I'm not sure how to answer.

"We worked together," Giada says to Elise. "We were lifeguards at a pool the summer after we graduated college."

"The summer you lived with your cousin?" Elise asks me.

"Yeah, in Oklahoma." I keep my eyes on Giada. "It's been a long time."

"It has," Giada says, her eyes going between Elise and me. "So you two are engaged? When's the wedding?"

"We haven't set a date yet," Elise answers. "But we're thinking maybe next summer."

Giada points to the bar. "Why don't we go inside? I don't have much time before I have to leave for the airport."

I hold open the door for Elise and Giada and follow them to a table near the back.

"How crazy that you guys know each other," Elise says, scooting her chair closer to mine. "Brad's never told me much about that summer," she says to Giada. "Must have been pretty boring, living in that small town out in the middle of nowhere?" She laughs.

"It wasn't boring," I say. "I actually liked living there."

"You did?" Elise asks. "Then why don't you ever tell me about it?"

"Why talk about it? It's the past." I look around. "Should I go get us some drinks? I doubt we'll see a waitress. The service here sucks."

"She's coming right now," Elise says as the waitress stops by.

After we order our drinks, I say to Giada, "So are you still in Texas?"

"No. North Carolina. Charlotte. That's where the sales office is, but I'm not in the office much. I'm usually traveling for sales calls."

"Pharmaceutical sales?"

"Medical equipment. New York isn't my territory, but the usual rep is out on maternity leave so I'm covering for her."

"I thought you were a psych major. Weren't you going to grad school for that?"

"I did, but after a year I decided counseling wasn't for me. I dropped out and got this sales job. I thought I'd just do it for a few months, but it's been about three years now. So how about you? Done with med school?"

"Yeah. My residency starts in the fall."

"In Charleston," Elise says with a sigh. "He didn't get placed in New York, so we'll be living apart." She kisses my cheek. "I'm going to miss him."

"But it's only for a year, right?" Giada asks Elise. "When your residency ends, you'll move to Charleston."

"We haven't decided that yet," Elise says.

"We haven't?" I look at her. "I thought you were moving."

"Maybe, but..." She scrunches her nose. "Charlston? I'm not really a southern girl."

"You'll be my wife by then. A husband and wife usually live together."

"Not always. Sara and Mark don't live together and they make it work."

Sara is a theater producer here in New York and her husband works in TV out in LA. They're married, but I don't know why. Whenever we're around them they argue, and I know Sara cheats. I saw her kissing another guy on the street one day. I wouldn't be surprised if Mark cheated too.

"You guys will figure it out," Giada says, seeming uncomfortable.

I'm uncomfortable too. It's bad enough I just found out my fiancé doesn't want to move to be with me, but it's even worse to find it out in front of Giada. She'll think Elise and I never talk about stuff. The truth is, we *did* talk about her moving to Charleston, and agreed she'd move down there in a year. Why wouldn't she? We'll be married by then, and she'll be done with her residency. Why would she even consider staying here?

"Are you single?" Elise asks Giada.

"At the moment, yes. I don't have much time to date and I'm always traveling. Makes it hard."

Elise grabs my arm. "You know who would be perfect for her? That friend of yours. James."

I laugh. "James is an idiot. And he drinks too much. I wouldn't set him up with anyone, especially a friend."

"He's exaggerating," Elise says. "James gets a little silly when he's drunk, but sober James is extremely intelligent. He graduated at the top of his class and is going to be a surgeon. And he's from a very good family."

"She means wealthy," I say. "It's not a good family. They're just as messed up as James."

"Every family is messed up," Elise says to me, before looking back at Giada. "Ignore him. James would be perfect for you. I could set something up for next time you're here."

"Thanks, but I think I'll pass. I'm happy being single for now. And I may not be back. Cynthia said she may cut her maternity leave short and come back to work next month."

Elise frowns. "So I won't be seeing you again?"

"I sometimes have meetings and conferences here, so I'll be back for those."

The two of them start talking about work stuff while I try to figure out how I can talk to Giada without Elise around. I want to ask Giada if she knows anything about Riley. I'm sure they're still friends.

"Didn't you need to confirm things with the caterer?" I ask Elise as she sips her wine. "You needed to let her know about the scallops."

"Oh, that's right." She gets out her phone. "I'll text her."

"Maybe you should go call her. Make sure we didn't forget anything."

She smiles at me. "Why are you suddenly so interested in this? You didn't seem interested at all when we were with the caterer."

"I just want to make sure you get what you want."

"I don't need to call her. I'll just text her about the scallops."

While she's texting, Giada says to me, "Do you talk to Nate much?"

"Not really. It's probably been a year since I talked to him. He works a lot, and I've been busy with school, so we don't get around to calling each other." I pause. "You still talk to Riley?" I say it casually, like I really don't care, but my heart's pounding just saying her name.

"I talk to her all the time," Giada says, smiling at me.

She knows. She knows I still think about Riley. But does Riley still think about me? Is that why Giada is smiling?

"Riley," Elise says as she texts. "There's that name again." She looks up at Giada. "You know her too?"

"She was another lifeguard," Giada says. "We all worked at the pool that summer."

Elise's eyes return to her phone. "Brad thought he saw her today and practically chased the poor woman down the street."

Giada's still smiling at me. "You thought you saw her?"

"Yeah, but it obviously wasn't her. So where's she living now?" I'm so nervous asking these questions, my palms are sweating. Why am I nervous? Is it because I'm worried Giada will tell me Riley is with another guy? Or is my guilt making

175

me nervous? I'm engaged to Elise, so why am I asking about Riley?

"She's in Florida," Giada says. "You know her mom died, right?"

"Yeah. Nate told me."

"That's sad," Elise says, still texting. "Why'd she move to Florida?"

"She wanted to live by the beach," I say.

Elise looks at me. "For someone you never told me about, you sure know a lot about this girl." She smiles. "Did you two used to date? Did you have one of those summer romances?"

My eyes go to Giada, who's waiting for me to answer.

"Yeah, actually we did go out a few times. Then I moved here and we broke up."

Elise looks at Giada. "I can't keep track of all the girls he's dated. And honestly, I'd rather not know," she says with a laugh. "He's with me now and that's all that matters, isn't it, sweetie?" She gives me a kiss, then looks back at her phone and sighs. "I never should've checked email. I have over a hundred new ones since this morning."

"You know, I should really get going," Giada says. "I like to get to the airport early." She takes out her wallet.

"I got it," I tell her.

"Let me," she says. "We talked business. I'll charge it to the company." She drops some money on the table. "It was good seeing you again, Brad."

"Yeah. Let me walk you out."

"We both will," Elise says, putting her phone away. "I wish you could've stayed longer."

"I'll call you next time I'm in town. Maybe we could get together."

176

"Yes, definitely. It'll probably just be us girls since Brad will be off in Charleston."

We walk Giada out to the street. I was really hoping I could get her alone to ask her more about Riley, but I didn't know how without Elise getting suspicious.

"Have a good trip," Elise says, giving Giada a hug.

I give her one too. "Good seeing you."

She pulls back and smiles at me. "Things will work out. They always do."

She knows my saying. How does she know? Did Riley tell her?

Elise and I go back inside.

"What was she talking about?" Elise asks.

"What do you mean?"

"That stuff about things working out. What did she mean?"

I shrug. "Could be anything. The wedding plans. The engagement party. The move to Charleston." I stop her. "Hey, were you serious about not moving to Charleston?"

"We'll talk about it later. Let's go finish our drinks." She continues to our table.

I sit across from her, where Giada had been sitting. "We're talking about it now."

"I have to answer these emails," she says as she looks through her phone. "There's a few here that can't wait until tomorrow."

"They can wait until after we talk." I put my hand over her phone. "Would you please put it down?"

She sighs as she sets her phone on the table. "What's so important that it can't wait?"

"Our plans for next year. You told me you'd move after your residency."

"I don't remember saying that."

"You did, and it's the only way this is going to work."

"The only way *what's* going to work?"

"Us. We're engaged. We're getting married. Being apart for a year is bad enough, but longer than that? That's not a marriage."

"Brad, you're being ridiculous. There's no rule saying married couples have to live together. Sara and Mark don't."

"And they don't have a marriage. They never see each other, and Sara cheats on him."

"That's over now," she says, picking up her phone again. "And Mark cheated too, so they're even."

"You seriously think that's a good marriage? Two people who cheat on each other and live on opposite ends of the country?"

"Brad, relax. Why are you getting so worked up about this? We have a whole year to figure this out."

"And your answer won't change. You've already made up your mind about this. You're just putting off talking about it like you do with everything else you don't want to talk about."

"That is not what I'm doing."

"It's just like with this engagement party. I told you I didn't want some big elaborate party and you agreed, saying we'd talk about it later. But later never came, and next thing I know we're meeting with caterers and the guest list is over five hundred people."

She leans across the table, glaring at me. "What do you expect me to do? It's impossible to reason with you. Everything has to be your way or nothing at all."

"MY way? Are you serious? If we were doing things my way, we would've had a simple wedding this summer and I would've postponed my residency until we were both able to move to wherever I ended up. But that's not what you wanted. You told me to go. To move away. And now you're telling me we may not live together for another four years?" I lean back and look at her, noticing for the first time that she doesn't look at me the way she should. The way someone would look at the person they love. I only saw that look one time, from one person, and it wasn't Elise. "Do you even *want* to marry me?"

"Of course I do!" She folds her arms over her chest.

"Are you sure about that?"

"Are YOU?" she shoots back.

"No." I shake my head. "I'm not. I'm not sure about anything right now, but especially this. Us. I can't see it. I can't see us working."

She looks to the side, not saying anything.

"You don't want this either, Elise. You know you don't. Your life is here. In New York. Going to big parties. Planning them with your mom. Hanging out with people like Sara and Mark, who I can't stand, by the way. I fell in love with your energy, your enthusiasm, but it wasn't real. It's just an act you put on to hide the stuff you don't want to deal with or talk about."

"I don't do that," she mutters.

"You do. I know because I did it too. For years. Until I met someone that finally let me be myself. Someone I could tell anything to, even the stuff I'd always been afraid to talk about. That's the person you want to be with, Elise." I pause. "I'm not that person. You and I both know that."

She takes a breath and looks down at the table. "So what are we saying?"

"We're saying we tried to make something work that wasn't meant to be."

She wipes a tear from her eye. "I love you, Brad. I really do. I just don't see us lasting."

"I don't either." I reach across the table for her hand. "I want you to be happy, Elise. I want us both to."

She nods, sniffling, then takes her hand from mine and stands up. "I have to go."

I get up and go around the table to her. "I'll call up James. See if I can stay with him until I figure something out."

"No." She shakes her head. "Take the apartment. You can have it for the summer. I'll stay with my parents. I'll stay there tonight and get my things later."

"Elise, we don't have to avoid each other. Do whatever works for you. If you want me to stay somewhere else tonight, I can. Whatever you need, just tell me."

She softly smiles. "You're a good guy, Brad. I'm going to miss you." She leans up and kisses my cheek, then hurries out of the bar.

It's over. She's gone. And although I should be sad and missing her, my mind is back on Riley. I need to see her. Even if it's just one last time, I need to see her.

CHAPTER FOURTEEN

Riley

"Sweetie, I'm so tired," I say after Bree begs me to read the book for the third time. I've been reading to her every night and she loves it. "Mommy can't read anymore. I can't keep my eyes open."

"Okay." She puts her tiny hands on my cheeks and kisses me. "Mommy go sleep."

"Goodnight, sweetie." I tuck her into bed and give her a kiss.

I go to my room, and just as I get into bed, my phone dings.

It's a text from Giada. *If you're still awake, call me!*

I really want to go to sleep, but Giada wouldn't ask me to call her unless she had something important to tell me.

Not wanting to wake up Bree, I get up and close my door, then get back into bed and call Giada.

She answers on the first ring. "You're not going to believe this."

"Believe what?"

"Remember how I had to go to New York to cover for the sales rep that's on maternity leave?"

"Yeah. I thought you were still there."

"No, I just got back. Anyway, while I was at one of the hospitals doing my sales pitch meeting with the physicians, I met this girl. She's doing her residency there. We had lunch and really hit it off."

"Yeah? So?"

"We decided to meet for a drink before I left for the airport. And guess who was there?"

"Where?"

"At the bar where I met her for drinks."

"I don't know. Who?"

"Brad."

My pulse immediately spikes and I bolt up in bed. "Brad? As in..."

"Bree's father."

She waits for me to say something, but I'm too shocked to form words.

"I couldn't believe it," she says. "Here am I in this huge city with millions of people and there he is. I mean, what are the odds?"

"How did he, um..." I don't even know what I'm asking. I have so many questions. I don't know which to ask first.

"How did he *what*? Look? Even hotter than before. He still looks like an athlete. Big. All muscle. He looked taller for some reason. And he has kind of a beard thing going. Not a full beard, but one of those stubbly beards that look really sexy on the right guy."

I can see him in my head as she talks. He was, and always will be, the hottest guy I've ever dated. It's not just his looks, but the way he acts. Bold. Confident. So incredibly sexy.

"Did you talk to him?" I ask.

"Yeah. We had drinks with him. He, um...okay, this is the bad part."

"What? What is it?"

"He and Elise, the girl I was meeting for drinks, are engaged."

"Engaged," I repeat to myself as I let it sink in.

"Yeah." She sighs. "I'm really sorry. I considered not even telling you I saw him, but I thought you'd want to know."

"I do. And hey, it's not like I didn't expect this. I figured he was either engaged or married by now. At least it's not to Corinne." I pause, my mind now imagining Brad with some girl. A girl he's going to marry. "So this Elise girl, you said you liked her?"

"Yeah. I mean, I don't really see her with Brad, but she's fun to hang out with."

"You don't think she's good for Brad?"

"I don't know. I guess I'm just not sure they're a match. She's from a really wealthy family and when I knew Brad before, he was trying to get away from that life. He thought it's what made his parents break up."

"Maybe this girl feels the same way. Maybe they don't plan to live that way."

"No. Elise isn't giving that up. She likes her designer clothes and expensive jewelry and going to nice restaurants. And she loves living in the city. I can't imagine her ever leaving."

"Why would they leave? Brad loves the city too."

"But he didn't get a residency there. It's in South Carolina. He's moving to Charleston in the fall."

"What about Elise?"

"She's staying in New York. Apparently, Brad didn't know this because he got kind of angry when she said she was staying behind."

"I don't understand. They're getting married, but she doesn't want to live with him?"

"Not if it's in Charleston. She wants to stay in New York. It was really awkward watching them. They were both getting angry but trying not to fight in front of me. I felt like I should leave so they could talk. I told them I had to get to the airport and they walked me out."

"So before that, did Brad seem...did he seem happy?"

"I couldn't really tell. You know Brad. He doesn't like people knowing about his problems. He used to always smile and say things were great when they weren't."

"He didn't do that with me," I say, remembering back to all the long talks we had about his family and all the stuff they were going through.

"Well, he did with everyone else. That's the Brad I saw today. The one who smiles and pretends everything's good. Oh, and he asked about you."

"He did?" I hear how breathless I sound. It's because my heart's going so fast talking about Brad.

"He asked where you're living now."

"What did you tell him?"

"I just said you're in Florida. I didn't say where. I didn't think you'd want me to."

"I don't. It's better if he doesn't know." I fall back on my pillow, staring up at the ceiling. "Brad's getting married. Do you know when?"

"They haven't set a date, but Elise wants it to be next summer. They're having a big engagement party in August.

The way she described it, it sounded more like a wedding. They've rented a hotel ballroom and hired some really expensive caterer. She said over five hundred people will be there."

"For an engagement party? That doesn't sound like Brad at all. He'd be happy celebrating with some friends at a bar. A champagne toast is as fancy as it would get."

"That's exactly what he told Elise. She laughed it off like she thought he was kidding, but I think he was serious. He doesn't want this party. He's just doing it for her."

"I hope he's happy," I say, my voice trailing off as I think back to our summer together. We were both so happy. Even with our messed-up family drama, we were still happy because we had each other.

"I should go," she says. "I have an early morning flight to Atlanta."

"But you just got home."

"And now I have to leave again. Good thing I get paid well," she says with a laugh. "Tell Bree goodnight for me."

"She's already asleep. I put her to bed early because I couldn't keep my eyes open."

"Are you feeling okay? Seems like you've been tired a lot lately."

"It comes with having a toddler. You'll see once you have your own."

"That's a long ways off. Have to find a boyfriend first."

I smile. "I'll talk to you later. Love you, G!"

"Love you, too!"

IN THE MORNING, I'm still feeling tired. I struggle to get

through the breakfast shift. During my break, I go upstairs to make Bree her snack.

"Riley?" I hear Sophia say from the kitchen.

I go down the stairs. "Did you need something?"

"This was in the storeroom," Sophia says, holding up Bree's doll. She smiles. "Should I go bring it to her?"

"I'll do it. I'm surprised she forgot it. She goes everywhere with that doll."

I run up the stairs, pausing when I suddenly feel faint. I grab the railing and wait for the feeling to pass, then continue up the stairs.

After snack time, I return to the kitchen with Bree, still feeling exhausted.

"Riley, do you have the breakfast receipts?" Sophia asks, coming out of her office.

"I left them at the register." I go out there to get them, then bring them back to her at her desk.

"You didn't have to run, dear," she says.

"I wasn't running," I say.

"Then why are you so out of breath?"

She's right. Why am I breathing so hard?

"I guess I'm just getting old."

"I'm three times your age and don't get that out of breath just from walking."

"You must be in better shape than me."

She gets up and comes over to me. "When's the last time you saw a doctor?"

"When I had Bree."

"That was three years ago. You haven't seen one since?"

"I haven't been sick."

She eyes me, her brows drawing together. "I want you to

go. Let me know when the appointment is and I'll find someone to cover your shift."

"I'm not going to the doctor. I'm fine."

"The dizziness? Being tired all the time? Having to catch your breath just from walking? That doesn't sound fine to me, especially for someone your age."

"I'm not sick. I just haven't been eating right or getting enough sleep. Don't worry. I promise I'll do better." I smile. "I need to go finish helping Hector."

She grabs hold of my arm. "Riley, please. Make an appointment. My husband was just as stubborn as you. He kept having chest pains but refused to see a doctor. He kept saying it was heartburn, and then one day he collapsed from a heart attack."

"Sophia, I'm fine. Really. If it gets worse, I'll think about seeing a doctor."

"If it gets worse, you WILL see a doctor."

"Sophia, I—"

"If Bree even has the sniffles, you take her to the clinic. Why is it any different for you?"

"She's a kid. She doesn't know if it's serious or not. I take her in to make sure it isn't."

"These symptoms you're having could be serious. You won't know unless you see a doctor."

"Who will want to run tests and do blood work. I don't have money for that. The insurance doesn't pay until I hit a certain amount."

"I'll pay for it. You make the appointment, I'll pay for it."

"I'm not letting you do that. I don't need to go. I'm fine." I turn to leave and hear her mumble something to herself as I go.

She's being overly cautious because of what happened to

her husband. He refused to go to the doctor and then collapsed one day and died. But he was old and had high blood pressure. I'm young and don't have any health problems. I'm not going to pay money for some doctor to tell me I need to rest more and eat better.

The lunch crowd arrives early and I race around the dining room trying to keep up. Just as it quiets down, a bus filled with tourists shows up and it gets crazy again. We're only an hour into lunch and I'm already exhausted.

"You okay?" Hector asks as he stands at the grill.

"Yeah. Just need to catch my breath. Where's Bree?"

"In the back with Sophia." He laughs. "She got her doing inventory."

"She can't even count yet."

"She's learning. Just wait. Sophia will have her doing inventory on her own soon."

I smile. "She might."

"Burgers are up." He points to the two plates under the warmer.

"Got it." I walk over there. "I can't wait for lunch to be over."

"Yeah, it's busy today."

As I pick up the plates, my vision blacks and my head spins.

"Riley?"

The plates drop from my hands as I reach for the counter to steady myself. I miss the counter and fall to the ground.

"Riley!"

Next thing I know, I open my eyes to find myself lying on the floor surrounded by Hector, Sophia, and some man I don't know.

"What's going on?" I ask, feeling lightheaded and weak.

"You passed out," Hector says.

The man I don't know hovers over me. "Do you know your name?"

"Riley. Who are you?"

"Dr. Stanwick. I'm from the bus tour. I was having lunch when your boss came out and asked for a doctor."

"We've called an ambulance," Sophia says, rubbing my arm. "They'll be here soon."

"Ambulance? I don't need an ambulance." I sit up. "Where's Bree?"

"She's fine. She's upstairs with Hector."

I'm glad he's with her. He's good at distracting her. I don't want Bree knowing what's going on down here. It would scare her.

"It'd be best if you laid down," the doctor says. "Until they find out what's wrong."

"Nothing's wrong. I just didn't eat enough and got lightheaded." I turn to Sophia. "Call the ambulance and tell them I don't need it."

Just then, the ambulance guys arrive. "Is this her?"

"Yes." Sophia stands up. "She was serving lunch and collapsed to the floor."

"It was nothing," I say. "You can go." I get up and my vision blacks, making me stumble and reach for the counter.

"Miss, I think we should have you checked out."

I feel large hands grasp both of my arms and when my vision clears, I see an EMT on each side of me.

It's no use trying to fight this. Everyone's looking at me like they're going to tie me down and force me to go if I don't go along with this.

A half hour later I'm in a hospital bed hooked up to monitors with Sophia by my side.

"This is so ridiculous," I say, rolling my eyes. "People pass out all the time."

"They'll run the tests and if it's nothing, you can go home."

"I can already tell you it's nothing. What could possibly be wrong with me? I'm 26. I'm in perfect health."

They keep me there all afternoon, running tests without telling me anything. Finally, around five, one of doctors I met earlier comes in. She's an older woman with dark gray hair and black-rimmed glasses.

"Can I leave?" I ask.

"You can, but you'll be back."

"What does that mean?"

She glances at Sophia.

"She can stay," I tell the doctor.

She sits next to me on the bed. "We found an abnormality with your heart."

"Um, okay. What kind of abnormality?"

"A faulty valve. You've probably had it since birth but didn't know about it because you didn't have symptoms."

"Is it serious?"

"Not always, but it can be over time. In your case the valve isn't closing properly so it's causing blood to flow backwards, which is why you've been experiencing dizziness, fatigue, lightheadedness."

"Can you fix it?"

"Yes. Valves can be repaired or replaced. You'll need to consult with a cardiologist to see which option is best. I already have an appointment made for tomorrow. Does that work?"

"Yes," Sophia answers, giving me a stern look. "She'll be there."

"What are they going to do?" I ask the doctor.

"They'll run more tests and go from there."

"What does that mean? Will I need surgery?"

"Most likely, yes. As I said, they'll go over options with you once they run the tests."

She's acting like this is no big deal so maybe it's not, although I don't like the idea of having surgery. On my heart!

"Is it a simple surgery?" I ask. "Would I have to be in the hospital long?"

"It depends on what they do. A repair could be minimally invasive, but a replacement would be more involved. Either way, it's not a long hospital stay if everything goes well. I'd suggest holding your questions until you talk to the cardiologist. He'll be able to tell you more. For now, I'd go home and take it easy." She pats my leg. "We'll see you back here tomorrow. Oh, and no driving. I don't want you passing out behind the wheel."

She leaves and I stare up at the ceiling, avoiding eye contact with Sophia.

"Go ahead," I tell her. "Say it. Say I told you so."

I hear her sniffling. I look at her beside my bed and see that she's crying.

"Sophia, don't cry. I'm gonna be fine."

"I know, dear," she says, gripping my hand.

"Then why are you crying?"

"I was hoping I was wrong." She takes a tissue from her pocket and pats her nose.

"You knew there was something wrong with my heart?"

"No, but I had a feeling it was serious. I don't know why."

"It doesn't sound that serious," I say, trying to stay positive so I don't panic. I know nothing about heart problems other than that people die from them. "The doctor said it could be fixed. I'll just get the surgery."

"Yes," she says, forcing out a smile as she squeezes my hand. "You'll get the surgery and be good as new."

"Exactly," I say, like it's no big deal, but now I'm panicking. What if whatever's wrong with me is worse than they thought? How did this even happen? How could I not know until now?

THE NEXT MORNING, I return to the hospital with Sophia. She stays in the waiting area while I have tests run. Then we wait for the results.

In the afternoon, I get the news I didn't want to hear.

"We think it's best to replace the valve," the cardiologist says.

"Meaning you'll cut me open?"

"I need to meet with my team, but I think we could consider a less invasive surgery in which we only open part of the breast bone to reach the valve."

"Wait—you're cutting my chest open? And the bone? How is that not invasive?"

"It's less invasive than cutting open the entire chest. It means you'll have a faster recovery."

"What else happens? After you cut me open?"

"We'll put you on a heart-lung machine, replace the valve, then restart your heart and close the wound."

"You'll *re-start* my heart?" I glance at Sophia. "Okay, I'm getting really nervous."

"In order to work on your heart, we have to stop it

temporarily and use a machine to do its job. I know it sounds scary, but this is actually a common procedure."

"But there are risks, right?"

"Yes, and we can go over those."

I'm not sure I want to hear them. I'm not sure I want the surgery. I *know* I don't, but it doesn't sound like I have any other option.

"What if..." I don't want to ask, but I have to. "What if something goes wrong? Could I die?"

"The risk is low, especially for someone your age with otherwise good health."

"But it's possible," I say, looking down.

"As I said, the risks are very low and we take every precaution we can. We've done this procedure many times and—"

"I have a daughter," I blurt out. "She's only three. She... she doesn't have anyone if, um..." I look up at the doctor. "If something happens to me."

"Is her father in her life?"

"No," I quickly say. "And my parents are gone. My mom died a few years ago, and I never knew my dad." I look over at Sophia, knowing she'd care for Bree, but for how long? She's in her seventies. What if something happened to her? What would happen to Bree?

Sophia looks back at me like she's thinking the same thing.

"Although this is a very safe procedure," the doctor says, "I would advise you to have at least one person assigned to take over your daughter's care should something happen. Perhaps a friend?"

A friend. Maybe Giada? I don't know if she'd do it. She probably would, but she'd have to find a different job. She couldn't be traveling all the time. I can't believe I even have to think about this, although I probably should've before now. Anything could happen to me, and if it did, who would take care of Bree?

When we get back to the restaurant, Sophia pulls me into her office and shuts the door.

"What are you doing?"

She stands in front of me. "You need to tell him."

"Tell *who*? What are you talking about?"

"You need to call that little girl's father and tell him about her."

Brad. I didn't even think about him. When the doctor told me to pick someone to care for Bree, I didn't even consider Brad. He's so far removed from her life, he didn't even seem like an option.

Sophia points her finger at me, her eyes narrowed. "Don't you start with all that talk about how it's over with you two. I don't care if it's over. It's not about you and him. It's about that little girl needing her father if something happens to you." She chokes on those last few words, then yanks me in for a hug. "Nothing's going to happen. You're going to be fine."

I hug her back, hoping she's right because I'm scared to death.

"Please tell me you'll call him," she says.

I nod. "I will. I'll call him."

Later that night, Sophia takes Bree out for ice cream so I can be alone to call Brad. I'm so nervous I'm shaking. What if he doesn't answer? Or if he does, what if he doesn't want to talk to me? Last time we talked, I broke up with him. We had a great weekend together, and then I broke up with him. What if he's still angry at me for that?

I sit on my bed and stare at the phone. I take a deep breath and then call him.

The phone rings and rings, and just as I'm about to hang up, he answers.

"Hello?"

My voice suddenly doesn't work. I try to speak but can't.

"Hello?" he says. "Is anyone there? Who is this?"

He doesn't recognize my number. When I moved to Florida, I got a new phone and new number.

"Okay, well, I'm hanging up."

"Wait!" I blurt out.

There's a pause and then, "Who is this?"

"Riley." I pause. "It's Riley."

CHAPTER FIFTEEN

BRAD

There's no way it's her. Why would she call *now*? After four years? It must be a wrong number. A different Riley. But it kind of sounds like her.

"I think you might have the wrong number," I say.

"Brad? Brad Whittaker?"

"Yeah, that's me."

"It's Riley. From Oklahoma? We used to—"

"Yeah. Riley, of course I know who you are. I just didn't think it was really you."

"It's me," she says with a nervous laugh. "So how have you been?"

"Good. And you?"

"Okay."

The phone goes silent. This is odd. She hasn't called me in four years, and when she finally does, she doesn't say anything.

"So...I haven't heard from you for a while," I say.

"Yeah, I um, didn't think I should call after I, well, after everything that happened."

"You could've called. Breaking up didn't mean we could never talk again."

"Yeah, I guess you're right."

She gets quiet.

"You seem nervous."

She laughs a little. "Is it that obvious?"

"I know you, Riley. I know when you get quiet it means you're nervous."

More silence.

"Want to tell me why?" I ask.

"Why *what*?"

"Why you're nervous?"

"It's just been a long time."

"It has, but you don't have to be nervous. It's me. Brad. The guy who taught you how to play darts?"

"That's right, you did. But I kind of already knew."

"You knew how to play? Then why'd you act like you didn't?"

"I wanted you to teach me. I didn't...I wasn't ready to go that night. After dinner. I wanted to stay."

"I did too."

She doesn't respond. I'm assuming she called for a reason, so what is it? Maybe Giada told her we met for drinks and it made Riley think of me and want to call me.

"I had drinks with Giada," I say.

"Yeah, she told me. She was surprised she ran into you."

There's another pause of silence. She's still not telling me why she called.

"Riley, don't take this the wrong way, but I'm a little confused why you called. It's not that I don't want to talk to you. It's great to hear from you again, but you're not really saying much and—"

"I need you to come down here," she blurts out.

"Where?"

"To Florida. I live just south of Tampa. I'll pay for your plane ticket. I don't have money for a hotel, but maybe you could—"

"Riley, hold on. You want me to come see you?" I ask, surprised and confused by her request.

"I need to talk to you. In person. It's kind of important. Actually, it's really important."

"What is this about?"

"I don't want to tell you over the phone. Would you do it? Would you come here?"

"Um, yeah. Okay. When?"

"The sooner the better. I'm sure you're really busy, but is there any way you could get here sometime in the next couple weeks?"

"I could probably be there this week if it's that important. I'm done with school and my residency doesn't start until the fall."

"So you could leave this week?" she asks, sounding both nervous and excited.

"Yeah, just let me check flights."

"I'll pay for it. Or I could even get the ticket for you."

"I'll get it. And I'm paying for it."

"Brad, no. I'm the one making you come here. I should pay for the ticket."

"Riley, you're not paying. Just tell me when to be there."

"As soon as you can. I can pick you up at the airport so you won't have to rent a car." She pauses. "Actually, I can't do that."

"Do what?"

"I can't pick you up. But I could see if Sophia could."

"I'll just rent a car. It's no problem."

She gets quiet again. She's never this quiet. She must be really nervous. Surprisingly, I'm not. I think I'm too in shock that she called to be nervous.

"Who's Sophia?" I ask.

"My boss. She owns the restaurant I work at, and my apartment. She's Giada's grandmother. That's how I ended up here."

"Giada got you the job?"

"And a place to live. Her grandma needed a waitress and someone to rent the upstairs apartment. It isn't much, but it's right on the beach."

"You're living on the beach." I smile. "You got your dream."

"Almost," she mutters.

"What was that?"

"Nothing. Anyway, we really love it here. It's perfect."

"We?" I ask, knowing she has a kid, but wondering if she has a guy living with her too. Maybe the kid's father?

"So you think you could check flights today and let me know?" she asks, ignoring my question.

"Riley, I know you have a kid."

The phone goes silent.

"Nate told me. And don't worry about it. I don't hold anything against you. It was a long time ago."

"Um, I don't know what to say. When did you find out?"

"About three years ago. But hey, you don't have to explain. I get it. I moved away and you weren't sure if you'd ever see me again. You met someone else. So are you guys still together?"

"Um...no. It's just me and my daughter."

How could that guy just leave them like that? Does he even see his daughter, or did he just take off? I can't imagine doing that. Leaving your kid? Never seeing her again?

"So you had a girl," I say, smiling. "What's her name?"

"Bree," she says in a breathy tone. She's so nervous she sounds out of breath. Why is she so nervous?

"Bree." I chuckle. "Sounds similar to Brad. Good choice."

"Yeah. So anyway, I don't want to keep you. You can just text me when you find a flight so I know when you'll be here."

"If it's okay with you, I'd rather call. I like hearing your voice again."

She's quiet and then, "Sure. Call anytime. Bye, Brad."

The phone goes silent and I see she hung up.

I can't believe this. Riley called me. After four years. She wants to see me. But why?

Getting up from the couch, I search the living room for my laptop. I find it and return to the couch to look for flights. There's one that leaves tomorrow at noon. It costs a fortune, but I don't care. I want to see her as soon as possible. I don't know what this is about, but maybe I'll finally get the closure I need. I can't go the rest of my life thinking about her. Loving her. I eventually have to move on. Maybe that's what this trip is about. Maybe she needs closure too.

I call her up.

"Tomorrow at three," I say when she answers.

"What?" she asks, sounding groggy. "Who is this?"

"Sorry. It's Brad. Were you asleep?"

"Yeah, but it's okay. What were you saying?"

It's only eight. Seems kind of early for her to be asleep.

"I got a flight leaving tomorrow at noon. It gets in around three."

"Oh. Okay," she says, sounding more awake. "That's great."

"Text me your address so I know where to go."

"I'm doing it right now so I don't forget."

"You didn't say how long you wanted me to stay so I got a flight back for Sunday. If five days is too much for you, I'll just go do my own thing. I can always hang out on the beach for a few days."

"Five days is good." I hear the smile in her voice. "It'll be good seeing you again, Brad."

"Yeah. You too. I'll let you get back to sleep. See you tomorrow."

I'm seeing Riley tomorrow. This doesn't seem real. I've thought about her every day for four years, wondering where she was, what happened to her. And then she calls me out of the blue and asks me to come see her.

I wish I knew what this is about. What's so important she has to tell me in person?

———

THE NEXT DAY, I arrive in Florida both excited and a little nervous about seeing Riley again. As I drive to her place, I think back to that summer. Those months I spent with her are still the best months of my life. We had something special, something rare, something I doubt I'll feel again with anyone else.

The address she sent me leads me down a small road that goes along the beach. I stop when I see the sign for the diner. With the upper level apartment, it looks more like a house than a restaurant. It's painted light blue, but the paint is peeling in spots and the sign is so faded I almost missed the turn.

Walking up to the door, my nerves kick in again. I'm just seconds away from seeing Riley. The girl I still think about. The girl I still love.

"It's seat yourself," a woman tells me as I come in. She's probably around thirty, wearing jean shorts and a light blue t-shirt with the diner name on it.

I walk up to her. "I'm looking for Riley?"

The woman was wiping down tables but stops for a moment. "Riley isn't here, but she should be back any minute." She checks her watch. "Actually, I'm surprised she's not back by now. She said she'd be back around two."

"Do you know where she went?"

"Sissy, look!" A little girl runs out of the kitchen and up to the waitress. She holds up a rag doll. "Pretty dress!"

The waitress picks up the little girl. "You made her a dress?" She laughs as she looks at it. "With a dishtowel. That's very creative. Good job, Bree."

Bree. She's Riley's little girl. I should've known. She looks just like her. Long brown hair. That same beautiful smile.

"She's adorable," I say, looking at her.

"She's not mine," the waitress says. "She's Riley's little one." She bounces Bree on her hip. "Tell him how old you are."

"Three," she says, holding up three tiny fingers.

The waitress smiles. "She loves to tell people how old she is. Oh, and my name is Missy, not Sissy. When Bree was learning to talk, she had trouble with her M's so she kept calling me Sissy. It stuck, and now I'm Sissy, but only to Bree." She kisses her head. "Sweetie, why don't you go play with your doll while I clean up?"

"Where's Mommy?" she asks, looking around.

"She's still out. She'll be back soon." Missy sets Bree down.

The little girl walks over to me, not at all scared, even though I'm a stranger.

"Hi!" she says, smiling up at me with her big brown eyes.

"Hi." I lean down to her level. "I'm Brad."

She hugs her doll to her chest and stares at me.

"Do you want to go sit down with me?" I ask her. "I'm waiting for your mommy too."

Missy had gone back to cleaning tables but stops briefly, eyeing me with suspicion. "Who are you again?"

"Brad. Brad Whittaker. Riley and I are friends. We were lifeguards at a pool a few summers back."

The door from the kitchen swings open and my heart stops when I see her. God, she's beautiful. More beautiful than I remembered. Her dark hair is shorter now, just past her shoulders, and it's not straightened the way she used to wear it. It's wavy and natural-looking, like her face, which has just a touch of makeup and is tan from the sun. She's wearing a faded orange t-shirt and jeans, her body slimmer than when I last saw her in New York. I liked those extra pounds on her, but I like her this way too. She still has a large chest for someone her size, although I'm trying not to look at it. She hasn't aged a day. It's like I've traveled back in time and am seeing the same Riley I knew four years ago.

But this isn't that Riley. She may look the same, but her life is completely different. She has a daughter now. A daughter she had with another man. Despite what I told her, that still bothers me. She said she loved me back then, so why would she be with someone else?

"Missy, did—" Riley stops when she sees me, her eyes locked on me like she can't look away. "Brad."

"Hey." I smile at her.

"When did you get here?"

"Just a few minutes ago."

"Mommy!" Bree runs up to her. "Mommy, look!" She holds up her doll.

Riley's gaze breaks from mine as she looks down at Bree. "You made her a dress?"

Bree nods really fast.

"It's pretty."

"Up!" she says, raising her arms to Riley.

Riley picks her up and the little girl hugs her, resting her head on Riley's shoulder.

I walk over to Riley. "She's beautiful."

Riley smiles at Bree on her shoulder. "She's my everything."

"Riley?" An older woman comes through the door, stopping when she sees me. "Oh." She smiles. "You must be Brad."

The woman is short and tiny and has Giada's smile.

"Brad Whittaker," I say, going up to shake her hand. "I believe I know your granddaughter."

The woman nods. "Yes. I'm Sophia. Giada said she saw you in New York recently."

"Yeah, it was good seeing her again."

"Can I get you anything?" Riley asks, walking over to me. "Something to eat? Drink?"

"I'm fine. Actually, I was thinking maybe we could go to dinner tonight, unless you have to work."

"She doesn't work evenings," Sophia says.

"Great!" I smile at Riley. "You'll have to pick the place since I don't know the area."

"Oh, um, maybe we could just eat here. I don't have a sitter for Bree."

"I'll watch her." Sophia takes Bree from Riley. "You want to be with Nonna tonight?"

Bree nods with excitement. "Read books!"

"Yes, Nonna will read you books." She looks at Riley. "Why don't you take Brad out to the beach? Walk a little. I'm sure he'd like some fresh air after being cooped up on a plane for hours."

"Sounds good to me," I say, smiling at Riley.

"Um, okay." She sounds nervous, like she did on the phone last night. "Follow me."

We go out the door past the patio and walk along some boards that lead down to the beach.

"I should've asked if you needed to change." She points to my brown leather shoes. "You'll get sand in those."

"It's fine," I tell her.

"We'll go this way," she says, pointing to my right. "The other way is a public beach. It gets crowded this time of day."

We continue a few moments in silence, then I turn to her.

"Riley, wait."

She stops. "What?"

"What are we doing here?"

"Taking a walk."

"I haven't seen or talked to you in four years, and the first time I see you, we just go out and take a walk?" I smile. "You don't find that strange?"

"What did you want to do?"

"Well, for starters, this." I pull her into my arms and hug her.

She laughs, hugging me back. "You could've done that earlier."

"I wasn't sure if I could." I let her go. "When we were in the diner, you were almost acting like you didn't want me here."

"It's not that," she says, shaking her head. "I'm just nervous, that's all."

"Why are you nervous?"

"I have a lot going on right now."

"So it's not me making you nervous?"

Her eyes drop down to the sand. "You're part of the reason."

"Why do I make you nervous?"

"Let's keep walking." She takes my hand and pulls on me to follow her. We take a few steps and she drops my hand. "Sorry. I didn't mean to do that."

"Do what? Hold my hand?"

"Yeah. Sorry."

"You can hold my hand."

She shakes her head as she walks.

"Why can't you hold my hand?"

"You're engaged," she says, keeping her eyes straight ahead.

"I'm not engaged."

She stops and turns to me. "What happened to Elise?"

"How do you know about Elise?"

"Giada told me. She said you're getting married next summer."

"You talked to Giada about me?" I ask with a smile.

Riley folds her arms over her chest. "I didn't ask. She told me."

"Giada has old information. Elise and I aren't getting

married. We broke off the engagement right after Giada left that night."

"Why? What happened?"

"We decided we weren't right for each other. We wanted different things."

"Like what?"

"A lot of stuff. For one, she wants to stay in New York. I don't. Did Giada tell you I'm moving to Charleston?"

"Yeah, but I thought you loved New York."

"I did at first, but after a few years it got old. The traffic, the crowds, the noise. And you were right about the smell. I don't know what that smell is, but it's good to get away from it and breathe in some fresh air."

"Aren't you two living together? You and Elise?"

"We were, but we're not anymore. She moved back with her parents and I'm going to stay in the apartment until I move to Charleston."

We start walking again.

"I'm sorry it didn't work out," Riley says.

"It's fine. I always had a feeling we weren't right together, but we got along okay and had similar interests so I just ignored the stuff that didn't feel right."

"You don't think you guys will get back together?"

"No. It's over. She wanted out as much as I did. We just didn't want to admit it to each other."

We continue along the beach, the only sound being the waves crashing against the shore. Riley's quiet again, like she was on the phone.

I reach over and take her hand.

"What are you doing?" she asks.

"Holding your hand."

"We probably shouldn't do that."

"Why not?"

"We just shouldn't," she says, and yet she doesn't let go.

"Are you engaged?"

"No."

"Married?"

She laughs. "No."

"Boyfriend?"

She shakes her head.

I hold up our joined hands. "Then I think we're good."

We walk in silence and all I can think about is how much I want her back. She obviously doesn't want that. She didn't even want to hold my hand. So if she didn't call me down here to try to rekindle our relationship, then what am I doing here?

CHAPTER SIXTEEN

BRAD

"We should probably turn around," Riley says as we approach a hotel. "That part of the beach is only for hotel guests."

We turn and start walking back. I take Riley's hand again, noticing the slight smile on her face when I do.

"So where are we going for dinner?" I ask.

"There's a sports bar about a mile from here. We could go there."

"Is there anything nicer than that?"

"There's a seafood restaurant, but it's expensive."

"Don't worry about the cost. Tonight's on me."

"Brad, I don't want you going broke from this trip. You already spent money on a plane ticket. I don't want you spending even more."

"Riley, I have money now. I've been bartending for three years. You know how much bartenders in New York make?"

"No. How much?"

"A lot. So I can afford to pay for dinner. And the plane ticket. And I'll probably need a hotel." I glance at her. "Unless I can stay with you."

"I don't really have room. It's a small apartment."

"Any suggestions for hotels around here?"

"Actually, forget it." She stops. "I don't want you spending more money. You can stay with us. I'll sleep with Bree in her room."

"You sure? I don't want to make you uncomfortable."

"You won't. It'll be fine." She continues along the beach.

"Hey, check it out." I reach down and pick up a shell. "It's pink. You should give it to Bree."

Riley stops and turns to me. "How'd you know about that?"

"About what?"

"How'd you know Bree collected pink shells?"

"I didn't. I just thought she'd like it."

"She'll love it. Every morning, she comes out here with Sophia and they look for pink shells. When she finds one, she puts it in a jar. She made up this story about fairies living in pink shell houses, and when they're done with them, they leave them on the beach."

I smile. "She just came up with that, or did someone tell her that?"

"It was all her. She's very creative."

"I used to be like that too. I made up all kinds of crazy stories when I was a kid."

"You did?" She tilts her head as she looks at me. "What kind of stories?"

"I don't really remember. My mom could probably tell you. She used to think I'd grow up and be a writer because I had such a vivid imagination. I eventually grew out of it."

"Huh." She smiles. "I never knew that about you."

"Guess we weren't together long enough to find out everything about each other."

We continue along the beach until we're back at the diner. As we walk up to the door, I hold the shell out to Riley. "Here."

"You give it to her. You found it."

We go inside the diner, which is now filled with customers. Almost all the seats are taken.

"Busy place," I say.

"A lot of locals come here," Riley says. "Tourists usually only show up at lunch."

I follow her to the kitchen, then up some stairs. She takes them really slow, giving me plenty of time to look at her round perky ass.

"Bree?" she calls out. "There you are."

I look up and see Bree running over to Riley. "Nonna take me for ice cream."

"She's taking you for ice cream? What about dinner?"

"We'll have dinner first," Sophia says, coming out of a room just off the living room.

Looking around, it's a very small apartment. The living room and kitchen are attached, and there's a bedroom on each side.

"I'd like to take her to my place, if that's okay," Sophia says to Riley.

"Sure. We can pick her up after dinner."

"Or she could spend the night." Sophia tries to hide her smile. I get the feeling she's trying to set up Riley and me. Giada seemed to be hinting at that as well when I saw her in New York.

"We can pick her up," Riley says. "We won't be out late."

"Hey, Bree," I say, getting her attention.

"What?" she asks, hugging her doll as she twists side-to-side.

"I got something for you. Come over here."

Her eyes widen as she runs up to me.

I crouch down to her level and hold out my hand. "I found it on the beach."

"Fairy house!" she squeals. "Mommy, look!"

"Yeah, I saw it. Brad found it and wanted you to have it."

She drops her doll and hugs me. "Thank you."

"You're welcome."

She pulls away but grabs my hand. "I show you."

"Show me what?" I ask, my eyes going to Riley.

"Her jar," Riley says. "She wants you to see it."

Bree keeps hold of my hand as I follow her to her room. It's barely big enough to hold her twin bed. Next to it is a nightstand made from a cardboard box.

"They go here," she says, climbing up on her bed.

"Need some help?" I ask her.

Instead of answering, she grabs my arm to steady herself as she reaches over to drop the shell in the plastic jar.

"You sure have a lot of them," I say, noticing the jar's half full.

"Down," she says, her arms aimed up at me.

I smile as I pick her up off the bed and set her on the floor. She runs off, back to the other room.

I laugh. She's funny.

"Cmon, little one," Sophia says in a sing-songy voice. "Let's go to Nonna's house."

I walk back to the living room and see them leaving.

Bree waves at me. "Bye!"

"Bye."

They disappear down the stairs, leaving me alone with Riley, who's in the kitchen.

"If you want to clean up, the bathroom's over there." She points to it.

"I need to go get my stuff from the car."

"I'm going to take a short nap, if that's okay."

Nap? She never used to nap. She barely slept when I knew her before.

"Yeah, go ahead. What time should I be ready?"

"Maybe around six?"

"Sounds good."

"Okay, well, make yourself at home." She goes in her bedroom, grabs a pillow, and takes it to Bree's room.

"Riley, are you sure about this? I feel bad kicking you out of your room."

"I don't mind. Half the time I end up sleeping with Bree anyway, so tonight won't be any different."

"She's a great kid. Really sweet."

"Yeah, she is." Her eyes look past me, avoiding my gaze. "Okay, well, let me know if you need anything."

She shuts the door.

I walk over to the back window that looks out at the beach. It's really beautiful. Just what Riley always wanted.

Turning around, I look back at her apartment. It's small, but all the light coming in the windows makes it feel open, not cramped and dark like the trailer she used to live in. There are pictures of Bree everywhere and some of Bree and Riley together. I pick one up from the table by the couch. Bree is just a baby and Riley is holding her, a huge smile on her face.

I'm happy for her. She got her dream, or most of it. She's

missing the husband part, but she seems okay being on her own.

———————

AT SIX, we head to the restaurant. I'm hoping during dinner Riley will tell me why I'm here. If she doesn't, I'm just going to ask. I can't keep waiting. I need to know.

"Good choice," I say as I look around. "I like this place."

We went to the seafood restaurant she mentioned earlier. It's right on the water and we're seated at a table by the window. If this were a date, it'd be very romantic.

"Do you come here much?" I ask.

"No." She smiles as she reviews the menu. "Bree hasn't figured out that not every restaurant is like the diner. She can't just get up and run around."

"She spends a lot of time at the diner?"

"All day. I don't have money for daycare so we all just keep an eye on her. Sophia watches her in the mornings as she does her office work and I take her on my breaks. Or sometimes the other waitresses will watch her if I need to run an errand. She's become like everyone's kid. They all love her."

"What about other kids? Does she ever have play dates?"

"Not really. Sometimes Hector will bring his son to the diner. He's four, but he doesn't like playing with girls, so Bree usually ends up doing her own thing."

"Maybe she could meet some kids in preschool."

"I don't have money for preschool. I'm trying to teach her stuff on my own so she'll be ready for kindergarten."

I set my menu down. "So that guy...her dad...he doesn't help you at all?"

She bites her lip and turns her head to look out the window.

"Riley?"

The waiter stops at our table. "Are you ready to order, or would you like more time?"

"We're ready," Riley rushes to say.

She orders as I hurry to look over the menu.

"And for you, Sir?" the waiter asks.

"Just a minute." I find the shellfish section and order the shrimp platter.

"I'll be back with some bread," the waiter says before leaving.

"Sorry," Riley says. "I didn't even give you time to look at the menu."

"It's fine." I place the cloth napkin on my lap. "We can keep this quick if you need to get home."

"I don't. I just..." She looks out the window again. "I'm just nervous, I guess."

"And when you're nervous, you hurry."

"You remembered," she says, her eyes gazing out at the ocean.

"I remember everything about you, Riley."

She doesn't respond.

"So back to my question...does Bree's father help you out at all? Is he even in her life anymore?"

She looks back at me. "I need to talk to you about something."

The waiter drops off the bread. "Your dinners will be out shortly. Can I get you anything else?"

"No, we're good," I say, wanting him to go away. I wait for him to leave, then say to Riley, "Go ahead. You said you had to tell me something?"

She takes a piece of bread and sets it on her plate. "Lately I haven't been feeling that great."

"What do you mean?"

She takes her knife and butters her bread. "I've been dizzy. Lightheaded. Really tired."

Those are symptoms that could be caused by a variety of issues, some serious, some not. I'm starting to think it's serious if she took me here to tell me. Is this why she had me fly down here? Now I'm getting worried.

"Riley, just tell me. What's going on?"

"I didn't think it was anything to worry about, but then I passed out during the lunch rush and ended up at the hospital. They ran all these tests."

"And?" I ask, getting more anxious by the second. "What'd they find out?"

She sets her bread down. "There's a problem with my heart."

I've now passed the worry stage and am in full blown panic mode. What the hell is she telling me? Is she dying?

"What kind of problem?" I ask.

"Something with one of my heart valves. It's not working right. I don't understand it all, but I could show you the information they gave me. You'd understand it better than me."

I relax a little, knowing from my medical training that heart valve issues are fairly common and can be treated.

"What's the issue? Do you know?"

"It's damaged to the point it's leaking. The blood is going the wrong way. That's why I've had the dizziness and why I'm always so out of breath."

That explains why she took so long going up the stairs and why she was walking so slowly on the beach. I thought she was trying to prolong our walk so we'd have time to talk, but then she didn't say anything. It makes sense now, but what doesn't make sense is why she's telling me this. We're not exactly friends anymore. She hasn't spoken to me in years.

"I'm having surgery," she says, picking up her bread and breaking it into little pieces. It's another thing she does when she's nervous. She tries to keep her hands busy and focus on that instead of what she's saying.

"To fix the valve?" I ask.

"They want to replace it. They said it's up to me to make the final decision, but that replacing it would be better than fixing it. And then they went over all this stuff about different kinds of replacement valves and..." She sighs. "It's all really confusing. I was never good at science. I can't understand most of the stuff they give me to read over. It's hard to make a decision when you don't understand it."

Is that why she called me? To help her figure out what to do?

"Riley, I can help you with that. Show me what they gave you and I'll do my best to explain it to you. We can also go online and find out what's worked best for someone your age."

"Really?" Her eyes lift to mine. "Because that would be a huge help."

"I'll do whatever you need. When do you need to decide?"

"Soon. They want to do the surgery in the next few weeks." She looks down at the table. "That's the other thing I wanted to talk to you about. The surgery."

"I'll be here," I say, putting my hand over hers. "I'll fly back whenever it is."

She's quiet.

I look at her, trying to read her face. "Is that not what you were going to say?"

"I didn't expect you to be there, but if you could, then yeah, I'd like that. I'd feel a lot better if you were there."

"Then it's done. I'm there." I rub her hand. "So if that's not what you were going to say, then what is it? What were you going to tell me?"

She swallows. "I'm sure you already know this but—"

"The halibut," the waiter says, setting the plate down in front of Riley. "And our famous shrimp platter." He smiles at us. "Anything else?"

"No, we're good," I say, annoyed at the interruption.

He leaves and I look back at Riley. "Finish what you were saying. About the surgery."

"I was just going to say you probably already know how it's done. How they hook you up to all these machines and cut you open and...stop your heart."

"Yeah?"

"I'm kind of freaking out about that. The stopping the heart part."

"It sounds worse than it is. I mean, it's major surgery, but they do it all the time. And in someone as young as you, the risk is low that something will go wrong."

"That's what the doctor said, but still...it's possible something *could* go wrong. Like maybe my heart wouldn't restart."

"When we get back tonight, we'll go online and research this procedure for women your age, but I'm telling you, the risks are low. And it's better to have this done now than when you're older."

"That's the other thing. They said these valves don't last

and that I'd probably have to have this done again in 20 or 30 years."

"Yeah, that's true."

"I'll be older then. It'll be riskier."

"Maybe, or maybe they'll have better techniques by then that are safer. Either way, you don't need to worry about that now."

"But I do."

"Why?"

"Because of Bree. If I'm gone, I need to know she has someone. I don't want her to be all alone."

"By the time you have another surgery, she'll be an adult. She'll have friends, maybe even be married. She won't be alone."

"I want her to have family. And I'm not just talking about in the future. I'm talking about now. When I have this surgery in a few weeks, if something happened and I...if I didn't make it, I would need someone to raise Bree. Sophia loves her, but she's too old to raise her, and I don't have any family who could take her."

"What about her father? Or do you not want him having her?"

"I *do* want him to have her. It's just that..." She looks down at her plate.

"What?"

"He, um..." She clears her throat. "He doesn't know about her."

"He doesn't? You never told him?"

"No."

"Why not?"

"A lot of reasons, but mainly because he had other things going on in his life. He had opportunities I didn't want him to give up. Opportunities that may never come again."

"He couldn't do those things and still be a dad?"

"No. He would've had to give everything up. Or put it off. And if he put it off, I was worried it would never happen. All the stuff he'd done up until then would've been for nothing." Her eyes lift to mine. "I couldn't do it. I couldn't take away his dream."

She's staring at me. She's been avoiding looking at me this whole time and now she's staring at me.

"Riley, what are you—"

"He always wanted to be a doctor." She pauses as my heart beats faster. "And live in New York."

I look at her, suddenly realizing what she's saying.

"Holy shit." I shove my plate aside and lean across the table. "Are you telling me she's mine? Bree is my daughter?"

CHAPTER SEVENTEEN

BRAD

"Yes." Riley avoids my gaze as she says it, seeming ashamed and embarrassed that she kept this from me. I can't believe that she did.

I have a kid. A daughter. That sweet little girl with the big brown eyes and beautiful smile is mine.

"I know I should've told you," Riley says, "but I couldn't. I—"

"So there wasn't some other guy?"

"No, and when you said that on the phone, I didn't know what you were talking about. Why would you even think that?"

I shove back in my chair, anger shooting through my veins. "Nate."

"Nate?"

"He knew, didn't he? He knew about Bree. He knew I was the father."

"Yes, but I begged him not to tell you."

I shake my head in disgust. "I can't believe I listened to him. Fucking bastard. He lied to me. Made me think you had someone else."

"Wait—what exactly did he say?"

"He told me you had a kid and that the father was some guy you met right after I left town."

"When did he tell you this?"

"I don't know. Right after you had her. Maybe June?"

"June? I had her in April."

"He said you had her the end of May."

Riley sighs. "He made that up so you'd think it wasn't even possible she was yours."

"I can't believe he'd do that."

"I do. I told him not to tell you. He was making sure you wouldn't find out."

"He didn't do it for you. It was because of him. What *he* wanted. He wanted to make sure I stayed away from you and never tried to contact you or get you back. He didn't need to tell me about the baby, but he did so that I'd stay away."

"Why would he think you'd come back? You had someone else by then."

"Someone else? What are you talking about?"

"Corinne. When I saw Nate after I had the baby, he said you were dating Corinne. He said you two had been dating for months and that it was getting serious."

"He lied," I say through gritted teeth. "I never dated Corinne. Never even kissed her. We lived together that summer, but we were roommates. That's it. Nothing happened."

"Does Nate know that?"

"Yes. I told him Corinne and I were only friends. I'm

222

telling you, Riley, Nate did this. He purposely told us shit to keep us apart."

"But we already *were* apart. He didn't need to lie to us."

"He knew we loved each other and that people who love each other don't just give up unless there's a damn good reason. You cheating on me with some guy and having his kid was reason enough for me to stay away."

"What are you saying? That you were going to try to get back together with me?"

"About a million times. Riley, I've thought about you every day since the moment I said goodbye to you in New York. After we broke up, I tried to think of every possible way to get you back. The week of Thanksgiving I was going to fly out to see you so we could at least talk about it and see if we could find a way to make it work."

"But you didn't."

"Because Nate told me you had someone else."

"Who? The guy who was supposed to be Bree's father?"

"I didn't know about the baby back then. All Nate said is that you had someone else. He made it sound like you were with this guy when you and I were still together."

"So you decided not to come see me."

"Yeah." I clench my fist, trying to contain my anger. "How could he do this? How could be so damn jealous of me being with you that he makes up lies to keep us apart? Makes me think you cheated? Had someone else's baby." I pause, my heart pounding. "I'm a dad. I'm that little girl's father." I look around for the waiter. "I've gotta get out of here."

"We just got our food."

"I'm not hungry. I need to leave." I stand up. "Let's go." I take out my wallet and drop some money on the table.

When we get outside, I head to the car.

"Brad, wait," Riley says from behind me.

I whip around to Riley. "I need to see her. I need to see Bree. Where is she? Where does Sophia live?"

"In town, a few miles from here. But I don't want you seeing her like this."

"Like what?"

"You're angry. You haven't had time to let this sink in. I don't want you seeing her when you're like this. You need to calm down."

I stop before I reach the car, running my hand over my jaw. I hear the ocean just beyond the parking lot. "Let's take a walk."

Striding past her, I head to the wood planks that lead to the beach.

"Brad, hold on." I hear her behind me, breathing heavy. "I can't go that fast. The doctor said—"

"Yeah." I turn back to her. "Sorry. I'm not thinking right now."

This is all too much to take in. Riley's sick. She's having open heart surgery. And I have a daughter. WE have a daughter.

Now I get why she wanted me to come down here. I'm glad she didn't tell me this over the phone.

We make our way to the beach. I slow my pace to a very slow walk. Riley still sounds out of breath, but not as much as before. I'm so damn worried about her. I tried to act like her heart surgery wasn't a big deal, and it's true it's a fairly common procedure, but it's still surgery, and surgery has risks. They're cutting her chest open. Stopping her heart. She could die. It's not likely, but it's possible.

I stop suddenly. "Shit."

"What?" She turns to me. She looks worried, like I'm

about to yell at her. Part of me wants to. Part of me wants to scream at her for not telling me I had a kid. But the other part of me wants to bring her into my arms and hold her, because she's here, and I love her, and because this is what I've wanted for years. To see her again. To hold her in my arms.

"Come here," I tell her.

She slowly steps up to me. "Yeah?"

I take her in my arms and hold her there, kissing her on the head like I used to do. "It's going to be okay."

Her body shakes as she breaks down in tears. "I'm so scared, Brad."

"I know." I hold her tighter.

"I'm not just scared for me, but for her." She sniffles. "I have to know she'll be okay."

"Nothing's going to happen. You're going to be fine."

"But if something *does* happen, I need to know she'll be okay."

"She will be. I promise."

Her head lifts. "I need to know what that means."

"It means I'll do everything I can to make sure she has the best life possible." I look into her eyes. "I want to do that anyway. Now that I know about her, I want to be in her life, Riley."

She pulls away. "We need to talk about that."

"Yeah. We do."

"I'm not sure I'm ready to yet. Telling you this, having you here...it's not something I ever thought I'd do."

"You were never going to tell me about her?" I feel my anger rising but try to remain calm.

"I wasn't sure. I wanted to. I just didn't think I should."

I take her hand and sit down on the sand. "Come on. Let's sit a minute."

She sits down in front of me. "I need more time to think before we talk."

"We both need time to think, but right now, I need answers. I need to know if you ever even considered telling me."

"Of course I did. I was going to tell you right after I found out, but then you got that scholarship and you were so excited about New York that I couldn't do it. I couldn't take all that away from you."

"You didn't know that's what would've happened."

"I know you enough to know you wouldn't go off and leave us. You would've wanted to take care of us."

"You're right. That's what I would've wanted, and what I would've done. But that wasn't your decision to make. It was mine."

"I didn't want you making that decision. I knew if you did, you'd never go to med school. You'd put it off and it'd never happen." She pauses, her eyes on the sand as she runs her fingers through it. "I almost told you when I was in New York. I knew I couldn't afford to live there with an infant, but I thought maybe I could live close to there. Someplace where you could still come see us but that wasn't so expensive."

"You were really considering that?"

"I was, but then I got home and found out about my mom. I couldn't leave her, Brad. I was all she had. That made the decision for me. I had to accept I was stuck there, back in that town, and that I'd be raising Bree alone."

"Her name is similar to mine. Was that intentional?"

"I wanted her to have a connection to you, even if she never met you."

"She looks like you."

"She does." Riley smiles, her eyes still on the sand as she

runs her hand through it. "But she has your eyes. And she acts like you. Sometimes I watch her and it's like I'm watching you."

"What do you mean?"

"She's so intense sometimes. If she's trying to figure something out, her face tightens like she's thinking really hard, and if you say something to her, it's like she doesn't even hear you." Riley laughs. "And the stories she comes up with. I didn't know where all that creativity came from. I didn't know you were that way too. Oh, and she asks a million questions, just like you do. And if I don't have the answers, she makes them up. She has to have an answer."

I smile. "Sounds like me."

Riley's eyes lift to mine. "I don't want her to know. Not yet."

"When do you want to tell her?"

"I'm not sure. But telling her this and about my surgery is too much. She's going to be really scared that Mommy's going in the hospital. I don't want to tell her about you at the same time. It's too much for her."

"I get that. So then what do you want me to do?"

She pauses. "I want you to get to know her. Talk to her. Maybe read to her. She loves books. And she loves playing on the beach. You could give Sophia a break. She loves their beach walks, but she has a hard time keeping up with Bree."

"I could do that."

"I know you need to get back to New York on Sunday, but if you could just spend some time with her before you go, I think it would help for when we tell her."

"Riley, now that I know this, I don't want to leave on Sunday."

"So then when would you go?"

"What if I didn't?"

"What do you mean?"

"What if I stayed? What if I stayed until I had to leave for my residency?"

"What about New York?"

"There's nothing keeping me there. I could find a job here. Rent a place close by. What do you think?"

"Um...I don't know." I see her mind working and can tell she wants to accept my offer, but is worried it's not what I want. She always worries more about other people than herself. It's why she didn't tell me about Bree. But I wish she had. I've missed three years of my little girl's life.

"You're going to need help after your surgery," I tell her. "You won't be able to pick her up or run after her. You're going to need someone to do all that, and like you said, Sophia just doesn't have the energy. And you'll need someone to take care of you. After having your chest cut open, it might be nice to have a doctor around."

She smiles. "It would be."

"So it's settled. I'll stick around for the rest of summer and spend it with you and our daughter."

When I said 'our daughter' Riley's whole face lit up. "I'd really like that."

"I wish you'd told me sooner, Riley."

Her head drops. "I know."

"I would've been there for you. For both of you."

She keeps her head down. "Are you mad at me?"

"Yeah. I am. You should've told me when you found out. But there's nothing I can do about it now. I just don't want you trying to take her away from me. I was serious when I said I want to be in her life. Even when I move away, I still want to see her. We can figure that out later. I just need to know you'll let me be part of her life."

"I will." Her eyes lift to mine. "It's what I wanted, Brad. I always wanted you in her life. I just didn't think that could happen without ruining everything for you. But I knew you'd be a great dad. And I know Bree's going to love you."

What about Riley? Does she still love me? She's not acting like there's anything between us anymore, or indicating there ever could be. I've made several comments to let her know I'm still interested. I even flirted a little and held her hand. But I didn't get signals back that she wanted anything more than a friendship.

If that's all she wants, I'll take it. At least I'm back in her life now. And we have a little girl. I'm a father. I still can't believe it. I'm a dad.

CHAPTER EIGHTEEN

Riley

I was so nervous telling Brad about Bree. I thought he might yell at me, or tell me I was a horrible person for keeping this a secret for so long. But instead, he asked me questions, trying to understand why I did it. He's so much like Bree that way. Asking questions until he gets an answer that makes sense. I don't know if my answers made sense to him, but at least he didn't yell at me.

The more we talked, the more my nerves calmed down, and by the time we left the beach, I felt a peace come over me. I'm still scared about the surgery, but I'm not as scared now for Bree. If something happens to me, she'll be sad and have to adjust, but she'll have her father. Brad's kind, loving, mature...and he's smart. He can answer all her questions.

I smile when I think of them together. Seeing them interact at the apartment earlier had me almost in tears one moment and laughing the next. Bree is a feisty, take-charge girl who sometimes orders you around before you even realize what's happening. Like when she was taking Brad to see her jar of shells. He didn't know what was going on, but she convinced him to follow her, then instructed him to help her get off the bed.

I've been trying to teach her to not be so bossy, but so far, nothing's changed. It might just be how she is. She also has a really sweet side. She's always trying to help people. If a baby is crying, she'll race up and ask what's wrong. She doesn't like seeing someone cry. It makes her sad.

When we get back to the apartment, Brad goes over to the window and looks out at the ocean.

"Must be nice waking up to this every day."

"It is." I step up beside him. "It was my dream, but I never thought it'd actually happen."

"Sometimes life works out the way you want it," he says, gazing out at the water. "Other times you have to make it happen yourself."

"Like you." I look at him and smile. "You graduated from med school. It was your dream and you did it. I'm really proud of you, Brad."

"I have to finish my residency before I'm actually a doctor."

"And then what? Are you still taking over that clinic with Todd?"

He chuckles. "No. That was never going to happen. His dad retired and sold what would've been my half to some middle-aged guy looking to expand his practice. I should've known he wouldn't sell his business to someone my age."

"What about Todd?"

"He'll work there after his residency and own his father's half. When the other guy retires, he can buy him out." He glances at me. "I'm surprised you remembered that."

"What?"

"The stuff about the clinic. I told you that a long time ago."

"When you told me, I remember thinking it didn't seem like a good fit for you, but I didn't want to say anything because you were really excited about it."

"Why didn't you think it was a good fit?"

"You said you wanted to live somewhere warm."

"That was part of it too. I didn't want to live in Boston. I'm tired of the cold and I didn't want to live in another big city."

"I also didn't really see you being partners with Todd. I know you guys are friends, but he seemed like the type of person you were trying to get away from, at least back then."

He nods. "Todd comes from money, but so did everyone else there. Being around those people, I got into that life again. It's hard not to when those were the people I saw every day. We had the same classes. The same study groups. It's not that they're bad people. They just had different priorities than me. They're all about making money and impressing people and I—" He stops suddenly and sighs.

"What? What were you going to say?"

His gaze remains on the ocean. "I didn't realize until just the other day that I was becoming one of them. I was turning into the person I said I didn't want to be."

"What do you mean?"

"I chose a girl like Elise. A girl with money. A well-known family. The right connections to get me whatever job I wanted. She's the type of girl my parents always hoped I'd end up. They didn't care if I liked her or not, or if she made me happy. What mattered is that she had everything on their checklist." He pauses. "I can't believe I fell for it. I did exactly what they wanted, even though I knew she wasn't right for me."

"What changed your mind?"

"Seeing Giada again. Her showing up at that bar to meet Elise for drinks? It was almost like a sign. A wake-up call reminding me who I used to be. The guy I was the summer I met you. That guy never would've gone out with a girl like Elise."

"But you loved her. You were going to marry her."

"I was going to marry her because I thought I should. Because it would please my parents. Get approval from my friends. Help my career."

"You didn't love her?"

"I told myself I did, but in my heart, I knew it wasn't the type of love I should feel for my future wife. I've felt that kind of love before and it—" He shakes his head. "Anyway, Giada showed up that night and it was like a light went on in my head. I realized it would never work with Elise. We got along okay and had similar interests, but we didn't want the same things in life."

"What things are you talking about? What do you want?"

"Same things I told you when you asked me four years ago. To be a doctor. Have a family. Live somewhere warm."

"You have some of those things. You'll be a doctor soon, and Charleston is a lot warmer than New York. And when you're done with your residency, you could move somewhere that's even warmer."

"Like Florida?" He smiles at me.

"Yeah." I look out at the water. "You could live on the beach, like me."

"Then all I'd be missing is the family." I feel his eyes on me, but keep mine on the ocean.

He keeps doing that. He keeps making comments that make me think he wants us to get back together, but then I think maybe I'm imagining it because it's what I've wanted for so long. Even if I'm not imagining it, I don't think it's a good idea to get involved with him so soon after he broke off his engagement. He says he won't get back with Elise, but what if he did? Or what if he's just using me to get over her so he can move on with someone else? I don't think he'd do that, but I also haven't seen him in four years. A person can change a lot in four years.

"You have Bree," I say, "so you actually do have a family."

He checks his watch. "Do you know when she'll be home?"

"No, but I could call Sophia and ask."

"I'd like to go get her if we could. Could you call her right now?"

"Yeah." I get out my phone.

The sun is setting, which would make for a very romantic setting if Brad were interested in me that way. I thought he might suggest we take a walk on the beach or stay here and watch the sunset, but instead he wants to go get Bree. Now that I think about it, he hasn't been making flirty comments or done anything to show a romantic interest in me since I told him about Bree. Is it because he's angry at me? Did telling him that ruin any chance of us getting back together?

"Hey, Sophia," I say when she answers. "Are you at home? Brad and I were going to come over and pick up Bree."

"I was just about to call you. I was reading Bree a story and she fell asleep. She was so tired I hate to wake her. I was going to ask if she could just stay here tonight. Would that be okay?"

It's not even eight. Bree rarely goes to bed this early. I

wonder if she really is asleep or if Sophia just told me that as an excuse to keep her overnight so Brad and I could be alone. I know Sophia wants me to get back together with him, but if it happens, it's not happening tonight. He just got into town. And I'm pretty sure he's angry at me, even though he's trying to hide it.

"What's wrong?" Brad asks as he stands beside me.

"Bree fell asleep," I tell him. "Sophia wants her to stay the night so she doesn't have to wake her up."

"I'm okay with that, as long as I can see her tomorrow."

I nod. "Sophia, you can keep her there. Just give her a kiss from me."

"I will, dear. Goodnight. We'll see you in the morning."

I put my phone away and sit on the chair by the window. It's actually a small inflatable sofa someone left on the beach. When nobody claimed it, I brought it inside and set it by the window.

"Will that thing hold me?" Brad asks, pointing to it.

"Yeah. You can sit down." I scoot over.

He chuckles. "I've never seen an inflatable sofa before."

"I found it on the beach. I don't have much money for furniture. I bought my bed and Bree's, but that's all I've been able to afford. The living room stuff is Sophia's."

Brad looks down, not saying anything. I hope he doesn't think I was trying to make him feel guilty for not helping me out the past few years. I'd never want him to feel that way. It was my choice to raise Bree on my own.

"I miss her when she's not here," I say, watching the sun lower, streaking the sky with oranges and pinks.

"Does she stay there often?"

"A few times a month. She'd stay there more if I let her. She loves her Nonna."

"What's Nonna? Is that a nickname?"

"It means grandma in Italian. Sophia taught her that. She thinks of Bree as her grandchild, which is good because she's the only grandma Bree will ever have."

"She has my mom."

I turn to him. "That's right. I didn't even think of that."

"I'm not going to keep this from my parents. You know that, right?"

"I assumed you'd tell them. Do you think they'll be happy?"

"That they have a grandkid? Hell yeah. My mom's been begging my brother to give her one, but I'm not sure he even wants kids."

"You didn't used to want them either."

"I did. I just wanted to have everything in place before I had them. A job. A house. Some money in the bank."

"Sometimes the timing doesn't work out the way you want it to," I mutter, more to myself than to him.

"Our first time. That's when it happened?"

"Yeah. We um, forget to use a condom."

"Only time I ever forgot. But I thought you were on the pill."

"I was, but I missed a few days that month."

"When did you find out you were pregnant?"

"A few weeks after you left. I was feeling really sad so I called up Giada and she invited me over. I ended up staying at her house that night. In the morning, I didn't feel good. I got sick, but I didn't feel like I had the flu. Giada asked if I was pregnant and I laughed, thinking there was no way. She made me take a test to prove her wrong." I sigh. "Turns out she was right. After I found out, I went back and forth about telling you and not telling you. I didn't want to take away your future, but I also didn't want Bree growing up not knowing her father. I grew up that way, and I didn't want the same thing for Bree. I'm sure my dad was some loser who didn't want to be a father, but I still wanted to know who he was and maybe meet him someday."

"When did you decide not to tell me?"

"When I got home from New York and found out about my mom. I took it as a sign that you and I just weren't meant to be. Things kept coming between us every time we tried to be together."

"That's not a sign. That's life. Things get in the way. You could've told me, Riley. We would've found a way to make it work."

"With me living halfway across the country and you spending all your time studying and in class? Even if I lived closer, you wouldn't have had time for us. And if I had moved, I wouldn't have had the support I had back home."

"But you ended up moving away. To a place you didn't know anyone."

"I had Sophia. I didn't know her until I got here, but she instantly treated me like family. And she loved Bree and took care of her whenever I needed a break. If it weren't for Sophia, I don't think I ever would've left Oklahoma."

"You would have. You would've done it for Bree."

"You're right. I didn't want her growing up in that town. I just don't know where I would've gone. Nate kept trying to talk me into moving to Dallas. Maybe I would've ended up there."

"Don't even say his name. I'm so pissed at him for lying to me. I can't even think about him right now."

"You should be mad at *me*, not him. I asked him not to tell you."

"It's not just that. It's the lies he told me about *you*. About how you were with some other guy."

"He never should've told you that. And he shouldn't have told you I had a baby."

"He told me so I'd never come back. He didn't think telling me you had a boyfriend was enough to keep me away. He had to say you had another man's baby. And that you cheated on me." Brad rubs his jaw. "I can't fucking believe he did that."

"He lied to me too. And you're right. He didn't do it to help me. He did it to keep us apart, and to get back at me for choosing you instead of him."

Brad moves, which makes the inflatable couch squeak.

I laugh. "Sorry. It can be kind of loud."

"You need some real furniture. How about we go shopping tomorrow? We'll get you some chairs for by the window and an actual nightstand for Bree's room instead of a cardboard box."

"I'll do it later, after I've figured out how much this surgery's going to cost. I have insurance, but it doesn't pay for everything."

"I'm buying the furniture. What time do you get off work tomorrow?"

"Three, but Brad, I don't want you buying us stuff. That's not why I asked you to come down here. I don't expect you to support us that way."

"And you never would. That's your problem. You don't like accepting help. But Bree is my daughter and I'm not going to have her living this way."

"What way?" I say, getting angry. "Just because I use a box for her nightstand doesn't mean I'm not a good mom. I'm doing the best I can and I don't need you coming here and—"

"Hold on," he says, taking my hand. His touch instantly soothes me, just like it did when we were dating. "I didn't say you weren't a good mom. I know you're doing the best you can, but I haven't been able to do anything at all. Three years have gone by and I haven't been able to do anything for her."

"You didn't know about her."

"And now I do, so let me do this. Let me get rid of this inflatable thing and buy her a chair. One that's just her size that she can sit in and look out at the beach. She can even pick it out. And let me buy her a table to put by her bed. It won't cost much, and she'll have a sturdier place to put all those fairy houses."

I smile. "She would love that."

"You're getting a chair too. I know how much you love looking out at the ocean and you can't keep sitting on this inflatable thing."

"I don't need a chair. I can sit on the couch and see the ocean."

"It's better by the window. Just let me do this. It's not a big deal. It's just a chair. Think of it as a housewarming gift."

"Brad, really, I don't need anything."

"But I do. I need to see you in front of this window, in an actual chair, looking out at the ocean."

"Why?"

"Because you love it. It's what you always wanted. It makes you happy."

"It does," I say, gazing out at the now dark sky.

"That's all I ever wanted, Riley...for you to be happy." I feel him squeeze my hand. "So you're getting a chair whether you want it or not. If you refuse to go shopping, Bree and I will pick it out for you."

"Bree would pick out something pink with flowers all over it. Trust me, you don't want her picking it out."

"Then I guess you'll have to go with us tomorrow."

"I can't. I have an appointment at the hospital. Do you think you could watch Bree for me?"

"Yeah, of course. Or we could go with you."

"She'd be bored, and I don't want her being exposed to all the germs there. She hasn't been sick in months and I want to keep it that way."

"Could Sophia watch her?"

"Yeah, but I thought you'd want to spend time with her."

"I do, but I'd also like to go with you to your appointment if you wouldn't mind."

"Why would you go with? They're just going to run some tests, and then I'll probably meet with the doctor."

"Tests can be scary. It helps to have someone there. And if you meet with the doctor, I'd like to be there to ask questions."

"What questions?"

"Questions about the surgery and what they plan to do, unless you're confident that what they're telling you is the best choice."

"I'm not. I'm just trusting they know what they're doing. They gave me all this information, but I can't understand it. I was just going to go there tomorrow and go with whatever they tell me."

"Where's the stuff they gave you?"

"In my room. Why?"

"Go get it. I'll read it over and explain it to you the best I can. If you still have questions, we'll write them down and you can ask them tomorrow."

I go to my room and get the packet from the hospital and bring it back to Brad. "Thanks for doing this."

"I'm happy to do it. And I want to go with you tomorrow." He looks into my eyes. "I'm here for you, Riley. Not just tomorrow, but for all of it. I don't want you going through this alone."

My heart swells with so much love for him. Love I've tried to bury deep inside and pretend no longer exists. But it's still there. It never went away. And in the short time he's been here, my love for him has grown. Seeing him with Bree? His offer to help me get through the surgery? It makes me love him even more.

Why would he do this for me? I broke his heart four years ago. I didn't tell him about Bree. And yet he's still here, wanting to help me.

"This one hasn't been performing well long-term," he says, pointing to something in the packet. It's the booklet that goes over the different types of artificial valves.

"That's the one they're thinking of using," I tell him.

"Are you serious? Have they read the research?"

"I assumed they had. Is it really that bad?"

"It's been failing after ten years. It should last twice that. And there were complications with this one. The company that makes it even got sued last year."

"So I shouldn't let them put that in me?"

"No. That's the worst of all the options they gave you."

"I don't think they'll listen to me. I don't know anything about heart valves."

"But I do, and I'm not letting them put something in you that's dangerous. If you really think they're going to fight you on this, I'll stay up all night and pull together the research that proves they shouldn't be using this one, at least not this version of it."

"If it's that bad, why would they recommend it?"

"They may not know. Sometimes doctors don't have time to keep up on the research. They rely on what their sales rep tells them, which is that it's safe and effective." He turns to a different page in the booklet. "This one here would be a better option. It's newer, and it's been tested in people your age."

"Brad, I can't thank you enough for doing this. I've just been trusting what they tell me."

"Which is what most people do, and usually everything comes out okay. But I'm not taking any chances here. I need you to be okay. Bree needs her mom."

So is that why he's doing this? Because he wants to make sure I'm here for Bree?

I can't tell what he's thinking. I know he's concerned for me, but why? Is it because of our daughter? Or because he still has feelings for me?

CHAPTER NINETEEN

BRAD

Riley fell asleep an hour ago while I was reading through the material from the hospital. Her head is resting on my shoulder and I'm afraid if I move, I'll wake her. She has to be at work at six and needs her sleep, so I decide to just stay here on the couch and let her sleep on me. Besides, it gives me a chance to look at her.

I've seen her face in my mind every day for the last four years and yet I didn't remember her being this beautiful. God, I've missed her. I never missed Elise like this. When she'd go away on trips, I never really missed her. I thought it was a sign of maturity, of healthy independence, that I could go a weekend without her and not miss her, but the truth is, I didn't love her enough to miss her. Now that I think about it, I've never missed any girl the way I missed Riley.

That summer we dated, I'd miss Riley when she was only gone a few hours. I missed her when I had to say goodbye to her at night. And when I moved away? I missed her so much it hurt. The hurt never went away. I just tried to ignore it, but then something would make me think of her and the pain would return.

Now I'm with her again, but the pain still lingers because I know this won't last. Soon I'll have to leave her again. And I'll have to leave Bree, which will break my heart even more. I don't know if I can do it. After missing the first three years of her life, I don't know if I can leave my little girl. I want her to know me, and I want to know her. I want to be with her as she grows up.

As I scoot down on the couch trying to get comfortable, Riley startles, then presses on my chest like I'm a pillow she's trying to adjust.

"Riley?" I whisper, thinking she must be awake.

She mutters something that doesn't make sense, then brings her legs up on the couch and lays her head on my lap. I grab the blanket from the back of the couch and drape it over her. The lamp is still on, but I can't reach it to turn it off.

I look down at Riley and gently move the hair off her face. "It's going to be okay. You're gonna be fine."

Even though I say it, I'm still so damn scared something will go wrong. What if she didn't make it?

Why am I even thinking that way? I need to stay positive, both for my own peace of mind as well as hers. But the fact that her doctor was going to use a valve that's known to have serious issues has me thinking she's not getting the best care. She may think I'm interfering, but I have to make sure she's making the right decisions for her health. Doctors make mistakes, but I won't let them make one with Riley.

That thought keeps me awake as I watch Riley sleep. Eventually, I doze off myself.

"Brad," I hear a tiny voice whisper.

I open my eyes and see a sweet little face with big brown eyes staring back at me. Bree's right beside me, standing on the couch, clutching my shirt in her tiny hand as she leans over my face.

"Hi, Bree." I lift my head and glance down at the couch. "Where's your mom?"

"Mommy at work." She smiles, then jumps up and down. "Let's go!"

As I open my eyes more, I notice it's light out now. "What time is it?"

"Breakfast!" She jumps around the couch cushions.

"Careful," I say, grabbing her and setting her down on the floor. She's so tiny. I haven't been around kids her age since I worked at the pool. I forgot how tiny they are and how much energy they have.

She plops down beside me. "You had a sleepover with mommy?"

What do I tell her? Riley and I should've talked about this last night. We never discussed what to tell Bree, other than we'd wait to tell her I'm her father.

"It wasn't really a sleepover," I say. "I just needed a place to stay while I'm here."

She frowns. "You have to go?"

"No. I'm staying here for a little while."

"What's little while?"

"A short time."

She tilts her head. "What's short time?"

"More than a week but less than a year."

"How long is that?"

Riley wasn't kidding when she said Bree asks a lot of questions. This could be a problem when I don't have answers.

"I might be here the rest of the summer," I tell her. "Would you like that?"

She nods really fast, then jumps up and hugs me.

I laugh as I hug her back.

"Mommy says wake you up."

"She did, huh?"

She pushes off me and smiles. "She says we get to play all day."

"You and me?"

She nods, then cocks her head. "Are you mommy's friend?"

"I am. From a long time ago."

"Then you my friend too." She climbs down off the couch, holding onto my leg for support. "Come on." She pulls on my hand.

I hear laughing and look up and see Riley at the top of the stairs, smiling but looking winded as she takes a moment to breathe. She's really struggling. I see why the doctors are insisting on doing this surgery sooner rather than later. Knowing Riley, she ignored her symptoms as long as she could. She doesn't want to be a bother, and to her, being sick is a bother to people. I wish she wouldn't think that way, but she does.

"Bree, what did I say about asking versus telling?" Riley says, leaning against the kitchen counter as she catches her breath.

Bree remains in front of me, looking at her mom and answering her with a shrug.

"We ask people. We don't just tell them." Riley walks over to us. "If you want Brad to do something, ask him, and do it nicely."

Bree turns to look at me, her bottom lip going over the top, then back down again like she's thinking of what to say.

"Try this," Riley says to her. "Brad, would you like to have breakfast with me?"

Bree looks at her mom, then back at me. "Breakfast?"

"Sure," I say, giving her a smile.

"It's a start," Riley says with a laugh. I love her laugh. I've missed it. "Did you get any sleep? Sorry you were stuck on the couch. You could've woke me up."

"You needed the sleep. And I was fine. I didn't even hear you get up."

Bree goes over to Riley. "Up!"

"I can't sweetie. Mommy can't pick you up until she's better."

"Mommy's got an owie," Bree says to me.

"The doctor said I shouldn't pick her up," Riley says to me. "I could black out and drop her."

"I can do it." I stand up and lift Bree into my arms. "How's that?"

She smiles really wide.

"You like Brad, don't you?" Riley asks her.

She nods, then rests her head on my shoulder. I still can't believe this. Bree is my daughter. I'm holding my daughter.

"Do you want breakfast?" Riley asks me. "The breakfast crowd is pretty much gone, but the kitchen is still open. Hector can make you anything you want."

"Let me take a quick shower and then I'll be down." I nod toward Bree. "What about this little one?"

"She'll come with me. Bree, let your da—" Riley freezes, realizing she almost said 'dad'. "Let go of Brad and come downstairs with me."

I set her down and she goes over to Riley.

"She has her snack around ten and then I'm going to see if she'll take a nap. Sophia said didn't Bree sleep much last night."

"It's ten? You should've woke me up sooner. I never sleep that late."

"Go ahead and shower. We'll be down in the kitchen."

After my shower, I go downstairs but don't see them in the kitchen.

"They're in the back," a guy says. He's tall and heavy-set, with short black hair, wearing a white apron.

"I'm Hector." He comes over to shake my hand. "I'm the day cook."

"I'm Brad. A friend of Riley's. So you said they're in the back?"

"The storage room, which is also the office. Sophia works back there." He folds his arms over his chest. "So you and Riley? You two got something going on?"

I'm surprised by the question. I just got here. Why would he think I'm dating Riley?

"We're friends," I tell him. "We used to work together."

"Yeah, she told me." His eyes narrow. "She don't have time for games. She's got a kid. And now she's sick. So if you're just here to mess around..." He finishes that thought with a look that says he'll beat me up if I mess with her. I'm actually happy about that. I'm glad he's looking out for her.

"That's not why I'm here," I tell him. "Like I said, Riley and I are friends. She asked me to come here."

"Brad!" I hear Bree's tiny voice, then the patter of tiny feet as she runs toward me. She's so cute in her pink shirt and little denim shorts and that Riley smile.

I pick her up. "Did you have your snack?"

She shakes her head. "Mommy said wait for you."

"Brad, tell Hector what you want," Riley yells from down the hall. "I have to finish helping Sophia and then I'll meet you guys out there."

"Is the restaurant closed?" I ask Hector.

"Just for an hour between breakfast and lunch. We open again at eleven. So what do you want?"

"Could I just get a few eggs? Scrambled with extra cheese and maybe some ham if you have it?"

He stares at me, not saying anything.

"If you don't have it, that's fine. I can get something else."

"No, I got it." He cracks some eggs into a bowl.

"I want some too!" Bree yells.

"You want this for your snack?" Hector asks. "Instead of a cookie?"

She nods.

He glances at me. "She loves this."

"What?"

"Scrambled eggs with extra cheese and diced ham. She has it for breakfast almost every day. It's funny you asked for the same thing."

Now I get why he was looking at me like that. He knows, or *thinks* he knows. If you really look, you can see parts of me in Bree, especially her eyes. And then I ordered her favorite breakfast. I think that's more personal preference than genetics, but who knows?

Riley appears again. "I need to help Sophia with inventory. Are you okay watching her?" She leans over to give Bree a kiss.

"Yeah. We're good." I bounce Bree on my hip. "Maybe after your nap we could walk on the beach. Find more fairy houses."

Her eyes widen and she nods really fast.

"You just won her over," Riley says with a laugh. "That's her favorite thing to do."

"Or books," Hector says. "She's just like my son. I read to him all the time, but it's still not enough."

"I'll read to you later," I tell Bree. "Would you like that?"

Riley smiles. "Sounds like you have a full day. See you guys later."

When she's gone, Hector comes over with my plate of food. "You got a girlfriend?"

"I did. We just broke up."

"Got any kids?"

I almost say yes, but catch myself. "No. Never married."

"You don't have to be married to have kids. I wasn't when I had mine. He was kind of a surprise, if you know what I mean."

I'm holding my surprise in my arms right now. If he only knew.

He hands me the plate. "You can take it to the dining room. I'll bring out Bree's."

Struggling to hold a plate of hot food and a squirming toddler, I carefully make my way through the kitchen to the diner. It's empty, but the tables need to be cleared. I find a clean one and set the plate down, and then Bree.

"You sit here," she says, patting the chair next to hers.

She may be bossy, but I don't mind. I'm sure she gets it from me. I can be bossy too, although I like to call it being assertive.

"Here you go." Hector sets a tiny plate in front of Bree.

"Thank you," she says, reaching over me to grab a fork from the bin on the table.

I grab one too. "Thanks, Hector."

When he's gone, Bree says, "Hector's a daddy."

"Do you know his son?

"Mario. He's four." She chomps on her eggs, her legs swinging back and forth. "My daddy is gone."

"Gone?" I turn to her. "What do you mean?"

"Mommy can't find him."

"She told you that?"

She nods as she pushes the eggs around her plate with her fork. "I wish I had a daddy."

Riley told her she couldn't find me? I wonder what else she told her about me.

"Do *you* have a daddy?" Bree asks.

"I do, but I don't see him much. He lives far away."

She takes a bite of her eggs, chomping on them until they're gone, then turns to me. "Are *you* a daddy?"

What do I tell her? I can't tell her the truth. Not yet. Why is she even asking? She just heard me tell Hector I don't have kids, or maybe she wasn't listening.

I can't lie to her, then tell her the truth later, so I say, "Finish up your snack. We have a lot to do and you still have to take your nap."

"All done." She pushes her plate away.

"Let's go." I pick her up and take her to the back to find Riley. She's in the storeroom, talking quietly to Sophia.

"Riley, Bree's ready for her nap."

"Hey!" she says, like I surprised her. I think she was talking about me when I walked in. "You can just take her upstairs and put her in bed. And if you wouldn't mind staying up there while she sleeps."

"Yeah, okay. Before we go, do you have a minute to talk?"

Sophia walks over to me. "I'll put her up." She takes Bree from me.

"Sophia, I can do it," I tell her.

"I've got her. You go ahead and talk."

When she's gone, I close the door and walk over to Riley. "Bree just told me you don't know where her dad is."

"I didn't know what else to tell her. I didn't think she'd ask until she was older. When she did, I didn't know what to say."

"I don't like this, Riley. I don't think we should wait to tell her. I don't like lying to her."

"We're not lying. We're just waiting to tell her."

"She asked if I was a dad."

"And what did you say?"

"I didn't give her an answer. I distracted her so she wouldn't keep asking." I sigh. "I felt really bad knowing I was her dad but not able to tell her. She was so sad, Riley. She really wants a dad, and she has one. One that wants to be part of her life. So why wait? Why keep this from her? Let's just tell her. Let's tell her tonight."

"Brad, I don't know." She turns and walks away from me.

"Don't know what?"

She turns back to me. "What if you decide this isn't what you want? Sure it's fun for a few hours, but she's a lifetime commitment. Are you sure you're ready for that? Because I don't want to tell her the truth and then have you change your mind."

"Riley, you know I would never do that. I just met her and already love her. There's no way I would ever leave her."

"I want to believe that, but..."

"But what?"

"Guys don't always stick around, even if they tell you they will."

"Who are we talking about here? Your own father?"

252

"Mine. Yours. Not every guy wants that kind of commitment."

"She's not a commitment. She's a child. And I'm not my father. I would never walk out on my family like he did. Do you really think I'm that type of guy?"

"No," she says, looking down. "I know you're not. I shouldn't have said that. I'm just scared. I can already see how much Bree likes you, and I don't want her getting hurt."

"I don't want that either, and I'd never let it happen."

"You're leaving at the end of summer. That's gonna hurt her, Brad. Just when she gets used to having you around, you'll have to leave. You and I understand why, but she won't."

"I'll be back. I'll come back as much as I can. Or you could come with me. There's no reason for you to stay here."

"Bree and I have a life here. We have Sophia. The beach. I have a job where I can keep Bree with me all day. If we move, all that would change."

"She'd have her dad. That's important, Riley. Maybe you don't think so, but it is. She needs her dad."

Riley walks over to the desk and picks up her apron. "I should go clean tables."

"Hey." I go over to her. "Why don't you let me do that? You can go up and stay with Bree."

"You're going to wipe down tables?" She laughs. "Go upstairs. I'll check on you guys during my break."

I hold on to her arm. "Riley, I mean it. You're doing too much. You're out of breath and I can see you're exhausted."

"I'm fine. I'll take a nap after my appointment today. Are you still going with me?"

"Yes. Can Sophia watch Bree?"

"She already agreed to it. And she's taking her for dinner,

so it'll just be you and me. I can make something if you don't want to go out."

"You're not doing anything but resting. We can go out or I'll get us takeout."

Riley motions to the door. "I should really get out there."

We leave the office, and when I get upstairs, I find Sophia in the kitchen wiping down the counter.

"Bree spilled her juice," she says. "I was just cleaning up."

"I can do it."

"I'm done now." She tosses the paper towel. "Bree is asleep in her room. She may only sleep a few minutes. She doesn't usually take a morning nap." Sophia walks up to me and smiles. "It's good you're here. For both of them."

She goes around me and down the stairs. It feels odd just waiting here with nothing to do. Riley should be the one up here, keeping watch on Bree and resting.

Going over to Bree's room, I see her tiny body under a pink blanket holding a stuffed bear. She's sound asleep and looks adorable. On the floor by her bed are two big stacks of books. I'd get her a bookcase, but her room isn't big enough. It barely holds her bed. Riley's room isn't much bigger. This apartment seems way too small for the two of them, although it's much bigger than the trailer Riley used to live in.

Walking back to the living room, I look around for something to do. I get my laptop and do a search for the artificial heart valve they want to put in Riley. I find the studies showing the flaws in the valve and bookmark them to show the doctor.

"Brad?" I hear a tiny voice say.

I turn around and see Bree there, holding her blanket and stuffed bear.

"What are you doing up? You've only been asleep a few minutes."

She walks over to me, dragging her blanket behind. "I sleep here."

"You want to sleep here?" I get up with the laptop. "I'll go in the bedroom."

"No. You stay." She climbs on the couch. "Sit."

Setting the laptop on the table, I sit back on the couch. Bree climbs on my lap with her blanket and bear. She puts her head on my chest and closes her eyes.

"You comfy?" I ask, smiling at her.

She doesn't answer. Her eyes are shut and her body's relaxed, like she's already asleep.

I put my arm around her and kiss her head. It's almost like she knows. Like she knows I'm her dad. Why else would she be this comfortable with me? I just met her and she already trusts me enough to crawl on my lap and sleep on me. Or maybe she's just so desperate for a father she's using me to fill that gap. But I *am* her father, and I want to tell her. I don't want to wait.

I'm not going to leave her. How could Riley even think that I would? I'm not that guy. The guy who leaves his kid because he's not man enough to stick around? After seeing my dad walk out on me when I was four, I promised myself that'd never be me. That I'd always be there for my kid, and yet I've missed her first three years.

I'm still angry at Riley for that. I'm trying to forgive her, trying to get past it, but the anger is still there.

CHAPTER TWENTY

Riley

"Given the latest test results," Dr. Green says, "we'd like to schedule the surgery for next week."

"Next week?" I ask, feeling more anxious by the second. I thought he'd just go over the test results, not schedule the surgery. I was hoping the surgery wouldn't be scheduled for a few more weeks. "Why the rush?"

"We think it's best to get it done and taken care of, especially since your symptoms seem to be getting worse."

"They're not worse," I insist, but it's a total lie. Just walking up a few steps makes me winded, and I'm so tired I can barely get through the day.

The doctor folds his hands in front of him on the desk. "The damage is rather extensive for someone your age. Waiting will only worsen your symptoms."

"Riley, just get it done," Brad says. "You'll feel better when it's over."

Unless I don't survive. I keep having these dreams where

I die in surgery and Bree is left without a mom while Brad takes off for his residency. I know Brad wouldn't leave her behind like that, and yet I told him I thought he might. Why did I do that? I know that's not him. That's just my own history with men getting in the way of me trusting Brad to care for our daughter.

I never should have questioned Brad's commitment to being a father, but I'm not thinking straight right now. I'm worried this surgery won't go well and worried about Bree. She's my entire world, and I can't leave her without a mom. She needs me.

"We'll determine recovery time from there," Dr. Green says. "Sound good?"

"What was that?" I ask, realizing I hadn't been listening. "I missed whatever you just said."

"I was talking about the surgery. We can schedule it for next Friday, if that works."

"How long will I be in the hospital?"

"Most likely a week, depending on how fast you're recovering."

"And then what? How long before I can go back to work?"

"Given the physical demands of your job, I'd say eight to ten weeks, but again, it depends on your recovery."

"I can't go that long without working. Is there a way to speed it up?"

"Riley, we've talked about this. Even though you're young and able to recover faster than someone who's older, this is still major surgery that you don't just recover from in a week or two. It'll take about two months before you're back to your normal activities, and even then you'll need to take it easy. Waitressing is a demanding job. You won't be able to lift heavy trays and you may find it too tiring to be on your feet that long."

He's told me all this before, but it didn't sink in until now. I can't work for two months? Or longer than that? What am I going to do? I need money.

"Do you have someone to help care for your daughter during this time?" the doctor asks.

"I'll be taking care of her," Brad says. "I'll be caring for Riley too during her recovery."

I look over and see the commitment on his face. He's really doing this. He's really going to stay here and help me. I wasn't sure if he meant it when he said he'd stay the summer. And when he said it, I assumed he only meant he'd take care of Bree. I didn't expect him to take care of me too. Before today, I never even thought about all the care I would need after surgery. Honestly, I've been trying to pretend this isn't really happening and I'll end up being fine and not needing the surgery. But now it's real. It's happening next week!

My heart's beating faster and I'm starting to sweat. Brad reaches over and takes my hand from my lap, holding it in his. He interlocks our fingers, making me feel like we're in this together. With Brad's hand linked with mine, I instantly feel calmer.

"Riley, I know this is an uncomfortable topic," the doctor says, "but should something happen, do you have someone in place to care for your daughter?"

That sick, anxious feeling is back, making my muscles stiffen and my stomach hurt. He's asking what happens if I die. I can't even think about it.

"Her father will care for her," Brad says.

Dr. Green looks at me, his brows drawn together. "You told me the father was no longer in your daughter's life."

"He wasn't," I say. "But he is now."

"And you've spoken to him about this? About caring for her should something happen?"

I glance at Brad. "Yeah, he knows."

"Riley, you need to do more than just talk to him. You need to make his responsibilities very clear. You may even want to put it in writing with the help of an attorney. If it's not clear where the child should go, the state will intervene."

I feel Brad's eyes on me. "It's a good idea, Riley. To get it in writing."

"Make sure he knows what's expected of him should something happen," Dr. Green says. "You don't want him being surprised by this. He needs to know he'd be getting custody."

"He knows," I say, my eyes on the doctor. "He's sitting right here."

"You're the father?" the doctor asks Brad.

"Yes. I don't live in the area, but I'm here for the summer and will be staying with Riley and our daughter until I have to leave in September."

"I see." The doctor turns back to me. "Given the timing, that's all the more reason to have the surgery next week. Next Friday will be eight weeks from September. He'll be able to care for you and your daughter during the majority of your recovery. You'll need that, Riley. You can't do this alone, especially as a single mother."

Having to rely on people is not a strength of mine. I've always had to take care of myself. Asking for help makes me feel weak. Now I have no choice. I have to depend on Brad. Sophia has to run the diner, and even if she didn't, she's too old to chase Bree around all day. Brad is my only option.

I sit quietly in the chair, not knowing what to say and

wishing we could leave. I've been here for hours now and just want to go home.

"Regarding the surgery," Brad says to the doctor. "I read through the information you gave Riley, and I'm not comfortable with your choice in valves. I just completed medical school in New York and although I respect your opinion and realize you've been practicing medicine a lot longer than me, I've done a lot of research on that valve and don't want you putting it in Riley."

"Every artificial valve has risks," Dr. Green says.

"Yes, but this one has significantly more than others. There are at least three lawsuits filed against the company because of problems related to this valve. I can show you my research if you don't believe me."

"I'm aware of the research."

"Then why are you using it?" Brad asks, raising his voice.

"We use what we feel is best."

"But it's not. It's dangerous. And I'm not letting you put it in my girlfriend."

Girlfriend? I'm not his girlfriend.

"Young man, I know what it's like to be fresh out of medical school and feel as though you know everything, but my team has assessed Riley's case and we believe this is the best option."

"Why? Because it's the cheapest? Because the company's paying you to use it to try to prove that's it safe?"

Dr. Green stands up. "I think it's time we end this meeting. Riley, I suggest you tell your boyfriend to stop reading medical journals in regard to your care. It'll only just frighten you both."

I stand up. "I agree with Brad. I don't want that valve. I want you to use a different one."

Dr. Green glances at Brad, clearly annoyed with him for bringing this up. "I'll discuss it with the team at our meeting tomorrow."

"Thank you," I say.

"I'll schedule the surgery for Friday. My nurse will follow-up with you regarding the details." Dr. Green goes around me to the door. "I need to see another patient. You can see yourselves out."

As he leaves, Brad gets up. "What an ass. He didn't even want to consider a different valve. He's one of those doctors who thinks he knows best without even doing the research."

"Thank you for doing that."

"I wasn't going to just stand by and let him put something in you that's proven to be dangerous."

"Not just that. All the research you did too. Thanks for doing that. There's no way I would've known all that if you hadn't told me."

He puts his arm around me. "That's why I'm here. To help you out."

"I never expected you to do all this. Helping me after the surgery? Caring for Bree? I wasn't thinking about any of that when I called you and asked you to come here."

"Riley, I know you're someone who hates asking for help, but you need it. There's no way you'd be able to do this on your own. This is major surgery."

"I still feel bad making you do this. You probably wanted to relax and have fun this summer, and now you're stuck taking care of me."

"There's nothing I'd rather do," he says, leaning down to kiss my forehead. It makes me feel like we're dating again and reminds me of what he said earlier.

I look up at him. "Can I ask you something?"

"Go ahead."

"Why'd you call me your girlfriend?"

"I thought it'd make the doctor take what I was saying more seriously."

So that's all it was. He doesn't really think I'm his girlfriend. I guess I knew that, but I wanted to make sure.

"You hungry?" he asks.

"A little."

"Let's go get dinner."

We leave the hospital and go to a restaurant downtown. It's a small downtown lined with shops and restaurants that reminds me of back home. It's one of the many reasons I like living here. It's near a big city but has a small-town feel like where I grew up.

"What do you think?" Brad asks, pointing behind me. We're at a sports bar and just finished dinner.

I laugh when I see where he's pointing. "You want to play darts?"

"When's the last time you played?"

"With you, so four years ago."

"C'mon." He gets up from the table, leaving some cash for the check.

We walk past the bar to the dart board.

"Remember how to play?" he asks, handing me the darts.

"Yes," I say with a laugh. "It's not that complicated."

"Go ahead." He stands back.

I toss the dart and am surprised I actually hit the board. Last time I played, I kept missing it. I toss the next two. Both hit the outer ring.

"Not bad," Brad says, stepping up to throw his darts. One hits the bullseye and two land in the ring next to it.

"Have you been practicing?" I ask.

"Not at all." He yanks the darts from the board. "Haven't played since our first date."

I smile. "That wasn't a date. We were just friends."

He walks back to me. "That's not how I remember it."

"It wasn't a date. We had dinner and played darts. It's not like we kissed."

"But we wanted to," he says with a smile.

"Yeah? So? We didn't, which means it wasn't a date." I throw a dart, hitting the outer ring again. "Why can't I get it closer?"

"Here." He comes up behind me, his hands going around my waist. "Move right a little." He nudges me over. "Stand there and try it. And keep your eye on the bullseye." I throw another dart. It hits the ring second closest to the outside.

"You don't have to kiss for it to be a date," he says as I throw the third dart.

"It wasn't a date. It was two friends having dinner." I go to get my darts.

"Is that what this is?"

"I don't know. You seem to be the expert on dates. What would you call this?"

"I'm letting you decide."

I walk back to him. "I think it's two friends getting to know each other again."

"Fair enough." He steps up to throw his darts.

Why was he asking me that? Does he want tonight to be a date? I still can't figure him out. One minute I think he's flirting with me and the next I think he's mad at me for not telling him about Bree. When she's around, he's not as friendly to me and I catch him giving me these looks like he wants to yell at me for keeping him out of her life for so long.

When it's my turn to play, my mind is so focused on

figuring out what's going on with Brad that I miss the board and the dart lands on the floor. My next two darts hit the board but on the outer ring.

"You need to aim lower," Brad says.

"Next time," I say, going to get my darts. I pick up the one that fell on the floor, and as I'm standing up, I get so dizzy I stumble back.

"Riley!" Brad says, coming up behind me, his arms steadying me. "You okay?"

"Yeah. I just got dizzy when I stood up."

"Maybe we should quit for tonight."

"Yeah. I'm getting tired."

We go out to his car.

"You don't have to keep renting this," I tell him. "Since you're staying, you can return this and drive mine."

"I'll take it back tomorrow."

As we're driving back, I realize we're close to Sophia's. "Do you want to stop and get Bree? Sophia lives just a few miles from here."

"What if they're not home?"

"I'll call her." I get my phone out.

"Hello, Riley," she answers. "How was your appointment?"

"They scheduled the surgery for next Friday."

"That's good! You'll get it over with."

"I guess. Hey, are you home now? We were going to come get Bree."

"We're out having ice cream. I can take her home. It's on my way."

"Okay."

"Oh, and Riley, I don't know what your plans are for telling Bree, but she needs to know soon."

"I don't think she'll understand. I'm just going to tell her Mommy hurt herself and has to go in the hospital for a week to get fixed."

"I wasn't referring to the surgery. I was talking about Brad. Bree is completely over the moon about him. She can't stop talking about him. You need to tell her he's her father."

I glance at Brad. "Yeah. Okay. See you soon."

"What'd she say?" Brad asks.

"She'll drop Bree off. They're out having ice cream."

"So we're going back to the apartment?"

"Yeah." I pause. "So, um, Sophia thinks we should tell Bree about you. She doesn't think we should wait."

"I agree." He glances at me. "So why don't we?"

"I guess I just don't feel ready yet. She just met you."

"And she's already bonding with me. She feels comfortable around me. She even came out of her room this morning just to be with me."

"She did?"

"Why are you so surprised? She's my kid. She probably senses something familiar about me. Kids pick up on stuff like that."

"She probably just wanted to play."

"She didn't play. She climbed on my lap and fell asleep. Is that something she'd normally do with someone she just met?"

"No. Never," I say, my heart warming as I picture her sleeping on him. "She usually stays away from new people until she knows them better."

"Maybe she's figured it out."

"I don't think so. I told her I didn't know where you were."

He shakes his head and mutters something.

"What?" I ask.

He doesn't respond as he turns down the road that goes to the apartment.

"Brad, I know you said something, so what is it?"

"Nothing. Just forget it."

He pulls into the parking lot and turns the car off.

"You're still mad at me," I say.

"Riley, let's not talk about this. Let's go inside."

"But we *need* to talk about it." I take my seatbelt off and turn to him. "You're angry, and pretending you're not is just making you angrier."

His head falls back on the headrest. "Don't start this, Riley. Bree's going to be here soon and I don't want her to see us fighting."

"We're already fighting. We've been fighting since I told you about her."

"What are you talking about?" he asks, taking his seatbelt off.

"Ever since I told you, you've acted differently. It's like you're trying to be nice to me, even though you're mad. You're holding it all inside, but it starts to come out whenever Bree's around. She's a reminder of what I did, so it's harder to hide your anger. She's going to start noticing that, if she hasn't already."

Brad gets out of the car and slams the door.

"Where are you going?" I ask, following him as he heads to the beach.

"Just leave me alone," he says, walking fast and kicking up sand everywhere.

"Brad, talk to me. Or yell at me. Whatever you need to do to get back at me for what I did." I struggle to breathe as I try to catch up to him. "Brad, please slow down. I can't go that fast."

He whips around and sees me bent over, trying to breathe.

"Dammit, Riley," he says, walking back to me. "I told you to leave me alone. Why are you doing this?"

"Because..." I take a breath as I stand up. "Because I want you to be honest with me, like you were when we were together. I know you're angry, and hurting, and feeling guilty you haven't been part of her life. And I know I'm the reason for that." I feel tears forming and blink them away. "I just want you to talk to me, Brad, about everything that's happened. About how you're feeling about all this. You used to tell me everything, the good and the bad. I want to have that again. I want us to be able to talk to each other."

"It's not the same, Riley."

"Why? Why can't you talk to me anymore?"

"Because this is about YOU. Don't you get that?"

"I know it's about me. I know you blame me for not being part of her life. So just tell me that!" I raise my voice because I'm so frustrated with him. "Just tell me how you feel!"

"I hate you, okay?" he yells. "Is that what you want to hear?" He drops his head, breathing hard as he stares at the ground.

"You hate me?" I ask, no longer able to contain my tears.

He doesn't answer, but he doesn't need to. I asked how he feels and he told me.

I thought he might still love me, but he doesn't. He hates me.

CHAPTER TWENTY-ONE

Riley

"I'm sorry," I whisper.

"Sorry doesn't give me the last three years back," Brad says, keeping his head down. "I missed seeing her birth. I missed her first birthday. Her first words. I missed seeing the first time she walked. I missed Christmases with her. I missed it all, Riley. Because of you."

I nod, tears pouring from my eyes.

"You see why I didn't tell you?" he says, motioning to me as I sob. "Dammit, Riley, why did you have to keep pushing?"

"Because I needed to hear it. And you needed to say it."

"I DIDN'T need to say it! Saying it hurts, and I didn't want to fucking hurt you."

"It hurts even more when you won't talk to me. When you won't tell me how you really feel."

"You want to know how I feel?" he says, throwing his hands up. "Betrayed. Lied to. Angry that I missed three years of my little girl's life. Angry that she thinks her dad left her, and pissed off that she still doesn't know who I am." He leans down to me. "And most of all, I'm angry that the girl I loved, the girl I trusted, disappeared out of my life without even talking to me." He backs away. "You say it hurts you when I don't talk to you? Don't tell you what I'm feeling? Try living with that for the past four years."

"Brad, I told you it wasn't working. I explained it. We couldn't keep dating from that far apart."

"That wasn't the reason you broke up with me. We could've found a way to make it work. We'd just had a great weekend together in New York. You said you loved me. You cried when you left. And then you call and tell me it's over? It didn't make sense. You wouldn't answer my calls. My texts. All I got was silence. And then I found out you'd moved and changed your number."

"Brad, I—"

"I've spent the last four years wondering what happened. Wondering if I'd done something wrong. Wondering how you could tell me you love me and then hours later, tell me it's over."

So that's why he's been acting this way. All the anger I've been feeling from him wasn't just because I didn't tell him about Bree. It's because of what I did four years ago, when I was pregnant and afraid telling him would ruin his life. I thought I was helping him, but instead I hurt him. And all these years later, he's still hurting.

"I wish I could change it," I tell him. "I wish I could go back and do it differently. At the time, I thought it was the right decision. I thought you'd go on with your life and forget all about me."

"Forget about the only girl I've ever loved? I wish I could have. It would've made my life a lot easier."

"I never forgot you either. Every day I'd wake up and wonder how you were and what you were doing. I imagined you with some other girl and would think how lucky she is to have you."

"You never thought that girl could be you?"

"Not after what I did. I knew if I ever told you, you'd never forgive me. That you'd hate me. And I was right."

He sighs. "I hate what you did. Not you."

"And you're still angry."

"I am," he says, his eyes on the sand as he kicks it around.

"You could've told me that."

"No. I couldn't."

"Why?"

His eyes lift to mine. "Because you're sick, Riley."

"What does that have to do with anything?"

"You don't yell at sick people. You don't get angry at them. You don't fucking tell them you hate them." He blows out a breath. "We need to go inside. I don't want to talk anymore." He goes around me, but I grab his arm.

"Brad, wait."

"Riley, I'm serious. I can't talk to you right now."

"It's okay if you're angry at me. It's even okay if you hate me."

He turns back to me. "I don't hate you. I could never hate you. Believe me, I tried, but I couldn't do it. Even now, knowing you hid Bree from me, I want to hate you, but I can't."

"Why?"

He pauses, then says, "Because I love you, Riley. Even after what you did, after all these years, I still love you. If I could make it stop I would, but I can't." He turns and takes off down the beach.

"Brad, wait," I say, trying to catch up. "Why would you want it to stop?"

He either doesn't hear me or doesn't answer as he continues down the beach. Struggling to breathe, I slow down and see Brad waiting for me. He didn't want to walk with me, but he waits to make sure I'm okay. Because he loves me. But he hates what I've done. I don't know what that means for us, and I'm afraid to ask. I've asked enough for now. He needs time to cool off, and I need time to think about what he said.

"Brad!" I hear Bree yell.

Brad turns around and I see Bree running up to him. When she reaches him, he picks her up, just like a father would. In fact, if anyone saw them together, that's what they'd think. They'd assume Bree is his daughter.

What Brad said is true. Bree just met him and she's already comfortable with him. Maybe she *does* know he's her dad, or maybe she just senses he's a good and kind person, like I did when I first met him.

Sophia goes up to Brad and says something to him, then gives me a wave and a smile before heading back to the parking lot.

I'm only about ten feet away, but it's taking me forever to get there. Brad walks toward me, still holding Bree in his arms.

"You okay?" he asks.

"Yeah." I smile at Bree. "Hey, sweet girl," I say, giving her a kiss. I'm out of breath from the walk and Brad notices, concern on his face.

"Why don't you go sit down?" He nods to the bench just a few feet away.

"I'll be fine. Let's go inside. Did Sophia leave?"

"Yeah. She said she wanted to get to the store before it got dark."

"Mommy, can Brad read me a story?" Bree asks.

"Yes, but you need to ask him first. And say please."

"Will you please read me a story?" she asks Brad, her little arms and legs wrapped around him.

"I'd be happy to. You want to pick it out?"

She nods really fast.

We go inside. Brad goes ahead of me up the stairs while I take one at a time, still feeling lightheaded from the walk.

"Go find a book," I hear Brad say. I look up and see him setting Bree down at the top of the stairs.

Brad walks back down to me. "Need some help?"

"I just need to take it slow. I don't know why it's getting so much worse."

"Because you need the surgery. You'll feel a lot better with the new valve." He holds my arm. "Just take a step at a time. Rest when you need to."

We slowly make it up the stairs.

"Go rest," Brad says. "I'll read to Bree and get her ready for bed."

I head to her room.

"Riley, take your own bed. I'll sleep on the couch."

I continue to Bree's bed. After all he's doing for me, I don't want Brad sleeping on the couch. As soon as I lie down, I fall asleep. I wake up when I feel Bree being laid down beside me. From the way she's breathing, I can tell she's asleep.

"Goodnight, Bree," I hear Brad say as he kisses her head. "I love you."

I almost cry hearing him say it. He just met her and already loves her. I feel so much guilt for not telling him. All those years I convinced myself I'd done the right thing, but now? Seeing him with her? I think I made the wrong decision. He got his medical degree and his life in New York, but he missed three years with his daughter. I thought if I told him, he'd regret missing out on the things he worked so hard for, but I think I was wrong.

THE REST OF THE WEEK, Sophia cuts my hours to part-time, saying we're not busy enough for me to work full-time. It's a total lie. She just wants me to rest and knows I won't do it unless she makes me. I'm guessing Brad had something to do with that. I'm sure he told her I was overdoing it. And Sophia, who keeps trying to play matchmaker, knows my extra time off will be spent with Brad. But there's no matches being made. The past few days, Brad has shown no interest in me. He hasn't even made any flirty comments. He's just been a friend, which is what I need right now. I've been telling him how scared I am about next week, and although he doesn't say much, just having him here to listen makes me feel better.

On Sunday, I have the day off. Brad and I take Bree to the park and out for lunch, then come home for her afternoon nap. While she's sleeping, I go over to Brad. He's sitting on the couch, looking at his phone.

"I think we should tell her when she wakes up."

He puts his phone down. "Why now? You keep saying you want to wait."

"I don't want to wait. I want to tell her today. And then we need to figure out what to tell her about my surgery."

"We're telling her together? I thought you wanted to be the one to tell her."

"We're her parents. We should tell her together. We don't need to go into detail, but she needs to know why I'm going in the hospital."

"Okay." He picks his phone up and goes back to whatever has was doing.

This is what I mean. He's changed since we had that fight on the beach. He's distant. He's here, but it's like his mind is somewhere else. I'm afraid to ask him about it because I don't want us to fight again.

When Bree wakes up, I take her to the couch and set her on my lap.

"Mommy, can I have a snack?"

"Yes, but not right now." I look at Brad. "I need to tell you something first."

She pushes off my lap and crawls over to Brad, sitting in his lap and getting comfortable.

He smiles at me, trying not to laugh.

"Bree, do you like Brad?"

She nods. "He's my best friend."

"I thought I was your best friend."

"You're my mommy." She picks up the string on Brad's hoodie and starts playing with it.

"Bree, I need your attention. Put the string down."

She drops it and falls back on Brad's chest.

"Remember when you asked about your daddy?"

She nods.

"What I didn't tell you that day is that he didn't know about you until just a few weeks ago. That's why you never saw him."

She chews on her lip, looking bored.

"Anyway, I asked him to come here, and he did."

She sits up. "My daddy's here?"

"Right here," Brad says.

She looks at him, then me, then back at Brad.

"I'm your dad," Brad says to her. "What do you think of that?"

She still seems confused. She looks at me to confirm it.

"Brad is your dad," I tell her. "We wanted you to get to know him before we told you."

Her eyes shoot back to Brad and she smiles. Then she hugs him, her little arms practically strangling his neck.

"I think she's okay with it," Brad says with a laugh.

"You want a snack now?" I ask her, not wanting to push her to talk about this. She needs time to let it sink in.

"I get snack with Brad," she says, climbing off him.

He chuckles. "You can call me Dad now. Brad's a little formal."

I smile as she drags him to the kitchen. I remain on the couch, watching them interact.

"No, Daddy, the blue bowl," Bree says.

"Got it. Blue bowl." Brad opens the cupboard and finds it. "Now what?"

"Mommy cuts it in circles."

Brad looks over at me. "Circles, huh? This is a lot of work."

I laugh. Watching them together is better than watching TV.

We spend the rest of the day at home. Brad makes dinner while Bree watches. She can't get enough of him. She follows him around, talks to him, climbs on him every time he sits down. It's like I'm not even here. But it's good. I want her to get to know him, to love him, although I think she already does.

Being together like this makes me feel like we're a family.

I know Bree wants that, but eventually I'll have to explain to her that we're not a family and that Brad has to leave.

Later that night, we tell her about my surgery. I had Brad do most of the talking because whenever I talk about it, I tear up. I'm not sure if it's because I'm scared for myself or scared for Bree. I think it's more about Bree. She depends on me for so much. I don't want her being left without a mom.

Over the next few days, I get more and more nervous about the surgery. I've never had surgery, and the only time I've been in the hospital was to have Bree.

"I don't feel well," I tell Brad as he cleans up after dinner. He's taken over all the cooking and cleaning, along with caring for Bree. He's been such a huge help. I feel so much better knowing he'll be here after the surgery, keeping up the apartment and taking care of Bree. That's one thing I won't have to worry about.

"You want to go lay down?" Brad asks as I sit at the counter, watching him dry dishes.

"It's not that kind of sick. It's the kind that comes from being scared of what's going to happen."

"You have nothing to worry about. Everything's going to be fine." He opens the cupboard and puts the plates away.

He's been so calm about this, almost indifferent. It's strange. I thought he would've been as nervous as I am. If he loves me, shouldn't he be more concerned?

He hasn't said he loves me since that day on the beach. He hasn't said much of anything to me. He's been really quiet, except with Bree. The two of them talk and play and go for walks on the beach, and he reads to her every night. He took her to the store and got her some new books. She was so excited. Her other books were old and used, the pages torn and pictures faded. I got them at the library where they sell old books for ten cents a piece.

"What if it's not fine?" I say. "I keep having these dreams where I don't wake up from the surgery. I see myself on the table and can't—"

"Riley, you're going to be fine." He comes around the counter and stands next to me. "Why don't you watch TV? I'll get Bree ready for bed."

He takes off for her room, leaving me wondering why he's acting so nonchalant about this, like it's no big deal. He knows the risks, and even though they're low, the risks are still there.

My phone rings. It's Giada. I take the phone in my room and close the door.

"Hey, Giada."

"Hey. How are you doing?"

"Same. Still scared to death."

"You're going to be fine."

"Everyone keeps saying that, but they're not the one having their chest sawed open."

"The doctors know what they're doing. They do this every day."

"Still doesn't make feel better."

"I know it's scary. When I had my appendix out, I thought for sure I wouldn't wake up. It wasn't so much the surgery, but the anesthesia. For some reason, I have a fear of anesthesia. I panicked when they were about to put me under, and then the next thing I knew I was awake and the surgery was over."

"That's not the same as heart surgery."

"I know," she says with a sigh. "I was trying to make you feel better."

"Just having you call makes me feel better. I miss you. When do you think you'll be down here again?"

"That's the other reason I was calling. I want to come down next week, but only if you're okay with it. I know you'll still be in the hospital, so if you want me to wait and come later, I can."

"Next week is perfect. Brad will be home with Bree and I'll be stuck all alone in the hospital. I'd love to have company."

"Great! I'll let my boss know and get the ticket today. So when do you have to be at the hospital?"

"Tomorrow. The surgery isn't until Friday, but they make you get there early to run tests and whatever else they're going to do. I'm so scared, Giada. I can't eat. I can't sleep."

"What about Brad? Is he a mess too?"

"No, and I can't figure it out. He's completely detached, like it's not even happening. When I try to talk to him about it, he tells me everything will be fine and then changes the subject."

"I guess that makes sense."

"Why? Because he's a doctor? Do they all see surgery as no big deal?"

"It's not about that. It's about him being in love with you. So in love that he can't even let his mind think about something bad happening to you."

"I don't think that's it. He hasn't shown any interest in me since I told him about the surgery. He made a few flirty comments last week, but that's just his personality. It's not like he tried to make a move."

"He won't until he knows you're okay. Right now, he's worried. He's shutting down. It's what guys do. If they can't handle feeling something, they just shut down. It's a classic response to stressful situations. And it's common when someone they love is involved."

"How do you know all this?"

"I was a psych major, remember? And I had a year of grad school courses in psychology. Believe me, Brad's behavior is totally normal and just confirms how much he still loves you."

"Giada, I need to tell you something. I haven't told your grandma this yet, so don't tell her. Let me do it."

"Okay. What is it?"

"I'm going with him."

"With who? What are you talking about?"

"When Brad goes to Charleston for his residency, I'm going with him. I'm going to move with him. I'm not saying we'll live together, but I'm definitely moving there."

"Riley, that's great! Have you told Brad?"

"Not yet. I think I'm going to wait until after the surgery. I've given this a lot of thought and it feels like the right thing to do. I didn't move to New York with him and always wondered if I'd made a mistake. But back then, I don't think I could've done it. I was too young. Too afraid. Now that I'm older and a mom, I'm not as afraid of change, especially if it's for Bree. She needs her dad. I tried to tell myself I was enough for her, but seeing them together, I see what she's missing. He's such a great dad, and he loves her so much. I want her to be able to see him. To grow up with him, even if Brad and I aren't together."

"I'm so glad you're doing this. Nonna will be upset about losing you and Bree, but she'll get over it. She wants the three of you to be family. I don't know if you've noticed, but she's been trying to get you and Brad together."

I smile. "I've noticed. She keeps trying to find excuses to take Bree so Brad and I can be alone."

"He's going to be so happy about this. And you will too, right?"

"I'll miss Sophia, and living on the beach, but yeah, I'm happy about it. I want Bree to have her dad in her life."

"And you want Brad in your life."

"I'm not going to think about that right now. I'd like to get back with Brad, but things have changed between us. We can't just restart where we left off. He hasn't forgiven me for not telling him about Bree. He may never forgive me. We can't have a relationship if he holds that against me."

"He just needs more time. He's only known about this for a couple weeks. Give him time. You don't have to rush into anything. For now, just be friends and see where it goes."

There's a knock on the door. "Riley, Bree wants to say goodnight."

"Okay," I yell back. "Be there in a minute."

"I'll let you go," Giada says. "Give Bree a hug for me."

"I will. I probably won't talk to you again until after the surgery so..."

"You're going to do great. They'll do the surgery and you're going to feel better than you have in years. You'll finally be able to beat my grandma up the stairs."

I laugh. "That's pretty sad when your grandma goes faster than me."

"Love you. We'll talk soon."

"Love you too. Bye."

Giada's the first person I told about the move. It feels a lot more real now that I've said it out loud. It's going to be a big change, but I know it's for the best. Bree needs to be with her dad. And I want to be with Brad. I don't want to lose him again.

CHAPTER TWENTY-TWO

BRAD

It's Friday morning and they're getting ready to take Riley to surgery. I've been trying not to worry, but my stomach's in knots. I just want this to be over.

Sophia and I brought Riley to the hospital yesterday so they could prep her for today. She was so nervous. I kept telling her funny things Bree said, hoping it would make Riley laugh and calm her down. I avoided any talk about the surgery, both for her sake and mine. Even though I keep assuring her she'll be fine, I'm still worried. Even young, otherwise healthy people can die in surgery, especially heart surgery. Doctors aren't perfect. They mess up on the job just like anyone else, except their screw-ups can kill someone or cause permanent damage.

"Brad." Riley reaches for me from her hospital bed.

"Right here." I hold her hand. "What do you need?"

"Give Bree a hug for me?"

"I will. I'll give her lots of hugs."

Riley asked Sophia to stay home with Bree this morning instead of coming to hospital. She wants to keep Bree's routine as normal as possible. She says it'll make her feel safe and not as scared. She's such a great mom.

"And make sure she takes her naps," Riley says. "Without me around she'll try to skip them, but don't let her. She gets cranky when she doesn't sleep."

"I'll make sure she naps." I rub Riley's hand. "Don't worry about Bree. I'll take good care of her."

She softly smiles. "I know you will. You're a good dad."

It's nice that she said that, but I really have no clue what I'm doing. I don't know anything about being a dad. I just know I love that little girl and don't want to leave her. I've been wanting to talk to Riley about that. About what happens when I leave at the end of the summer. When will I see Bree? Will I fly down every couple weeks? Would they fly up to see me? Would Riley be willing to stay longer than a few days? These are all things we need to discuss, but that'll have to wait until later.

"Can I ask you something?" Riley says.

"Go ahead."

"Back when we had that fight on the beach."

"Riley, let's not talk about that."

"I just need to know something. About what you said that day."

I keep quiet and wait for her to continue.

"You said you wished you could stop." Her eyes go to my hand, which is still wrapped around hers. "Stop loving me."

"Riley," I say, wishing she would forget that day. I was angry and said things I shouldn't have said, like that I hate her. I never should've said that. It's not even close to the truth. I hated what she did, but I never once hated her. I wish I could take it back.

"Why did you say it?" Riley asks. "Why do you want to stop loving me?"

This is not what I want to be talking about, not now, just minutes before her surgery. I didn't even think she heard me that day.

"Brad, I need an answer."

I pause, my eyes going to hers. "I said it because loving you hurts. It hurts because you're not mine. Because I can't seem to hold on to you. It's hard to love someone and not be with them. Thinking about you, missing you...it hurts. And now you're having this surgery and..." I shake my head.

"What? You don't think I'll make it?"

"I think you'll be fine. But just the idea, the possibility, that something could go wrong, hurts worse than I can describe. I can't lose you, Riley. I lost you once, but I can't lose you again."

"You're not losing me." She smiles. "Everything's going to work out. It always does. Isn't that what you used to tell me?"

"I was younger then. I didn't know the world like I do now."

"You don't believe it anymore?"

"I'd like to, but it's not realistic. Sometimes things really don't work out. You just have to accept that and move on."

"You met Bree, and that worked out well."

"Yeah, but I'm going to lose her soon. I'm going to move away, and who knows when I'll see her?"

I shouldn't have said that. This isn't the time to bring that up.

"About that."

"What?" I say.

"Bree. You seeing her."

"Riley, we'll talk about it later."

"I need to say this now. I was going to wait, but I changed my mind."

"What is it?"

"I'm moving."

"Moving where?"

"To Charleston."

I don't respond, thinking I either heard her wrong or this is some kind of side effect of the meds they gave her. Maybe she's not sure what she's saying.

"Brad, did you hear me? I'm moving to Charleston."

"Are you serious?" I ask, still not believing her.

She nods. "There's this guy there I really like. Well, actually I love him. I've never *stopped* loving him. And my daughter is crazy about him. When he's around, she acts like I'm not even there. So the only logical choice is to move to Charleston to be with him."

I look at her. "You're really doing this? You're not just thinking about it?"

"I've already thought about it. This is what I want. I want Bree to grow up with her dad. I don't know what that means for us, or if there will even *be* an us. We can figure that out later. I just want you to know that you'll see her. You'll see her as much as you want."

I'm shocked, and still not sure that she means it. She said she'd move to New York and it never happened.

The door opens and a nurse pops her head in the room. "They'll be in shortly to get you."

"Okay," Riley says.

"We'll talk about this later," I tell her.

"Brad, you didn't say anything. What do you think of me moving?"

"I don't know. I mean, I'd love it if it actually happened. I just don't want to get my hopes up."

"I'm not going to change my mind this time. I've already started looking for apartments there. And jobs. Daycare centers for Bree. I'm really doing this, Brad. I'm moving to Charleston."

I'm starting to believe her. She seems determined to make this happen. And happy. She actually seems happy about it.

"One condition," I say.

"What?"

"Move in with me. I have an apartment already rented. It's a two bedroom. I was going to use one room as an office, but we could make it Bree's room."

"What about me? Where am I going to sleep?"

I don't answer, because this is another topic that should wait until later.

"Brad, I don't know what you're thinking, but as for me, I'm not ready to even try getting back together until you've forgiven me."

"I've already done that."

"But you haven't. This past week you've been distant and quiet. I know it's because you're still mad at me."

"That wasn't the reason."

"Then what was it?"

I hesitate, then just say it. "I was worried. And when I'm worried I avoid the thing I'm worried about it."

"You avoided me because you were worried about me?"

"I get that it's not the best way to deal with it, but it's what I had to do to get through it."

"So you're not still mad at me?"

"No." I smile and rub her hand. "I probably should be, but I've never been someone who can hold a grudge. I'm ready to try this again. I know we're different people now and can't just start where we left off, but I think we need to at least give it a try."

She smiles. "I think so too."

The nurse walks in. "Sir, you'll need to leave now."

I lean down and give Riley a kiss. "I love you. See you when you wake up."

I leave her room, then watch as they wheel her away.

The surgery will take several hours, so I head back to the apartment to check on Bree. As I'm driving, I call up Nate. I've been debating whether or not to call him but decided I just need to do it, even though I'm still furious with him for lying to me about Riley. He's the one I haven't forgiven, and I'm not sure I ever will.

"Brad," Nate says. "Haven't talked to you forever. How've you been?"

"I've been better, that's for sure."

"What do you mean?"

"Well, let's start with the fact that you lied to keep me away from Riley."

"What are you talking about? I didn't lie."

"The fake boyfriend. The kid you said was his and not mine. I could go on, but those are the big ones."

The phone is quiet.

"What? You didn't think I'd find out?"

"She didn't want you knowing about the kid. I had to tell you that stuff so you wouldn't find out it was yours."

"You told me that shit so I wouldn't show up there."

"Because it's not what Riley wanted. I was doing what Riley told me to. I was being a friend."

"She never told you to make up a story about some other guy."

"It was the only way I could convince you to not fly out there."

"And what about Corinne? What's your excuse there? You told Riley I was dating Corinne."

"So she could move on. If Riley knew you had a girlfriend, she could stop thinking about you. She could go be with someone else."

"Like you?"

He laughs. "You really think I'm still hung up on Riley? I gave up that dream a long time ago."

"If that were true, you wouldn't have tried so hard to keep Riley and me apart. You wanted her and couldn't have her, so you made sure I couldn't have her either."

"Is this why you called? To blame me for why you're not with Riley? You really need to get a life, Brad. She was some girl you dated for what? A few months? Go find someone else. Actually, didn't you already find someone? My mom said you're engaged."

"I was. I'm not anymore. And Riley wasn't just some girl. As for why I called, I just wanted you to know that Riley and I both know you lied to us and we know you did it to keep us apart."

"If that's what you want to think, fine. I don't care." He pauses. "How do you know Riley knows? Have you talked to her?"

"I'm with her right now. Well, she's not in the car with me, but I'm here with her in Florida."

"You're with Riley?"

"I'm staying at her apartment. I've been staying there for weeks now."

"You guys are back together?"

"We're working on it. And I finally got to meet my daughter. I could've met her three years ago if you'd told me the truth."

"That was Riley's decision, not mine. I'm surprised you'd want to be with her after she lied to you like that."

There he goes again, trying to break us apart. If I let him, he'd try to talk me out of giving her a second chance.

Ignoring his comment, I say, "She's having surgery."

"Who? Riley?"

"Yeah. It's serious. A valve in her heart is being replaced."

"Holy shit. Do they have to cut open her chest, or what?"

"It's open heart surgery, so yeah. Because of where the valve is, they're only cutting open part of her chest, but it's still serious surgery. They have to stop her heart, put her on a machine."

"How did this happen? She's young. Healthy. How could she have heart problems?"

"It was there when she was born and got worse over time. Usually people don't get symptoms until their thirties or forties, but it can happen earlier. Anyway, I just thought you should know."

"Can you give me her address? I should send flowers. Or maybe I'll come down there."

"I don't think that's a good idea. And I'm not sure if she'd be okay with me giving you her address. I'll ask her later and let her decide."

"Riley and I are best friends. She's not going to say no. Just give me her address."

"You're not her best friend. Not anymore." I pull into the diner parking lot. "Nate, I gotta go. Take care."

I end the call, not waiting for him to say goodbye. If he

288

calls back, I'm not sure if I'll answer. I said what I needed to say and don't care if I ever talk to him again. I'm sure I will, given we're family and attend the same family functions, but I don't want to talk to him outside of that. We were like brothers when we were kids, but that's over. It'll never be like that again.

"Daddy!" Bree yells as I come through the back door to the kitchen. I love hearing her call me that. It always makes me smile.

"Hey." I lift her up and spin her around, which makes her laugh. "Did you have breakfast?"

She nods. "Where's Mommy?"

"At the hospital, remember? We talked about it yesterday."

"She's getting an owie fixed."

"That's right. And then she'll be all better."

Sophia appears, her face covered in worry. "How was she this morning?"

"Okay. She just wants it to be over."

"I think we all feel that way."

"Nonna's taking me to find fairy houses," Bree says.

"You can take her," Sophia says. "I wasn't sure when you'd be home."

"Actually, I'd kind of like to go back to the hospital."

"You'll just be waiting," Sophia says. "The surgery will take hours and then she'll have to recover before they let us in to see her."

"I know, but I still want to be there. It feels wrong not to be with her, even if she's not fully aware that I'm there."

Sophia smiles. "I understand."

"You okay watching this little one?" I ask, kissing Bree's cheek.

"I'm happy to." She takes Bree from me. "Let's go find those fairy houses."

"What about Daddy?"

"He's going to be with your mom."

Bree smiles, almost like she knows her parents are getting back together. I don't know if that'll happen, but it's what I want. It's what I've always wanted, but didn't think would happen when she left. Now we have a second chance. She just needs to make it out of this surgery.

CHAPTER TWENTY-THREE

Riley

I wake up feeling groggy, and my chest feels like someone hit it really hard.

"Riley, I'm here." I feel a warm hand wrap around mine. "I'm right here."

I flutter open my eyes and see Brad beside me.

"Is it over?" I ask, my voice hoarse and weak.

"It's over. You did great." He smiles but also looks a little sad.

"It went okay?"

"There were a few issues, but it all worked out. You're gonna be fine."

"What issues?"

"We'll talk about it later."

I try to sit up, but don't have the strength to move.

"Tell me," I say, opening my eyes more. "I want to know."

"They um..." He looks down, then back up at me. "They had to try a few times to get you off the machine."

"The heart machine?"

"Yeah, but it all worked out."

He's saying they couldn't get my heart going again? So that's why he looks sad. I could've died. I don't want to think about that.

"What else?" I ask.

"Everything else went smoothly. They ended up using a different artificial valve."

"Yours?"

He nods. "The one I suggested."

Last Monday, Brad printed out all his research on the heart valve they were putting in me and brought it to the cardiologist. The doctor said he'd look at it, but I didn't think he would. I also didn't think he'd listen to Brad, who recommended an alternative.

"Why didn't they tell me?" I ask.

"They didn't have time. While they were prepping you for surgery, they found out the valve had been recalled. Someone died from it and the company had to take it off the market."

"You were right all along." I try to smile, but even my mouth feels too tired to move.

"I knew it had problems, but the doctors refused to listen until they got the news about the recall." Brad leans down to kiss my forehead. "I'm going to let you rest."

"Where's Bree?"

"Still at home. You need to recover more before they'll let her see you. We'll come by later, when you're more awake."

My eyelids droop, but I force them back open. "Brad?"

"Yeah?"

"Thanks for being here."

He says something, but I'm not sure what. My eyes fall shut and I'm out.

―――――

"MOMMY," a little voice whispers.

My eyes open and I see her tiny face next to mine. "Bree."

She's all smiles, not at all afraid. I was worried she might be. It can be scary to see your mom hooked up to machines in a hospital bed. I saw my own mom like that and it freaked me out. But not Bree. She's probably too young to understand.

"Mommy all better?" she asks, kissing my cheek.

"Almost." I look up and see Brad there, along with Sophia.

"Hey, Sophia," I say, my voice still hoarse.

She smiles and comes up to my bed. "You look good."

"She does," someone says from the other side of the bed. I look over and see Giada.

"Giada!" I want to sit up but can't, so I just smile at her.

She smiles back. "Surprise!"

"I thought you weren't coming until next week."

"I decided to come a little early. Besides, it's the weekend. What else am I'm going to do? It's not like I have a date."

"What happened to the pilot?" Brad asks.

She rolls her eyes. "Found out he's married."

I look at Brad. "How'd you know about that?"

"I might've called her recently to get some advice."

"Advice about what?" I ask.

"This girl he really likes," Giada says. "She can be hard to figure out so I gave him a little help." She smiles at Brad.

"Not much," he says. "I had to figure out a lot on my own."

"Mommy, come home," Bree says, laying beside me.

"I can't yet," I tell her. "But you have your daddy. He'll take care of you."

"Can Daddy stay with us?" she asks, her big brown eyes looking up at me.

"He already is staying with us."

"What if he leaves and we can't find him?"

She's remembering what I told her before. About how I couldn't find him.

I wasn't going to tell her this yet, but I don't know how else to answer her question.

"Daddy has to leave, but we're going with him." I glance at Brad.

"You're moving?" Sophia asks, sitting beside me.

"Sorry. I was going to tell you later."

She smiles. "No need to be sorry. I think it's the right decision. For all of you."

"Nonna come with?" Bree asks.

"She can," I say, "but I think she might stay here. I bet she'd let us visit though."

"You better," she says, shaking her finger at me. "I need to see my girls." She turns to Giada. "That includes you. You need to see your Nonna more."

She laughs. "I'll work on it."

Sophia stands up. "Well, I suppose we should let you rest."

"But you just got here."

"You're only allowed visitors for short periods of time," Brad says. "We'll be back tomorrow."

Everyone walks to the door except Brad.

"I'll just be a minute," he says as they leave.

"What's going on?" I ask.

He sits beside me. "I called Nate."

"You did? Why?"

"When you said all that stuff about me seeming angry, like I hadn't forgiven you? I realized it was Nate I was angry with. So I called him up and told him we knew what he'd done. How he tried to keep us apart."

"And what'd he say?"

"He said he was just doing what you told him. Keeping me from finding out about Bree."

"It's kind of true."

"Riley, you and I both know Nate only said that stuff to keep us from getting back together. He wasn't doing it to be your friend."

"What else did he say?"

"That he wants to fly out here to see you. I told him about the surgery. I also told him I had to check with you before agreeing to let him come here. I know it's your decision, but I don't want him here. I don't trust him. I don't want him ever coming between us again. I think it's best if we keep him out of our lives."

"He'll always be part of our lives. He's your cousin."

"That doesn't mean I have to talk to him. And you don't either. You don't owe him anything. You guys were friends a long time ago. That doesn't mean you still have to be friends. And there's nothing wrong with telling him you don't want to see him."

"I'll think about it." I take a breath. "I'm so glad this is over."

"The surgery's over, but this problem with your heart isn't something that just goes away. You'll still need to be aware of any symptoms. Those valves don't always last, and with the kind you're on you'll be on blood thinners, which have their own set of risks."

"Good thing I'm living with a doctor."

"Only for a few more weeks. Then you'll need to—wait, did you mean..." I wait for her to answer.

"I'm moving in with you." I smile. "If that's okay."

"You just made my fucking day." He leans down and kisses me. "I love you."

"I love you too."

CHAPTER TWENTY-FOUR

ONE YEAR LATER

BRAD

"She's going to be up any minute now," Riley says, smiling as I kiss her neck.

"She can play with her toys." I undo the button on Riley's shirt. It's actually mine, the one I was wearing last night on our date.

It was such a great night. Dinner at our favorite restaurant, then a concert downtown, followed by late night dessert. When we got home, Bree was sound asleep. Tillie, our sitter and next-door neighbor, who bears a striking resemblance to Sophia, went back to her place and I was left alone with my beautiful wife.

We went to our room and made love, then she slipped into my shirt and fell asleep in my arms. Now it's morning and I want her again, but she's right. Bree will be up any minute now.

"We'll be quick," I say to Riley, her shirt now fully unbuttoned. I slide the fabric aside so I can look at her. The scar from her surgery runs halfway down her chest. She hates it and used to get mad when I looked at it, but I finally convinced her it's not ugly. It's beautiful. A beautiful reminder of what led us back together. If she hadn't needed that surgery, we'd still be apart. She never would've called me. I'd still be wondering where she is, not knowing I had a daughter.

Riley's heart surgery is what got us to where we are now —married, and living together as a family. She and Bree moved here last September. I arrived a week earlier to get the apartment ready. At first I was worried about living with them, mainly because Riley and I would be sharing a room after we'd just started dating again. But it didn't feel awkward at all. In fact, we both agreed it felt like we'd been together for years. It was like that summer we met. We immediately clicked and felt like we'd known each other much longer than we had.

Last Christmas, I asked Riley to marry me. The wedding was in March on the beach outside the diner. Sophia planned it for us so all we had to do was show up. It was a small wedding. Riley's friend, April, flew in for it, along with Todd, my friend from med school. Giada was the maid of honor and my brother was best man. I had some other friends there, and of course, my parents, who were too preoccupied with their granddaughter to fight with each other. My mom is obsessed with Bree. She calls her every day and comes out to visit all the time.

Nate planned to come to the wedding, but then changed his mind. He said he had to work, but I think the real reason is he couldn't watch Riley marry a guy that wasn't him. He says he's over her, but I don't believe him. Riley doesn't either.

She decided it's best if they're not friends anymore, and I agree. If Nate can't be happy for us, we can't be friends.

Riley moans as I slip my hand under her panties. "God, I want you. But she's going to wake up."

"The door is locked," I say, pleasuring her with my hand as I kiss her. She continues to softly moan as I kiss my way down to her chest, along her scar, down her stomach. Just as I'm about to go lower, there's a knock on the door.

"Mommy?"

"Damn," I mutter, rolling onto my back.

Riley laughs. "Told you." She quickly buttons her shirt. "Mommy will be there in a minute!" She gives me a kiss. "It was good while it lasted."

She gets out of bed and opens the door.

Bree runs in and jumps up on the bed. "Hi, Daddy!" She kisses me all over my face like she does every morning.

"How's my girl?" I ask, tickling her.

"Daddy, no," she says, giggling as I tickle her.

"C'mon, Bree," Riley says. "Let's get your breakfast."

Bree hops off the bed and runs to Riley, following her to the kitchen. It's not a big apartment, but it's bigger than their old one. I'd love for us to get a house, but that'll have to wait until I'm done with my residency and we've picked a place to live. We've talked about going back to Florida or maybe Arizona, where my parents live. For now, we're enjoying Charleston. The weather is warm for most of the year and there's lots to do here. Riley works part time at the children's museum, which is a much less strenuous job than waitressing. Even though her heart is better now, I didn't want her having a job that tires her out like waitressing did. She likes the museum, and working part-time gives her more time to spend with Bree. We enrolled Bree in preschool, so she goes there in the mornings and is home with her mom in the afternoons.

"She's having breakfast and watching cartoons," Riley says, laying beside me. She gives me a kiss. "We can try again during her nap."

"She needs something to keep her occupied. Maybe we should get her a dog."

"Or a sister."

I laugh. "Yeah, she'd love that. It'd be like a real-life doll, and you know how much she loves her dolls."

"So what do you think?" Riley asks.

"About what?"

"About Bree having a sister. Or brother."

"Well, sure, eventually. I mean, we both agreed we want more kids. We just need to figure out when."

Riley lays on her back and looks up at the ceiling. "I think it should be soon. Bree's already four, and you don't want them to be too far apart in age."

"How soon were you thinking?"

"I don't know. Maybe eight months?"

"You want to try in eight months? Why eight months?"

"Not try." She turns back to me. "I was thinking we'd have it in eight months. Or maybe more like seven and a half."

"To have a baby that soon you'd have to be—" I smile at her. "You're pregnant?"

"Just found out." She bites her lip. "What do you think?"

"I think it's great!" I grab her and kiss her. "You're really pregnant? You went to the doctor?"

"On Friday. I kind of had a feeling I might be, so I did a home test and then went to the doctor to confirm it."

I kiss her again. "We're having a baby! And this time I'll actually be there."

She frowns. "Brad, I'm sorry. I wish I could go back and let you be there for Bree's birth."

"Riley, I didn't mean it that way. I'm just excited. And happy. I'm so freaking happy."

"Mommy, I need more milk," Bree yells from the kitchen.

"I'll be right there." Riley gives me a kiss. "Meet you back here at nap time."

I love her so much. And I love being a dad. I can't wait to have another.

Just over a year ago, I didn't think I'd ever see Riley again, and now we're married with a child and another one on the way.

I guess what I told Riley all those years ago was true after all. Everything really does work out.

Made in United States
North Haven, CT
23 July 2023

39407654R00182